WEIGHTLESS

ST. MARTIN'S GRIFFIN ⚋ NEW YORK

WEIGHTLESS

SARAH BANNAN

WEIGHTLESS. Copyright © 2015 by Sarah Bannan. All rights reserved. Printed in the United States of America. For information, address St. Martin's Press, 175 Fifth Avenue, New York, N.Y. 10010.

www.stmartins.com

Designed by Anna Gorovoy

The Library of Congress Cataloging-in-Publication Data is available upon request.

ISBN 978-1-250-05092-2 (hardcover)
ISBN 978-1-250-07898-8 (trade paperback)
ISBN 978-1-4668-5188-7 (e-book)

St. Martin's Griffin books may be purchased for educational, business, or promotional use. For information on bulk purchases, please contact the Macmillan Corporate and Premium Sales Department at 1-800-221-7945, extension 5442, or write to specialmarkets@macmillan.com.

First Edition: July 2015

10 9 8 7 6 5 4 3 2 1

for Niamh

august

1

They came out in groups of three, wearing matching shorts and T-shirts, their hair tied back with orange and black ribbons. Their eyes were wide and they yelled and clapped and turned, precisely, rehearsed. They smiled and their lipstick was pink and smooth, their teeth white and perfect. They sparkled.

We sat in the bleachers, towels underneath our legs, trying not to burn our skin on the metal. We wore our Nicole Richie sunglasses and our Auburn and Alabama baseball caps and our Abercrombie tank tops and shorts. The scoreboard on the left of the field displayed the temperature—97 degrees—and the Adamsville morning news said that the heat index made it closer to 105. This is something we had learned to get used to, to air so hot and sticky that you felt like you were moving through liquid, to summers so hot you moved as little as humanly possible, and even then, only to get into air-conditioned air. The temperature flashed away and the time appeared—5.24 P.M. The sun would set in two, maybe three hours, but the sky was already turning a deeper orange; some clouds gave a little shelter, softening the glare. We sat and we let the heat do what it had to; sweat collected underneath our knees, between our legs, on the backs of our necks.

Three more moved to the field, all spirit fingers and toe touches and back handsprings. Thin, tanned and golden: they were smiling and they did not sweat. They looked fresh and impossibly clean and their mascara didn't run and their foundation didn't melt and their hair didn't frizz. We clapped and we cheered and we watched and we waited. The marching band played in the bleachers across from us: brass, drums, Adams High's fight song. We sang along to the parts we knew, we screamed during the parts we didn't. And it always ended the same way:

"ADAMS HAIL TO THEE."

The pep rally would have been indoors, would have taken place in the gym on the basketball court, like always, like we were used to, only a bunch of seniors had vandalized the walls the day after graduation, and they hadn't turned up to do their punishment, to remove their spray paint with paint thinner and methyl chloride: the administration couldn't do a fucking thing now, until the day before the school year began. But Mr. Overton refused to give in, refused to have the janitors paint over it. So, here we were, a week before that, a gym full of expletives or some kind of soft core porno crap or something. Our parents had been told that the whole school was being fumigated for asbestos, but we knew better. We knew the real story. We'd heard it from Taylor Lyon, and she'd told everybody, and eventually, it was something that everybody knew. Or everybody who was anybody.

We watched the girls run to the side of the track, but Taylor Lyon stayed in the center and we watched her cheer. All on her own. The faculty sponsors sat in the front row—Miss Simpson, Mr. Ferris, Coach Cox—and we watched them watch her, watch her as she jumped and clapped and touched her toes and yelled. She yelled so much louder than you could imagine, a deep voice from an almost invisible body:

"Jam with us! You've got to, got to, got to jam with us! Go AHS!"

Taylor had hair that was just a little red—mostly brown, but with fiery glints—and when the sun hit it, the little glints looked supershiny, like something out of a Crayola box. When we were in kindergarten, Mrs. Cornish picked her for everything: to be Snow White in our end-of-year production, to be the line leader, to be the Pilgrim who said grace at Thanksgiving. Mrs. Cornish loved Taylor, and said her red hair was her "crowning glory." And when she said that, or when she picked Taylor for another honor, for another role, Taylor's face would burn deep, a red that looked like it stung her cheeks, like it ran through her whole body. It was strange to watch her now, and we wondered if she thought it was strange too, how much she had changed.

The heat was still unbearable, and we took out bottles of Gatorade and tried to focus on Taylor as she did her back handsprings, as she tumbled across the track. She came back to the center again, gave us spirit fingers and a smile, picked up her pom-poms, and she ran to the side. Her solo was over.

Gemma Davies moved to the center, and a cloud started to drift over the sun, putting half of Gemma into the shade. Gemma's hair was blond, almost peroxide, but we knew it wasn't, that was her natural color, it had been since preschool. We watched as her ponytail rose and fell with each toe touch. Gemma's gymnastics were the best—she could jump higher than any of the others, and she was the captain and probably always would be. Gemma smiled at everybody, or that's what everybody said, and she had been voted "Best Personality" our freshman and sophomore year. Now she was going to be a junior, just like us, and her boyfriend, Andrew Wright, was going to be a senior. You'd think things like this were lame, that only in Hilary Duff movies did crap like this make a difference, but it was weird how much it meant to us, even if we didn't say it out loud.

We'd heard that Gemma's dad was freaked about Andrew at first—Reverend Davies was our preacher—and everybody knew that he used to come with her and Andrew to the movies and to Olive Garden for their Saturday night date. Whether he sat with them, or a few rows or tables back, we weren't sure. We imagined he drove his own car, and that Andrew at least got to be alone with Gemma for the drive, but even that wasn't entirely clear. Gemma's life was a series of rules, this much we knew, and she wasn't some preacher's daughter who went against things, who flouted authority, like Ashlee and Jessica Simpson. Gemma did as she was told, or at least for the most part, and for that and maybe because of how she looked, she was popular. Popular and good.

We thought that Reverend Davies should have been happy about Andrew. He was good too, probably a lot nicer than Gemma. Andrew Wright was tall and thin and gangly and kind. He opened doors for girls and said "yes, ma'am" and "no, sir" and he never laughed during prayers or when somebody dropped their tray in the cafeteria. He had sandy-brown hair and freckles and our mothers used to tell us he was "darling," whatever that meant. He wore khakis and New Balance sneakers and his face was as smooth as a little boy's, he probably didn't even have to shave. He was so tall compared to Gemma we said it was actually gross to watch them kiss, her on her tippy toes, him hunching over. He had a thing for tiny girls, we said later. The tinier, the better. Gemma could have fit in his pocket, he could take her home and nobody would know.

Gemma Davies wasn't allowed to wear a bathing suit—a religious thing—and when we were in fourth grade, and we took a field trip to the water park in Moulton, she had to wear her giant culottes and an old T-shirt in the water. Nobody laughed at her—not that any of us remember—but when we went again a year later, Gemma was sick, and she didn't come at all.

We looked at her uniform now—the top like a corset, the skirt no bigger than a postage stamp. Her navel popped out every time she raised her arms. She was toned and her body was tanned and she must have waxed her legs and everything 'cause when she did her arabesque, everything was all perfect and clean. She was so pretty. So pretty and light.

We were always surprised that Reverend Davies allowed her to cheer. We guessed he didn't mind 'cause there were so many rules for cheerleading in Alabama, so many things they couldn't do, most of them involving the hips and the ass. You could do stuff above the waist, but none of the hip-hop stuff that you'd see in *Bring It On*. But the cheerleaders still danced, they still moved more than you'd think girls who couldn't wear bathing suits would be allowed to. We wondered what the difference was between the uniform and a bathing suit—from where we were sitting we couldn't tell—but there must have been something, 'cause Reverend Davies was there in the bleachers, with Mrs. Davies, near the front, right behind the teachers. Gemma's mother had been a cheerleader at Adams back when she was in school, and Gemma had the old yearbooks to prove it. Mrs. Davies still kinda looked like a cheerleader, we thought, or like a Desperate Housewife, and the guys in our class called her a MILF. We wondered if they really meant it, and even though it was disgusting that guys said shit like that, we were still kinda jealous of Gemma and her mom: you'd see them walking through the mall together any time you were there, bags like accordions, from Banana Republic and Abercrombie and Parisians, and the next day in school Gemma would be wearing something new.

We watched Gemma's miniature frame as she tumbled across the track—she was no more than five foot two. Her makeup sparkled—Benefit or Stila, we guessed—and her eyes were so blue you wanted to dive into them. Her eyes were wide and big, bigger than a Disney character's, and new teachers, teachers who hadn't grown up in Adamsville and didn't know that Mrs. Davies used to be captain of the cheerleading squad and Reverend Davies used to be captain of the football team, they thought that Gemma might be a little bit slow, her eyes seemed so empty. In sixth grade, when a new social studies teacher started, Gemma had been asked who the current president of the United States was and she hadn't answered. At first, Mr. Abbot thought she was being fresh and, as the seconds and minutes passed and she continued to sit still and silent, he thought she might suffer from a form of retardation. He sent Gemma to the principal's office and, later, we found out Mr. Abbot had suggested she be given a basic aptitude and IQ test. She didn't even get to the principal—the secretary, Mrs. Bullen, she knew the Davies and knew this was a misunderstanding. She sent Gemma home sick.

Gemma was the nicest girl in our class, that was what everybody said. But when you thought about it, when you really tried to remember the nice stuff she did, it was kinda hard. Looking back, we wondered if it was because she was so dumb, if that was the reason we let the label stick. Or maybe because she was so pretty, her hair so blond and smooth and her skin so perfect and tanned. Being honest, it was probably just because we said it so many times. Sometimes you will something to be true.

Gemma did her chant and while she clapped and turned and pivoted and jumped, some of the senior guys in the back started shouting.

"*Hot.*"

"I want Davies to have my babies!"

"One more handspring, Gemma!"

"*Hhhhhhooooottttttt!*"

"Take it off!"

We turned and watched the guys throw their arms around, hit one another on the back, cover their mouths as they spoke to muffle the sound. We turned back to watch Reverend Davies—

he didn't move his head. But he lifted his arm around his wife's shoulder and held her next to him. She pushed him off. It was too hot.

Gemma ran to the end of the track and gave Taylor a hug. We watched as Brooke Moore moved to the center, now fully in the shade.

Brooke's eyes were so brown they were nearly black, and she wore white eyeliner that made them pop—we could see that even from where we were sitting, even with her covered in shadow. She had freckles, thousands of them, but she smothered them with liquid foundation. When she started to cheer, you could hear the murmuring start, the speculation from the guys and the girls, and maybe even from some of the parents, the alumni scattered around us.

"Baby got back."

"That's at least ten pounds."

"Fifteen, easy."

"She went on the Pill."

"I think she looks better."

"You're such a liar."

"Y'all be nice."

"Just saying."

"Summer of Twinkies."

"Summer of sex."

"Shut up."

The uniform was two sizes too small, that much was for sure, and we heard later that her mother had bought it as a kind of motivation for her to drop the weight. Brooke was tall, her legs were longer than Gemma's whole body, we guessed, and "when you're five foot eight, and you put on a few pounds, a cheerleading uniform isn't kind," we overheard Miss Simpson saying later. Whatever, we thought.

Her routine was faultless, really. Arms tight and rigid, clapping in straight lines, just below her chin. She did Candlesticks and Raise the Roof and an arabesque, but her size was distracting.

Brooke was still beautiful, this much we knew. She'd even done some modeling for our local department store, Parisians, and a couple of years ago, in the Galleria in Birmingham, she was scouted by an actual agency who wanted her to come to New York for some interviews. Why she didn't go, we weren't sure. Some people said this proved that the scouting never happened, and other people said it wasn't a modeling agency at all, and that she hadn't been scouted, but that she'd gone to Birmingham to audition for "Survivor" or "Big Brother" or "Paris Hilton's BFF" or some other reality show, and that she had gotten a call back, but that they couldn't afford the airline ticket to New York. But that didn't seem likely either, we thought. Brooke Moore wasn't that poor. It was just something people said.

Whatever the truth, Brooke's features were flawless, her skin had never seen a zit, not even a whitehead. She was a Neutrogena ad, we said. She hadn't always been tall—in elementary school, she'd been one of the smallest in the class, and she looked even smaller because her hair was always long, almost down to her waist, and she wore it in braids sometimes, and you could be hypnotized by the cords of brown, some parts glimmering like pennies, other parts smooth like a Hershey bar, weaving in and out of each other and tied with a perfect purple bauble.

Brooke always wanted to have it cut—she begged her mother to let her get a bob, something short she could tuck behind her ears. But her mother refused, insisted that girls were meant to have long hair, that Brooke's prominent chin, her slightly crooked nose, all of this would be exposed with the wrong haircut. "A bob would be unforgiving," she was overheard saying in Winn-Dixie, in church, at the country club, to whomever had just complimented her on her daughter's beautiful hair.

When she was ten, Brooke rode her bike to a hair salon—to

Cutting Edge or Just Cuts or maybe it was even Sam's—her allow-
ance for the past six months stashed in her pocket. She brought a
photograph of Jennifer Aniston's bob and one of Tiffani Thies-
sen's shag. Her mother had arrived before the scissors came out
and the cut had been aborted. Her braids stayed for years.

We watched Brooke now, her hair just shoulder length—a bat-
tle had obviously been won, somewhere in the last five years. And
her chin didn't jut, we didn't think, her nose looked perfect to us,
but we'd heard that Mrs. Moore had been exploring plastic sur-
gery options for Brooke over the summer, had even been to the
bank to see about a loan. Something about a deviated septum. And
we wondered now if liposuction had been added to the list. She
was the fattest of all the cheerleaders, that was obvious. She'd
probably go back to her pseudo-bulimia, we said to each other.
Not enough self-control to be rexy.

The uniform was too tight all over but it looked the worst in
her chest—she was huge, had gotten even bigger over the summer.
We'd heard before that she had to special-order her bras from the
Web, nobody carried a 32 triple F or whatever freaky size she was.
We wondered what she was doing for underwear now. Somebody
behind us said, "Her boobs are like something out of *National Geo-
graphic*," and we laughed a little, because we knew what they meant.
When we were twelve or thirteen, when everybody was just getting training bras, Brooke was already stocked in Victoria's Secret and she'd come into school wearing a white shirt with a red
bra you could see underneath.

Brooke finished her chant and people yelled and clapped and
called her name—fat or not, she was still popular, people loved her.
We looked around and we could see Mrs. Moore—not sitting in
the bleachers, but standing on the side of the parking lot, a cigarette in her left hand, a Diet Coke in her right, platinum hair
catching the sun, and even from a distance you could see it was
perfectly set. She wore huge sunglasses that obscured half her

face—we couldn't tell if she was even looking at the field. She didn't clap. Her hands were full.

We shifted on the bleachers. Wiped the sweat from the backs of our necks, let out breath that lifted our bangs from our faces. We tried to cool down however we could.

We looked out at the field in front of us. We sat in front of the fifty-yard line, straight down the middle, and we said we had never seen the field looking so green, so polished, the white lines sharper than anything in HD. In the center, the letters "AHS" and a bear, our mascot, our hero. We looked across the field, to the other set of bleachers, to the band playing away, in a sea of black and orange. And then, beyond the bleachers, you could see a couple of telephone poles, the parking lot, half a dozen pine trees. And empty pink sky. It looked like our football field had been dropped in the middle of a wasteland, that's how little you could see beyond it, the bleachers, the parking lot.

Lauren Brink turned to us. "I may actually die from this heat. This might actually be how I, like, go."

We laughed and Nicole pulled her T-shirt up to her face, wiping the sweat. "I am literally sweating buckets. Literally."

Lauren rolled her eyes. "Really? Like literally, literally?" Nicole's lip might have trembled, we couldn't tell.

Jessica Grady put her hand on Nicole's arm. "Brooke in training," she whispered. And Nicole laughed, even though we thought this might be true and that probably wasn't something to laugh about. Another Brooke.

We looked over at Brooke's mother, smoking another cigarette, drinking yet another Diet Coke. "I don't even think that woman has sweat glands," Lauren said. "Or tear ducts." We smiled, and wondered what it would be like to have Mrs. Moore as your mother, your actual mother—not your leader in Girl Scouts or your parent rep at a youth group field trip. Your actual mother. We imagined we wouldn't like it. At all.

The only thing that Mrs. Moore liked about Brooke, from what we could see—and from what she told our mothers at PTA meetings or in the Winn-Dixie—was Shane Duggan. Shane was popular, beautiful, a good student—not smart, but not dumb—his dad a former quarterback, a star, had molded Shane into his image. And Shane had been into Brooke for years before she agreed to go out with him. That's what we heard, or that's what people said. He was going to be a senior, and over summer vacation, Shane and Brooke had been seen at the movies together—at *Salt, Iron Man 2, Prince of Persia*—and they'd been seen at Wendy's, sitting in the same side of the booth, sharing a Frosty or something like that. And Shane had been seen picking up Brooke from the country club, where she lifeguarded.

Nobody could say for sure that they were a couple—they never went to parties together—but people were pretty sure they were having sex, and that was why she'd gone on the Pill, and that was why she'd piled on the weight. Brooke and Gemma had taken the virginity pledge at church the previous year, wore rings on their wedding fingers just to prove it, but once she started hanging out with Shane, everybody was sure that was over. When we were freshmen, a thing had gone around on text about Brooke being a prick tease, and some people said that Shane was only into her to get her to give it up. Whatever, we thought. Pledge or no pledge, Shane Duggan was hot.

We watched as the eight girls performed together, the varsity cheerleading squad: we had watched them, along with twenty others, the last week of our sophomore year, and we had voted, voted for the most talented, yes, but also for the prettiest, for the most popular, for the ones that we knew the very best. And now here they were, representing the best of us, who we wished we could be.

We clapped and we yelled and the band played the fight song

again and the football team took to the field, behind the cheer-leaders. We watched Coach Cox come to the center, with his orange hair, orange cap, ears so big we could see light shining through them. What a dork.

"We have a real exciting year ahead of us, y'all." The microphone squealed, we covered our ears, the senior guys booed, the parents grimaced. Coach Cox stepped back and waited and leaned forward again, speaking more softly now. "We've got here a real talented bunch of boys, boys I believe in, boys that I've known since they were in diapers, boys I saw the first day they threw a football, the first day they caught one too." He paused, looked down at his hands—he wrote on his body always, had done this for years, and tonight it looked like he'd written stuff all the way up his forearms, probably reaching up to his shoulders. "I'd like to thank these boys for their dedication this summer. They've played through some mighty hot weather and they haven't complained. But they need your support over the next few months to keep them strong, to keep them focused. I'd ask all y'all to come to all the games—home and away—and cheer on a team I think can go unbeaten. We only lost two games last year—and I know—I *know*—we can do it. If we trust in ourselves, if we trust in the Lord, if we stay focused, stay strong. Praise the Lord."

Coach Cox stepped back. We clapped, the band beat the drums, and we watched as Reverend Davies came to the microphone.

He put his hand up and we got quiet. An ambulance siren could be heard a few streets away, the sound of cars just barely audible. "Let us pray."

And then it began. The prayer, the prayer for the year. In Adamsville, we didn't pray that we'd graduate, that we'd get along, that we'd get good jobs or get into Ivy League schools. We didn't pray that some of us would manage to get out of here, that some of us might have a life outside of this town. We prayed for our foot-

ball team, that they'd go undefeated, that we would get to State.
That we would win.

We were meant to keep our heads bowed as we prayed. And we
did, mostly, only it was so hot and the prayer was so long, we
couldn't help but look around, and something drew our eyes to
the parking lot, just to the left of the field. We could see somebody emerge from a red car—a Honda?—and begin to walk toward
the bleachers. As Reverend Davies spoke, we watched this figure,
this girl, move closer and closer to us. Even from a distance, we
knew we had never seen her before.

The prayer finished and people clapped again. The sun was beginning to set. The air was five degrees cooler, maybe more. We
picked up our towels, and we headed down to the field—we would
say hello to Taylor, if she saw us, and then we would hang around
to see where people were going.

We searched the crowd for that girl—it should be easy to notice something new, we thought, when everything in our town was
always the same—but we couldn't see her. We thought she had disappeared. And then, as we got closer to the field, as we filed down
the bleachers, we saw her again: tiny, beautiful. She had brown
hair, long and shiny and curled just at the ends. She was wearing
jeans—how could she stand the heat?—and a white tank top that
was so white it nearly blinded you. Perfect.

It's important to remember how weird this was—a new girl
coming to our town—how unused to it we all were. And not just
us—our parents, the teachers, the coaches—them too. Adamsville
wasn't a place that people came to. It was a place you were from,
where you were born, where you were raised, where you stayed.
And in spite of this, or because of this, everybody tried really hard
to make things work with Carolyn, with her mom, and that's
something that nobody seems to remember or realize or know.
We wanted to make things work and we wanted to know her. But

it's a two-way street, you know. It wasn't just up to us. We couldn't be the only ones responsible, the only ones to blame.

The girl looked uncertain, unsteady, staring at her feet, and then she took out a phone and started to type, real fast, like we would. And then Reverend Davies yelled, "Lynn." She looked up and then she was steady. He walked over to her and she walked toward him and he called out again and this time we heard it right: "Carolyn." He put his arm around her, and led her down the track.

We stood still and didn't talk and we watched her walk, her hair swishing back and forth, her hands in her back pockets. Reverend Davies got a little bit ahead of her—they were dodging the band—and she stumbled a little, on what we didn't know. She disappeared behind Michael Morrison and his tuba and then she reappeared, flip-flop in one of her hands, putting it back onto her foot. Even from where we were, we knew that everything about her was perfect, manicured, groomed. The reverend looked back and gestured to her again—and he pointed her toward the girls' locker room. He waited outside. She walked toward the door, running into Ken Phillips, the school's janitor—we called him Janitor Ken—on her way in. His mop, his broom, his pail of soapy water: we watched all of it tip over to one side as this tiny girl disappeared through the large double doors.

We'd think about this moment later: the first time we saw her, her flip-flop in one hand, her silky smooth hair, her perfectly small body. Later, when they showed the pictures of her on TV, we thought she looked older, and not in a good way. And her eyes: we especially noticed her eyes. They looked tired. Tired and sad and bored and fed up. And tired.

But all of that was later, after everything had been said and done. That day, the day on the football field, along the track, we saw Carolyn Lessing for the first time, with a flip-flop in one hand, nervous but smiling. We saw her the way she really was: perfect.

2

After the band had cleared off, after the football players and the cheerleaders had gone into the locker rooms, we were still standing around in the bleachers, trying to decide where to go.

"There's a party at Morris's."

"Nah, that was last night."

"Where are people going?"

"It's so fucking hot."

"I wanna go swimming."

"I wanna go eat."

"Let's leave."

"Let's go."

"Where are we going?"

And round and round and round it went, the same conversation as always, the same indecision, nobody to tell us what to do. Looking back, we can see that we cared so much, that we were so conscious of how we were standing, who we were next to, how our hair looked in the light, after the humidity, the sweat. The trick was always to look like you didn't care, didn't give a shit. To hide yourself away and present somebody else, somebody who was as similar to everybody else without looking like a clone, like a wannabe stalker. It was hard.

We got into our cars. Lauren had driven us, had just gotten her license, couldn't stop talking about it, and we followed a couple of the guys—Blake Wyatt and Dylan Hall—and we drove to the Hardee's parking lot. There were a few cars there when we arrived: other juniors, a couple of seniors. None of the football players was there yet, none of the cheerleaders. We hoped we were in the right place.

The heat from the day was still trapped in the parking lot, in the asphalt, but the air was bearable, now that the sky was turning black. We stood outside Lauren's car, and then walked over to Dylan's, and then walked back to Lauren's, pretending we had to get something out of the trunk. We used it as a chance to reapply our base. Humidity sucked.

We went in and ordered—milk shakes and Diet Cokes and cheese fries and crispy curls. We got it to go, so we could sit in the back of Dylan's truck, watching whoever came in, trying to look busy.

Coach Cox and some parents with their elementary school kids passed us by, and we hid our Marlboro Golds and smiled and waved and made small talk about our parents. "Y'all kids be good," Coach Cox said, and the parents said something like that, and we yelled back, " 'Course we will," and waited till they got out of sight before we passed around a bottle of Absolut.

We wondered if the new girl would come, whether Reverend Davies had forced Gemma to bring her along. We asked the guys if they thought she was hot, and they said they thought she should be a model. This made us flinch, just a little, but we also thought it was true. Even though she was too short, we said, she could still be a model. But just for catalogs. For catalogs, height just didn't matter—or at least that's what Tyra Banks said.

Tiffany Port pulled into the parking lot in her mother's Suburban, and we looked in the windows and saw Taylor in the passenger seat, like a Skipper doll in the Dream Bus.

"Look who's gracing us with her presence." Lauren let out a puff of smoke. She passed the cigarette to Jessica.

"Do you think they're, like, lesbians together or something?" Jessica wasn't looking at the car, just looking at us, half smiling, half scowling.

"Definitely," Nicole said and we laughed, only we weren't really sure if it was that funny.

Taylor's face was illuminated by her phone, and she was talking and laughing and Tiffany rolled her window down as they approached the drive-thru, her long, blond hair flying out the window. Even from where we were standing, we knew it was perfectly straight, impossibly smooth, like Tiffany's hair had always been. Blake reached into the front seat of his car and honked his horn, but they ignored him: they were bitches that way.

When we were little, we were friends with Taylor. Tiffany, too. We went to one another's birthday parties and we made up stories and we organized yard sales and we designed elaborate imaginary games and we jumped on giant trampolines and we stayed outside playing cartoon tag until it was pitch dark and we laughed until our sides hurt, until we were afraid we might actually explode. And then our parents would call to us and call to us, and after we'd ignored them for forever, they'd haul us indoors, threatening to ground us as we walked in.

Taylor Lyon liked the Beatles. She liked Monty Python and could do all the accents. She was funny, and she had the best sleepovers of anybody because her mother was divorced and drank red wine at three in the afternoon and didn't really care what we did. We watched R-rated movies and called 1-900 numbers and we ate Breyer's ice cream straight out of the tub. We loved being with Taylor and she loved being with us, or at least this is what we remember.

Tiffany was quieter, her voice like a whisper, but she had followed us around, and we remembered spending afternoons at her parents' gas station—they owned three in Adamsville—and, if we were good, Mr. Port would let us check somebody out, scan their cereal boxes and cigarettes. Tiffany was allowed to pump gas sometimes, and if her parents weren't looking, she'd let us do that too. We never went to Tiffany's house, not that we could remember, but we didn't care, so long as we could hang out at the gas station, as long as we could all play together, play like grown-ups.

Things changed in middle school. Not gradually, like we might have thought, or like our mothers said, but all of a sudden, as soon as we walked into Fairview Middle. All of a sudden things mattered: who had shaved their legs, who had pierced their ears, who had gotten a bra, how our thighs looked in a bathing suit, in skinny jeans. It mattered where you'd been on Friday night, and who you'd talked to at the mall, who you ate lunch with, who you'd texted over the weekend, whose numbers were in your phone, what was on your Myspace.

Taylor got the first period. She got it at the Adamsville Country Club the summer between sixth and seventh grades, when we were at the pool. It was in July—just after the Fourth, 'cause the American flags were still dotting the sides of the deep end. We had been playing Marco Polo and when Taylor jumped out—"Fish Out of Water"—we saw a pink stain forming around her crotch, rising up her yellow Speedo, threatening to wrap around her butt. Taylor didn't notice, not at first.

"Oh my God, what is *that*?"

"Keep your eyes closed!"

"We're playing Marco Polo! Stop cheating!"

"Taylor, you got Kool-Aid on your bathing suit."

"That is so not Kool-Aid."

And Taylor looked down and we all looked as she looked, swimming in closer to the side of the pool, hoisting ourselves up to inspect her bathing suit, the stain, the blob, whatever it was. Taylor's face flushed, and her chest went red too, and she turned toward the locker room. She had only started when the lifeguard blew his whistle and yelled, "No running." And she blushed again and slowed herself down and walked into the locker room and we watched her take every step. We said it took her five minutes to walk five feet. Tiffany followed her, a few moments later, like Taylor's shadow, that's what Tiffany was. We gave up the game after that, and tread water in the deep end for an hour, waiting on Taylor to come out, until we finally decided to go. We dried ourselves off and took our bikes home. Jessica Grady says she remembers leaving a note for Taylor, but Lauren Brink says we decided not to. Who knows and who cares, it was so long ago. In any case, Taylor stopped coming to the country club after that. She quit swim team too. And it was then that she got really into cheerleading. Her and Tiffany, together.

Taylor's hair calmed down that summer, but we didn't notice that until we saw her on the first day of seventh grade: she had grown it long and it hung straight and her freckles had softened too. And the baby fat that filled her cheeks, that made even her elbows a little pudgy, that pushed over the sides of her monokini, that had melted away and suddenly Taylor was thin. Suddenly Taylor was pretty. She was wearing makeup and it wasn't Revlon or Maybelline or some other crap from Walgreens or CVS or Winn-Dixie. It was department store stuff: Nicole Willis had seen her in the mall at the Clinique counter with her mother the week before school started and she assumed they were buying stuff for her mom, but then Taylor got into the chair at the side of the counter, next to the Skin System charts, next to the Clinique Bonus Time display, and the woman in her white medical coat started to wipe down Taylor's face with cotton balls. Nicole said hey, but Taylor must not have heard her, because she didn't say anything back. Mrs. Lyon smiled, and Nicole pretended as if she hadn't seen them either.

Taylor started seventh grade as a new person. Gemma Davies, Brooke Moore—all of a sudden they were interested in her. And then Taylor hardly spoke to us at all. She brought Tiffany with her, or Tiffany followed her, we weren't sure. Maybe 'cause Tiffany got boobs before us, or maybe 'cause she knew when not to talk; maybe because of all that Tiffany was cool enough to be part of Taylor's new life. Or the coolest of all of us. Whatever that meant. We watched them now and we wondered if they remembered these things and we guessed they probably didn't. It was so long ago. And they looked so different.

We watched Tiffany as she called her order into the loud-speaker—we wondered if they could even hear her inside, with her mouse-quiet voice, her inaudible whisper. We wondered if Tiffany still worked at the gas station—we hadn't seen her there in years—wondered if she still liked to wash people's windshields, if she still liked to count the money in the register. Probably not. Plus, only one of the gas stations was open now. Business was hard, our parents said.

They waited a few beats and then the Suburban moved forward, turned around the corner. They were out of our view, collecting their food, probably going someplace cool, someplace with seniors, someplace we knew nothing about.

We texted other juniors to see where everybody was, and people said they were on their way, or just hanging out, or had driven by and thought that nobody was there so they had already gone home. At 7:25—we heard the DJ from Blake's car radio—Blake's mother called him and he said he had to go home for dinner. Dylan followed Blake. And then we decided we should go too. Nothing was happening, same as ever. But maybe next time.

Over dinner, all our parents asked us about the pep rally, Coach Cox's prayer, the cheerleaders' routine, the football team's lineup, the band's new sequence of songs. When we said grace, we prayed for the team, and we knew that this happened all across our town, at dinner tables up and down Adamsville. Our parents had gone to Adams too, and they knew how important all of this was. Made sure we remembered it too.

That night, after we'd cleaned our plates and hugged our parents and kissed our younger brothers and sisters before bed, we started texting. Lauren Brink texted Blake, who texted Dylan, who texted somebody and found out that the new girl's last name was Lessing. First name Carolyn.

We all got on Facebook, messaging back and forth, posting pictures from the day—trying to tag as many people as we could in the bleachers. We found Carolyn eventually, and a lot of her page was public—not her wall, but her friends and her profile and her pictures, they were all there for us to see. Either she didn't understand privacy settings or she was some kind of exhibitionist freak. Whatever the case, we could see a lot this way. And we could figure out more.

She had 1,075 friends and 409 pictures in nine different albums. Some of them, like "Boredom is a sin," just had pictures of her body: her arms and legs, nothing sexual, just limbs. But she'd taken the pictures at funny angles and put on henna tattoos, or something like that, so they looked kinda cool.

There were pictures of her with guys—"Leaving party 2010"— and we looked at these for a long time, and we sent them back and forth to each other as jpegs to make sure we were texting about the same thing. A tanned girl with four guys—two on either side—her wearing shorts and a tank top—the same white one we saw during the day?—and the guys like Abercrombie models. Shirts off, shorts low, bodies like we were only used to seeing on those soft porn shopping bags. The guys looked older, like maybe even in college, and Carolyn looked cool and relaxed and we said you could tell that they were really friends, that the guys really liked her, just from the way they were standing. There were dozens like these. Carolyn and guys, all different and all the same: her pretty and smiling, standing next to or sitting on top of or leaning against guys who were hot. There was only one other girl in that whole album—number twenty-two of thirty-one—and the girl was a foot taller than Carolyn, at least, with hair that was blond and short and choppy—and she was pretty too. And underneath, a caption: "Me and my bestie!" and the girl was tagged: "Kourtni Kessler." We tried to find her, but her profile was blocked. Not even a picture. Weird, we said. Weird and annoying.

Carolyn's music likes: Vampire Weekend, Chemical Brothers, The Strokes, The Donnas, Vivian Girls, REM, Beastie Boys, Slumber Party. She was cool, we said. Some of those we hadn't even heard of, so we Googled them and found the stuff on iTunes and we downloaded and listened to what we could.

Her page listed her school—St. Bernard's—and the name of her town—Haddington—so we Googled them to find out more. Her school had an actual entry on Urban Dictionary. We couldn't believe it:

2,600 New Jersey kids fill the hallways of this elite New Jersey high school each day. If you haven't heard of us already, first thing you need to know is: we're awesome (25 percent brains, 25 percent class, 25 percent looks, and 25 percent beast,

which equals 100 percent awesome). Who are
we: mostly we're upper class, white (except for
the diplomats' kids, you know?), and we either
commute from plush brownstones in Manhattan or
we live in upscale towns like Haddington or Royston.
Girls roll into school at 8 am wearing North Face,
Uggs, Burberry scarf, carrying their Venti Skinny
Starbucks. Vineyard Vines and Sperrys are the
bomb, Lily Pulitzer scouts for models on campus.
We get into the best colleges and make a shitload
of money when we get out (unless we decide to
mooch off Mommy and Daddy).

We stayed on Carolyn's profile for at least thirty minutes: we
liked the way she looked and we liked the way she stood and we
liked the things she wrote in her profile. We wondered who she'd
want to hang out with, who she'd sit with at lunch, whether she
was as smart as her page made her look (she liked J.D. Salinger,
Jonathan Franzen, Virginia Woolf—people our parents read, or
who were on the AP reading list).

She didn't have a relationship status—this bugged us a lot—and
we thought it meant that she was single, and then we thought it
meant she had a boyfriend. The most important piece of information, we thought. And we couldn't uncover it, no matter how
many tabs we opened.

Carolyn Lessing had 1,075 friends. We would have gone through
them all, to figure out how many were guys, how many were rel-
atives, how many were old people who were friends of her parents. But we didn't have time that night. Our parents set timers
on Internet Explorer, so we got cut off before we were done, always. We thought about asking Reverend Davies for the new girl's
phone number or something—maybe we should ask her to go to
the mall?—but we didn't, not in the end. We didn't want to look

too needy or like lesbians and, plus, we didn't really know what we'd say to her.

Her location was still down as New Jersey and we watched the page for the next few days, the days before school started, and as soon as the location changed—from Jersey to Alabama—we texted each other. She'd made it official. She was one of us.

Adamsville Daily News—Weekend Edition

Thousands flock to Adamsville for Annual Balloon Festival

AUGUST 7, 2010

Hot air balloons took to the sky early on Saturday morning in the annual Sky Sprint, which marks the beginning of the Annual 3M Adamsville Balloon Festival in Harper's Memorial Field.

Jeffrey Grady, president of the annual festival, said the race, which involved 72 hot air balloons, began as the sun rose on Saturday morning, at around 6 a.m. Conditions were described as "near enough perfect" and the winning balloon, from the festival sponsor 3M, narrowly won the race, beating off competition from Texaco and Stewart's Coffee Shop. The prize is a trophy in the shape of a hot air balloon, along with $1,000 to the charity of choice. 3M announced that the prize money would be donated to Ronald McDonald House. Reverend Jim Davies, who has observed the race since it began 30 years ago, noted that the wind "seemed to make the journey somewhat smoother." Reverend Davies has been attending the festival since he was a boy and noted that it continues to fill him with a "deep sense of wonder and awe."

It is estimated that close to 40,000 people will attend the festival over the weekend, which will culminate in the annual balloon light show on Sunday evening. "It's been very successful and Adamsville needs it," said Grady, who noted last year's event was affected by the inclement weather. "It's a community thing where we give back to the community and say thanks."

When asked about how the festival was planning on dealing with disorderly conduct or the use of illegal substances, he noted that the local police would have a strong presence in the park but that he was also relying on members of the community to "be vigilant and report any inappropriate conduct."

Last year's festival was marred by the fact that several local high school students were hospitalized due to alcohol poisoning.

Although alcohol cannot be purchased on the premises, it is common for festival attendees to bring coolers with beverages, both alcoholic and nonalcoholic, to enjoy at the event. Grady noted that the festival had always encouraged "families to bring a picnic lunch or dinner with them" but that alcohol must be "consumed responsibly," particularly since so many young people attend the event.

Reverend Davies, whose daughter Gemma was one of the six young people to be hospitalized at the 2009 event, further underlined this point, advising his congregation to abstain from alcohol altogether during the festival weekend.

Grady was insistent that alcohol does not form a central part of the event. "We have a strong lineup of entertainment, in addition to the obvious draw of the hot air balloons." Local bluegrass band the New South will play, as will country singers Avery Avis and Donald Dillard. The Azalea Avenue Church of Christ Gospel Choir will perform and local artists will be displaying their work in various tents across the field. A farmers' market has been established this year, in an attempt to highlight the incredible locally grown produce available to Adamsville residents. "What we tried to do this year is have great entertainment and atmosphere," said Grady, "and we continually try to grow that every year. The festival is an important part of our local economy and, given the stress that everybody has been under over the past few years, we'd encourage as many people as possible to attend."

3

The last weekend of summer vacation, the balloons filled Harper's Field—we watched them arrive, coming in on the back of trucks along the Stripline—deflated silk in red and purple and orange and blue, silk that looked so thin you could tear it with a fingernail, the grit from the ground could rip it into shreds. Those who were afraid of heights would point to this—the casual way the balloons were brought into town—and explain they wouldn't get into one of those death traps if they were paid to. The same went for the rides—the Circle of Destiny (called The Circle of Hell in towns up North, but not around here), the Chamber of Mirrors, the Twirling Coffee Cups—all variations on better rides we'd seen at Six Flags or at Disney World, but shipped into town and put together on a weekend in late August for the balloon festival.

   Our parents said it was the oldest hot air balloon festival in the world and when we were little, we would beg and beg and beg to get there before 6 A.M., to see the race, to get the first balloon ride, and stay until the field closed at midnight. We waited all year for the funnel cakes and the corn dogs and the skee ball and the spot prizes and the picnics. And the balloons. Of course, the balloons.

When we turned thirteen, we begged to go alone, to arrive later, to get rides with our friends, for our parents to stay on the opposite side of the field so we could walk around the grounds and sneak Southern Comfort into our iced tea and snow cones. We would gather behind the balloons and share joints and then run to buy cotton candy in buckets and then feed each other, laughing, smiling.

That year, when we were sixteen, we got there around ten. The field was so hot you would want to wear your bathing suit but you couldn't, so we wore sundresses and flip-flops and tied our hair up so it didn't stick to our necks. By eleven, you tried to stay in the shade—the tans that we had were already extreme from the three months at the country club and the river, and to go any darker wouldn't be good—too dark a tan was redneck.

The field was divided into three parts—the rides to your left, the food to your right and the balloons straight in front of you, rising up into the air like notes on a piece of sheet music, all uneven and up and down. They were every color you could imagine and we picked out our favorites—the ones that had no advertising on them, mostly—deep purples and fluorescent orange and ones with seventies-style rainbows. Some said ADAMSVILLE in huge letters, some had the names of people on them—ROSA, PENELOPE, TERRY—the way you would name a boat. From far away, they looked light and gentle and sometimes we forgot how amazing this all was—these hot air balloons that came to our town—but when you watched them all in the air, you had to admit it was kinda cool, even if you'd seen it before.

Jessica Grady's dad had the 3M balloon and Jessica invited us to come with her for a ride, just after ten thirty. This was good—we were already hot and tired and cranky and the wind was still calm—and Jessica's dad waved us over. "Hurry up, y'all. I gotta long list of folks who are due to get their turn." Up close, the noise of the fire and the hot air and hammers nailing the ropes to the ground—all of this was louder than we remembered. The gas made a screeching sound and we screamed and covered our ears and Mr. Grady rolled his eyes and told us to hold on to the edge—he would go up with us, we'd get fifteen minutes. He released the ropes and the balloon started to lift, faster than we thought possible, and Mr. Grady leapt from the ground and into the balloon, closing the straw door behind him.

We passed balloon after balloon after balloon as we rose up—some were going up, some were coming down, some were moving to the side—and we checked to see who was inside those, if there was somebody our age, somebody we knew, but eventually, we got so high, and the balloons got so far apart, you couldn't make anybody out. So we looked down.

You'd think it'd be like being on an airplane—that the ground would look like it did when you were taking off and landing for vacation—and it was, just a little bit. But it was different too. We could see things more clearly: people looked all Fisher-Price, cars were from "Thunderbirds." And all of a sudden, the town was in squares and rectangles and straight lines. From where we looked, from however many feet above the ground, we looked at our town as a series of shapes, like an exercise in geometry. Plots and plots of land, subdivision after subdivision, roads that were straight and long. The pieces of road that curved and twisted, even they looked orderly—some of them like parabolas, a rounded line that could be made only with a compass, other ones like those up-and-down lines you'd see on the life support machines on "Grey's Anatomy." The ground was brown and red and just a little green, and on the edge of the town, past the Old Courthouse, past the Stripline and the country club and Fifth Avenue, past that, you could see the river—the Tennessee River—and it wasn't straight at all, not like we had expected. It curved and jutted and it went all over the place—a disruption to all the squares and lines. And it wasn't blue, not like water should be. It was dark gray, with strokes of white: "That's the river moving," Mr. Grady told us, "that's what the white comes from." It was funny to us then—and confusing too—that the white spots stayed completely still.

We didn't look at one another—we looked up and down and around—and we held on to the sides of the basket, our bodies light like paper when we were up there; you could be blown away. We couldn't talk—the sound of the wind was too much—and once we reached a certain height, after the people below us became un-recognizable, and after it was impossible to tell what was a per-son and what was a building, after that we held our breath, not wanting to add any weight or bring us closer to the ground: we wanted to be up high forever. When the ground below us was still and we felt like we might fly through a cloud, Mr. Grady lifted up the blankets that were at our feet and he wrapped one around us. We huddled together and we linked arms: we were smiling, laughing.

As we started to come down, people were clearer—first just col-ors, everything blue or red or yellow or green—and then we could pick apart male and female, kids and adults. We approached the ground slowly, but we picked up the detail quick—there was Dylan Hall and there was Miss Simpson and there was Reverend Davies. We saw Tiffany Port and Taylor Lyon and somebody else, some other girl—and then we saw Shane Duggan, standing close to her. We scanned the ground for Brooke—and nobody could see her, find her—and we looked back to where the girl had been stand-ing, near the funnel cake cart, and she was gone, just Tiff and Tay-lor, standing alone, mopping up grease from a funnel cake and then picking it apart with their fingers. We didn't know who we'd seen.

"I bet it was the new girl."

"Standing with Shane?"

"No way."

"How would he even *know* her?"

And we scanned the crowd again, everything confusing and big and distorted as we made our way down. And then Jessica saw Shane again, all broad and muscular, walking toward the trees, and he was with the new girl, we were pretty sure, and he was holding her hand, pulling her away. Tiffany and Taylor disappeared, just like that, and then we thought we saw Andrew Wright sucking on Gemma Davies's face, but we couldn't be sure it was him, not at first. Andrew had changed so much in the past year.

"If it's Andrew Wright, he looks weird." Lauren yelled to be heard, the wind was so loud.

"It looks like he's wearing makeup." Jessica gestured to her eyes. "Like they're all black and blue?"

"It's Andrew Wright, I know it," Nicole said. And we believed her. Her vision was, like, crazy good. "He looks hot."

"Vomit." Lauren pretended to retch. "Too skinny. Like Dan from *Gossip Girl* skinny. And tall. Like freakishly tall." And we laughed, even though we were pretty sure we shouldn't, even though we knew Andrew was actually kind of hot; people said so.

Andrew Wright was Shane's best friend. We guessed it was because their mothers were friends, and 'cause they lived next door to each other. We heard that when they were in kindergarten, Andrew cried during naptime, as soon as Mrs. Cornish turned out the lights. In music class, he covered his ears when Mr. Olsen clashed the cymbals. His hair was dirty blond and silky. He grew his hair out really long when we were in middle school, and people told him he'd be a pretty girl. He would have been. He was an athlete, like Shane, but never quite as good, always the tight end, never the quarterback. Still, he hung out with Shane and so it didn't really matter what he did. It made him popular.

His mother had cancer or something the year before, and we found that out during the first week of our sophomore year—he was a junior—and she died only a couple of months before school ended. Lauren Brink and her mother ran into him in Winn-Dixie over the summer, after his mom died. He was standing in the soft drink aisle, loading a cart with three-liter bottles of Coke and Dr Pepper and Mountain Dew. Lauren told us her mother had mortified her, asking him what he was doing. Lauren told us they came back to the same aisle twenty minutes later and he was still there. Standing in front of the soda, like some kind of zombie.

We tried to look at him now, and we remembered what we had heard people say at the pep rally—how it was a "tragedy" and he was "very brave" and that his father was "not coping well." We wondered what he was thinking as he stood in the field making out with Gemma Davies, the preacher's daughter, whether he knew what everybody was saying about him. We wondered if he cared that Gemma had made out with Jason Nelson over the summer, or if he knew what Shane Duggan was doing with the new girl or if he knew that Taylor and Tiffany had told people over the summer that he "should get over himself." We wondered if he'd say hi to us if we ran into him and where he and Shane would be sitting for the light show and whether we could sit near them. We wondered how long anybody could kiss for—he and Gemma were setting a record.

We landed. The field was busier than before and the New South band played in the gazebo at the center, the Azalea Avenue Church of Christ Gospel Choir waiting in the wings. They started a square dance and the senior citizens' dance club stepped into place, perfectly timed. We stood back, watching, laughing, waiting. The caller called us and the guys pulled us up—we did the dances we'd known since kindergarten, do-si-do and four-ladies chain—and we were laughing and the blue-haired ladies smiled back at us.

We hung out. We drank. We ate. We waited around and walked

around and we filled up a day moving around the field until the light started to fade, the techno pounding from the Chamber of Mirrors subsided, the Twirling Coffee Cups and the Circle of Destiny closed, the DJ by the dunking machine dismantled his decks. The New South came back to the gazebo and the fiddle and the banjo and the harmonica made people lower their voices, made them start to take their places on the field, with their blankets and their plastic chairs and their six-packs of Bud and liters of Mountain Dew. The field was on an incline, like a natural amphitheater, and we could hear the music, and our parents hummed along.

We stood on the edge, behind the parents and all the kids—versions of ourselves years from now and from years ago—and we watched the balloons. A football field away from us, they began to collapse as the air was released from them. They were hard and big and strong and then gradually limper and limper. From where we were standing, they made no sound and we thought it was incredible, watching these big things lose their power, lose their weight. It was cool, though we would never say this out loud.

We saw them: Andrew Wright and Brooke Moore and Gemma Davies. Andrew looked even taller from far away, and he had his bony fingers laced through Gemma's. Gemma, all blond and petite, looked up at Andrew, and then up at Brooke, in platform sandals that made her legs look like they went on for miles. They started to walk closer to the balloons, to the area where we weren't supposed to go. We stood away from them, but even from way back, we could see Brooke's face was red and blotchy. Gemma moved away from Andrew, put her arm around Brooke's waist. Andrew stood back, took out a cigarette. We didn't even know he smoked.

Gemma Davies was always consoling Brooke Moore, from what we could tell—and that was funny, 'cause Brooke had always been the one who got everything, Gemma always second runner-up, except for "Best Personality" and who cared about that anyway.

Even when Gemma had come in second place in the Miss Teen Tennessee Valley Authority Beauty Pageant, when she'd been beaten by Tiffany Port, who didn't even have a talent, even then Gemma was comforting Brooke. They'd been at the after-party at Shane's and Shane had ignored Brooke the whole night—he'd done a keg stand and then made out with Tiffany "as a joke"—and Brooke just stayed the whole night, watching it unfold, until Andrew Wright found Brooke sprawled out on the tiles in the Duggans' master bathroom, puke around the toilet seat, a little on her chin, down her shirt. Andrew got Gemma and she pulled back Brooke's hair and let her throw up some more, and then she took the bottle of vodka from Brooke's purse, along with her car keys. Andrew helped lift her up and they loaded her into Andrew's mom's Ford Escort. Brooke had been yelling the whole way out—it was kind of sad, and would have been really sad, if she hadn't made such a scene at church two weeks earlier, going on about the evils of alcohol, the weakness of those who partook. Until that night, Brooke had never had a drink—not even a sip of crappy champagne at New Year's or a glass of red wine when her parents weren't looking—and we never saw her take a drink after that night either. Pure and perfect. That was Brooke, so everybody said.

The day of the balloon festival, Brooke looked tired. Lauren said it was 'cause she was freaking out about Shane but Jessica said that that was crazy. He was the one who was obsessed with *her*. We wondered if that's just what she wanted us to think: maybe he wasn't really that into her. Or maybe he was pissed that she'd gotten all fat, or that she had worn the same outfit after the pep rally that she'd worn to the festival. We didn't know. But we knew that they weren't together. That she was alone.

We stayed and watched her for a little while, until the light show began. The balloons, which had been deflated just an hour or two ago, were inflated again, but they stayed on the ground. In the darkness, it was hard to tell which one was which, which was the blue one and which was the red and which was the rainbow and which was the silver. Once the light show started, everything would be clear.

The music came first—some instrumental song we were meant to know, but didn't—and then the first flash of fire from one of the balloons. The sound of the gas, the fire and then the color and then out again and then to the next balloon and then to the next and we moved our eyes with each of them and then there were two lit together, then three, then four. Like punches, explosions of yellow and pink and red and orange and gold. We had never known a show better than this—there'd been an article in the paper last year saying balloon light shows were a thing of the past. But we didn't think so, there was no way this could be forgotten, no way it could become extinct. We watched the fire pop and fade in each balloon and, as the show went on, the fires stayed on longer, the colors from the balloons got more intense. The music sped up and then each balloon was keeping time and then more and more, like they were on top of one another, like the balloons controlled the music, not the other way around. People, even us, let out "oooh"s and "aaah"s and sometimes somebody would shriek or scream or laugh. We watched the color—and we watched the smoke linger in the air after each fire was extinguished. We held one another's hands when we thought the sound was too close, afraid the fire might burn us. And we watched the balloons so closely that we didn't notice right away that Brooke and Gemma had left—and that Andrew was sitting on his own. We wondered how long he had been there, if he wanted us to join him, and we stared at him for a while, talking about him, his mother, his "depression."

And then Shane and Carolyn walked right in front of us—blocking our view for a second—and sat down next to Andrew on the grass. Even from behind him, we could see Andrew's shoulders stiffen, you could swear you saw his whole body freeze. And the finale began—and we looked back toward the balloons, just as Shane put his arm around Carolyn, for everybody to see.

We stared at the balloons—twenty or thirty of them lighting up and then going dark, and they were no longer pretty, just loud and terrifying, color and music and fire all at once. The music was going so fast now, we didn't think the balloons could keep up, didn't think the fire could be lit and put out so quickly. And then we watched the light disappear and the smoke fill the air—if you didn't know any better, you'd think there'd been a fire. People clapped, the guys manning the balloons came out and took a bow, and we clapped and screamed some more. It was dark without the fire from the balloons and we took out our phones and used them as flashlights, just to try to see where we were going.

The DJ came on again and played "I'm Proud to Be an American" and some of the dads sang along, loud and off-key. Families around us started pulling together their blankets and lawn chairs and Styrofoam coolers. And we looked in front of us again, at Shane and Carolyn. Their bodies were close together and he was leaning back, holding himself up with his elbows. We couldn't tell if they were holding hands anymore, not really. Andrew got up and brushed himself off—we thought he'd gotten a grass stain on his ass—and he said something to Shane. We couldn't hear him, but we watched him walk away, toward the parking lot. We started to gather our things too—we felt lame sitting around, listening to shitty music—but we kept our eyes on Shane, on Carolyn. We had gotten everything—our bags, our bottled water, our secret stash of Marlboro Golds—and made our way to Jessica's car.

We were fifteen or twenty feet away when Lauren remembered she didn't have her iPhone. And if she hadn't gone back, we never would have seen anything, maybe nobody would have ever known. If we hadn't gone back with Lauren to where we'd sat, to the place we'd laid our blanket for the evening, Lauren never would have been there with her iPhone in her hand, ready to take a picture, to save it. And we never would have seen Carolyn lay her head on Shane's shoulder. We never would have seen Shane put his hand through her hair and place his lips on her forehead. We wouldn't have known anything. And a part of us wished we knew nothing at all.

But we did see it: Carolyn and Shane, like a couple, like Brooke and Shane were supposed to be. Close to each other, not hooking up, nothing like that, but close, touching. We stared with our mouths open: this girl had been here for ten minutes, and already she was where everybody wanted to be. Close to Shane, close enough to smell him, feel the heat from his sunburn, the stubble on his neck. We weren't jealous—or at least we didn't think so— but we wanted to make sure what we saw was real, wanted to look at it later, to analyze their body language, like they did in every month's *Allure*. Lauren picked up her phone. She put the backs of their heads in her image finder. She clicked. She saved.

Lauren kept the picture to herself—she sent it to us, of course, but we didn't send it around, not immediately anyway. And even then, we didn't send it to very many people. That didn't seem to matter, though, when all was said and done.

But all of this came later, once we thought we knew what it all meant. That day in the field, nothing had happened. A new girl had come to our town and we saw her in a field with a football player who may or may not have been dating somebody else. You wouldn't have thought that it meant anything. But, in the end, we guessed it did.

But not yet. Not yet.

4

Living in Adamsville, Alabama, was embarrassing. It was embarrassing that you had to travel to the adjacent county to buy hard liquor; that Adamsville had the highest number of fast-food restaurants per capita in the United States that our mothers wore holiday sweaters and our fathers wore socks and sandals; that if you abbreviated our city and state you got AA. It was embarrassing that our department store was called Parisians, and that we called it Perish Anne's. It was embarrassing that our parents attended our Homecoming dance to watch Lead-Out, and that we wore corsages made of streamers and plastic, so heavy you had to make sure your dress didn't rip during the course of the night. It was embarrassing that we had known each other since kindergarten, and that we were all members of the same Baptist church. It was embarrassing that the sermons were about sex and drinking and their dangers, and it was embarrassing to watch our former nap

mates make out in the church parking lot immediately following service. All of this was embarrassing and all the more so when
someone from the outside looked in. We didn't like it.

The night before school started, we picked out what we would
wear and took pictures and texted them to one another to make
sure we weren't wearing the same thing. We needed to look dressed
up, but not so dressed up it looked like we were trying too hard.
We needed to look different, but not so different that people didn't
recognize us. It was hard to make much of an impression, really,
since we saw one another so often over the summer: at the river,
at the country club, at church, at the pep rally, at the balloon festival. And even though we would have seen people the week
before—or maybe even the night before—the way you looked on
the first day of school made a difference.

We wore jeans, mostly. Parisians had done a sale on Sevens in
July, and a bunch of us had bought them, but we tried to get different washes, so we didn't look like clones. We wore sandals that
showed off the French manicures we had managed to put on our
toes, and we wore white and black—colors that would show off our
tans. And what we wore was brand-new. This was important.

Over the past week, news about Carolyn had spread. Gemma
Davies was the main authority; her dad made her make friends
with anybody new to the congregation, if only in a totally fake and
superficial way, and Gemma obeyed. Brooke met her by extension,
and then so did Andrew Wright and Shane Duggan, and that was
why they were all together at the balloon fair—Gemma's dad had
made her invite Carolyn along. At the time, Gemma told people
that the new girl was really cool, that she was glad to have her with
them. Later, she told people she was sorry she'd ever invited her.
Things would have been simpler if she hadn't.

Taylor Lyon's mother had done the window treatments for Carolyn's house on D'Evereux Drive, so Taylor had seen her and talked
to her. We heard they had gone to the mall and a movie together,

along with Tiffany Port (who else?), and that Carolyn had worn J Brand jeans and an Abercrombie top and that she had seen Lady Gaga in some small and exclusive nightclub in New York. Taylor told people that Carolyn had had a boyfriend back home, but they had split up before she moved, or that they had an open relationship or that they would get back together over the summer or something like that. We heard she didn't have a dad, or maybe that her mom and dad were divorced, and that she and her mom lived in a one-story house on D'Evereux Drive. Brooke Moore's mother had sold them the house. They'd paid a fortune for it, apparently, but real estate is crazy in the North. You can get more for your money down here.

We wondered if Carolyn would be in any of our classes and we heard that she might join the swim team—Coach Billy had told Nicole's mom, who had told all of us. We wondered if she'd be fast or slow and what we would talk about in the locker room and if she would think we were lame. This is what we thought about as we ate our breakfast and packed up our bags and headed out the door on our first day of school.

There were no buses in Adamsville and everywhere was too far to walk, so we carpooled with Lauren Brink and she drove her parents' old Volvo. She'd put in an iPod deck over the summer to make it feel less lame, but it was better than being dropped off by our parents and we drove with the windows down until we noticed what it was doing to our hair, and we rolled them up, turning the air-conditioning vents to face us directly.

The parking lot was insane on the first day—everybody trying to get their place for the year—so we got there early, before seven fifteen, because we didn't want a space out in the middle of nowhere and, plus, we had volunteered to work in the office in the mornings—our mothers made us. We parked near the library, in the side parking lot, 'cause we'd heard this was where the seniors were gonna park, and some of the popular juniors. There were only a dozen cars there when we arrived—an Oldsmobile, an SUV, a brand-new Ford pickup right next to two beat-up Dodges, a few Japanese hatchbacks and a burgundy station wagon that we had seen sitting in the parking lot all summer. And then we saw Blake Wyatt's minivan—a hand-me-down from his mom—and we thought his car was a good sign. Blake usually knew stuff. We sat in Lauren's air-conditioning and reapplied our makeup, our deodorant, and looked in the rearview mirrors to see who we could see.

We saw a red Honda pull up and drop somebody off, and we heard later that that was probably Carolyn, but we missed it, 'cause we were busy trying to light a Marlboro Gold and pass it around and inhale a drag and then swallow some mouthwash so that we wouldn't reek when we talked to people later.

We checked the weather on our phones—97 degrees, heat index 102—and even though thick, puffy clouds were eclipsing the sun, the air was like soup, heavy. Our parents had called the heat "oppressive" and we thought that sounded about right. We sat in front of the air-conditioning vents, cooling down our faces, blasting our armpits, and we looked at the school. Since they already had to deal with the spray paint in the gym, they'd gone ahead and painted the outside of all the buildings too—and everything was so white it was almost blue—and we wondered how long it would stay that way before somebody put something obscene on the side.

Our school was single story—the PTA had insisted on this when the school was being constructed: there are more fights in two-story schools, more chances for students to hide underneath landings, lurk in corners and sneak cigarettes, that's what the research says. Banners were flying in between the different buildings—WELCOME CLASSES OF 2011, 2012, 2013 AND 2014—and a huge sign covered the front of the main building, GO BEARS! TAKE STATE!, in perfect bubble letters, the work of the cheerleaders, for sure.

A bunch of kids stood in front of the library, in orange and black T-shirts—the "welcome committee" in charge of guiding around lost freshmen, reassuring parents that their fourteen-year-olds would be safe in this new place, that there was nothing to fear. The welcome committee was made up of band kids, mostly, and Taylor Lyon volunteered to do it, but had backed out at the last minute, had said it was "too mortifying" and, plus, you were required to speak to "legions of social rejects." We wondered if she meant us.

At 7:35, the first bell rang, and we walked to Mr. Overton's office. The principal, Richard Overton—Tricky Dick—had graduated from Adams High twenty-four years ago, and had joined the coaching faculty four years after that. He was promoted from baseball to health to civics to history until landing in the vice principal's chair in 2006. Several other alums were part of the staff—Coach Cox, Miss Simpson, Miss Matthew—and there were even a few who had taught him way back, he'd told us.

"Some of them even tried to flunk me," he routinely explained, laughing, as if this were funny at all.

We imagined he wasn't a good student then, and he wasn't good at his job now. Especially now. We worked in his office every morning, had done this freshman year too, before homeroom and first period, for extra credit. And to keep our parents off our backs.

"You kids move too fast," he'd tell us. "Nobody enjoys the journey." He wore glasses with a safety bar and a clip-on Auburn tie with short-sleeved dress shirts. He'd lost twenty-five pounds last year with the Zone, suggested we try it. Mr. Overton was tall and tanned and our mothers said that he was "handsome" back in high school. His breath smelled like coffee and Fritos. We tried not to look him straight in the eye.

When we weren't listening to Mr. Overton, we checked our email and updated our Facebook statuses and studied our vocabulary and practiced for our SATs. And when we were done with that, we filed tardies and sick notes and did whatever we were asked to do. And then, if no one was watching, we snooped around.

"Welcome back," he grinned at us, as we stood in a line in front of him. "My loyal assistants are here. What would I do without you girls?" He called Lauren "Lori" and Jessica "Jessie" and he ignored Nicole entirely, we were never sure why. "I have a little project for you girls this morning. We have a new student."

"We heard."

"Carolyn Lessing?"

He nodded and pointed to his office and we imagined Carolyn inside with her ear pressed against the door, or maybe just sitting and reading a book, or walking around and examining the weird collection of photographs in Mr. Overton's office, turning her nose up at his junior college degree. Mr. Overton looked at us and he beamed—as if he were responsible for somebody new moving to our town—and we looked down.

"If you could go ahead and print out her schedule and dig out her file from the cabinet, that'd be just great." And he walked back into his office. He turned back to us before he entered—debating whether or not he would shut the door, we guessed—and then he looked at our faces, still staring at him, and he shut it hard behind him.

Our last new student was back when we were in eighth grade—Jennifer Bunn from Oklahoma. Before that, it was Brandy Benson, who had moved from Moulton or some place really close. That was back when we were in fourth or fifth, we thought, but nobody could really remember.

Nicole looked Carolyn up on the database and the rest of us huddled around the filing cabinet and we found the hard copy folder with notes from teachers and a guidance counselor. When we talked about it later, we said we wished we hadn't seen it, that we shouldn't have looked at it, that Mr. Overton never should have asked us to look into those files. But they were just there and we were doing what we were asked to, and the cabinet wasn't even locked. And, plus, nobody was ever new. We read what we could.

Her transcript:

English (Honors)	A
Algebra 2	A−
Biology	A−
History	A
Civics	A+
PE	B

A letter from a guidance counselor:

Re: Carolyn Lessing

Skipped first grade, in light of strong reading ability. Teachers tend to agree that she is a hardworking student and attentive in class. She has exhibited some behavioral problems in the past number of months, and used profanity in the classroom following some provocation from—

The office door opened; we stood still and Mr. Overton walked out. Carolyn was behind him, her long, brown hair covering half of her face. She looked like her pictures, we said later, only maybe she was prettier, if only we could see the rest of her. Her body was petite and she wore her clothes like a miniature Giselle and her skin was perfect—we all agreed. It was hard not to stare. He asked for the draft schedule.

"I know you'd like to be in Honors English, but there are a lot of bright students here. We'll have to see where you fit in." They had her in classes with the remedial kids, but he didn't say it.

Carolyn stared at him. She opened her mouth but didn't say anything, we thought she kind of smirked, and we said later that this was weird. Maybe she was shy, or maybe she was conceited or maybe she just wasn't as smart as the transcript had said. He hesitated and his face softened. "You'll have the opportunity to take some placement tests in a couple of weeks."

He turned to us, then back to Carolyn, then back to us again: "Lori, Jessie. . . . uh . . . girls, this is Carol Lessing. She's starting at Adams today."

Carolyn cleared her throat, reddened a little. "It's Carolyn."

We nodded and smiled and somebody said she was glad to meet her. And then Mr. Overton ushered her out the door.

Carolyn's first day of school was legend. What people had heard about her turned out to be true—she was beautiful, she was different, she spoke with a Yankee accent. She walked through the halls, seeming nervous and lost, looking down at her schedule and smiling when people passed—everybody said hello.

We could see that she was trying to find her way and at every water fountain somebody would offer her directions, a place at their lunch table, a stick of gum, a Hershey's Kiss. It was the girls that were most excited by her—probably due to Taylor Lyon's endorsement—and we all wanted to be her first best friends, responsible for "discovering" her.

She wore a blue sweater dress—from the cover of the first fall J Crew catalog—and thick black tights and patent leather ballet pumps—French Sole, we guessed—and she carried a Kate Spade bag, black and plain. Nobody carried real brand bags at our school and you could tell hers wasn't a fake. Tiffany Port had been to Boston over the summer and had been to the Kate Spade store and confirmed that Carolyn carried the real thing. She probably thought what she'd worn would make her inconspicuous, but her dress, her hair, her skin, the perfectly matte, opaque tights, all of this made it impossible for anybody to look away.

Plus, it was still 97 degrees outside—we thought she must be burning up.

In study hall, Lauren Brink told us Carolyn had gone to a private school in New Jersey, and the girls were all "bitches" and "vindictive" and "insecure." All the guys had been in love with her, and she had tried to make them stop asking her out, grinding with her at the semi-formals, but she couldn't help it. Carolyn had told somebody that girls here were different. Less bitchy, less controlling, less insecure. We weren't sure what this all meant, but we believed it. If only in the beginning.

We heard later she was surprised by how nice everybody was, how interested everybody was in her moving, in being her friend. This wasn't what you expected when you come to a small town, not at all, and she was happy, surprised, relieved, when the day was over—things were different here.

INTERNAL PROGRESS REPORT: Carolyn Lessing

Carole Matthew—August 23, 2010

Carolyn Lessing joined the junior class last week, coming to Adams High School from a large, suburban New Jersey high school. Only a few weeks into the school year, Carolyn's class schedule already seems inadequate for her academic ability. For example, her English teacher (Stephanie Simpson) has indicated that Carolyn submitted an essay on the short story "The Most Dangerous Game" which demonstrated senior-level ability and aptitude (e.g., she referred to the "protagonist" and "antagonist" in the story even though these terms have not been introduced in vocabulary). I have spoken to Carolyn's other teachers and, particularly in the area of math, she is also performing at a very high level. On this basis, I would recommend that Carolyn is moved into Honors English and trigonometry as soon as possible.

I understand that she has been encouraged to try out for the cheerleading squad later this year, and will be joining the swim team later this month (following tryouts with Coach Billy). I am happy to report that Carolyn is settling in well into the junior class.

No need for follow-up.

September

5

What we knew of Carolyn was pieced together little by little those first weeks, day by day, minute by minute. She was pretty, that was clear, but whether she knew or understood this wasn't. Her eyes were her best feature, but it was her hair we wanted the most—she looked like she'd had it professionally blown dry every day and then curled just so, like somebody on reruns of "The Hills" or "Pretty Little Liars." She wore less makeup than anybody, but her eyes, lips, cheeks, smile—they looked bigger, bolder, better. Our teachers called her a "breath of fresh air." We followed her movements, watched her fall right into place. People who had lived here all their lives hadn't achieved what she had in two weeks. She was a part of things.

Her town in New Jersey was small, even smaller than Adamsville. The houses were older, there wasn't any fast food, just restaurants and coffee shops. She complained that the bread in

Alabama was too soft, that there wasn't any decent Italian, and she said that Marshmallow Creme was called Marshmallow Fluff. When she told a story, her eyes got bigger, they looked right through you, and she smiled and laughed. It made you want to smile and laugh too. The cheerleaders told her she had to try out next semester—she laughed at that, and nobody understood why.

Her voice was quiet, but her accent always took us by surprise. It was like nothing we'd ever heard before—and not harsh like people had expected—but soft and round. Over time, that changed. She started to talk a little bit slower, started to say "y'all" instead of "you guys." Still a Yankee, but not as much.

She turned assignments in on time, she never wore skirts or shorts too short and everything she wore looked expensive. We tried to calculate what she cost from head to toe, tried to keep track of how many new things she wore, how many times she repeated her tops, her jeans, her boots. She wore skinny jeans that made her look even skinnier, but she still had an ass. And the guys really liked her.

"Shane Duggan is into the new girl."

"I hear he dumped Brooke Moore."

"He's taking Carolyn to the movies."

"He's taking her parking."

"He just needs to get laid."

"He doesn't even know her."

"They were together over the summer."

"How is that even possible?"

"Just don't tell Brooke."

"Yeah, don't tell Brooke."

The third week of school maybe, Shane Duggan started meeting Carolyn at her locker every day, after first, third and fifth periods. Three lockers down from Taylor Lyon's. He was six feet tall, Carolyn five foot three. He towered over her, and if he moved in the right way, you couldn't even see she was there. We said later he must have liked that—and that it made a big change from Brooke, who was all legs and height and hair. He could make Carolyn disappear. Like magic.

When we were freshmen, Shane Duggan's locker had been near Lauren Brink's and, on the first day, she couldn't figure out the lock, had spent fifteen minutes trying to get it to open, and she turned red in the face and was getting all sweaty and freaked and afraid that she'd miss all her classes and everybody would see her and send her back to Fairview Middle. Then Shane came up behind her, asked her for the combination and opened it up in, like, five seconds. Lauren had smiled and said thank you, under her breath, and he kind of laughed and patted her on the head, like she was a little girl, his little sister. We'd had fantasies back then that he might ask Lauren out, that he had done that 'cause he liked her, that he liked the way she had grown her hair over the summer, had put in some caramel highlights, had lost a couple of pounds. And if Shane Duggan asked Lauren out, then Lauren would be able to tell us what his house was like inside, if his parents were as strict as we'd heard, if he worked out on a Nautilus to keep him looking like Taylor Lautner.

Shane was tan all year round. Even in the winter, when everybody else was pasty and pale. He and his dad were "outdoorsy," that's what people said, and what they meant was that they hunted and fished and did things that good ole boys did, like they were auditioning for "Dukes of Hazzard." Shane wore his hair kind of long; it got in his eyes and it was brown but bleached by the sun in streaks. You would have almost sworn he had highlights, or that he poured lemon juice on his hair, only that wasn't the kind of guy he was. Shane was tall and we thought he might be the strongest guy we'd ever seen: his muscles were like something from the cover of *Men's Health*, like the guys' who advertise Soloflex. You could see his biceps under long-sleeve shirts; if he got hot he'd wipe his face with the bottom of his T-shirt, and he had an actual six-pack. He might have been vain, we wondered about that, might have thought he was too good-looking for his own good. We didn't know, and we didn't care. Shane Duggan was hot and his eyes were blue and they sparkled. Literally.

After we'd heard Shane Duggan had been meeting Carolyn Lessing at her locker for over a week, we rearranged the way we walked from class to see if we could see them. And we stood around the water fountain and watched them and tried not to get caught. When Shane stepped away from her, when he let her out from underneath his arms, we could see her face. And she was making crazy eye contact with him, and holding it for what seemed like forever, like she was playing Blink. People talked about this thing she did: she always looked people straight on, right in the eyes. Especially guys. He was talking to her really low, so low that we couldn't ever make out what they were talking about, and Carolyn whispered things back. She looked happy. But, back then, she always did.

Jessica filled up her water bottle and Nicole checked her watch and we said we needed to go and then Lauren got a text: "Duggs driving new girl to school!!!!!!!!!!!!" But we knew this already. Nicole had seen her getting into his car a couple of days before. Weeks later, Dylan Hall posted on Facebook that Carolyn sucked Shane off every morning and that was why he did it—her house was totally out of his way. Whatever. We figured Shane drove her because she was pretty, and also 'cause it would piss off Brooke. And this is what we told people. But we didn't know, not really. We didn't know much of anything. But we said a lot of things, and, eventually, we sent them round and round and round, texting, Tweeting, until everybody was sure they knew what was going on.

It was a Tuesday, the day Shane officially asked Carolyn out, and everybody saw it, and even if you didn't, you still felt like you had. He crossed the cafeteria to where Carolyn was standing, at a table with Alicia Cooper and two other black girls. Carolyn didn't seem to understand how it worked, didn't understand that we sat in the same place every day, we sat with people like us. Shane came over and said something to her and she laughed and started to sit down, and then he pulled her hand, and she was up again, following him. Alicia and the girls at the table rolled their eyes and then watched her walk away.

Shane led Carolyn over to the center of the cafeteria: "Come with me."

"I left my lunch there—" Carolyn was looking back at Alicia, shrugging her shoulders.

"Don't worry—you can share mine." He pulled Carolyn into him, close. She turned away from Alicia again and her body disappeared against Shane's.

And then Shane whispered, "I'm rescuing you, you know?"

Carolyn smiled. "Oh, I see." And then she stood on her tiptoes and kissed him on the cheek. "Well, thank you." She took her seat next to Shane, across from Taylor and Tiffany. She had arrived.

Nobody was sure what Brooke thought about all of this—at least not at the time. And people weren't sure if she had dumped Shane, or if Shane had dumped her. Nicole said she followed Brooke into the bathroom that same afternoon and heard her crying in the stall, but that was nothing new. Brooke was always making drama—she didn't need a breakup for that. No matter what Brooke felt, people thought Carolyn was lucky, thought Shane was cool for asking out the new girl. She'd only been at school a month. And she was already dating Shane. This made her popular, even if nobody knew her.

There are things that only make sense now—things that are only clear once the story is finished, once the past is the past. If we had realized what was happening, we might have stood up, shouted or at least cleared our throats. But you have to understand how quickly things move, how blurry your vision is as a car passes you by, how fast a balloon can fly out of your hands and get caught somewhere you cannot reach or even see—we didn't know what we know now. We couldn't have. If we had, things could have been—would have been—different.

From: Ssimpson@adams.mccounty.edu
To: Alessing@gmail.com
Date: September 12, 2010 19:42
Subject: Carolyn

Dear Mrs. Lessing:

I'm so sorry you were unable to attend the first parent-teacher conference of the Adams High School year. As part of our agreement with the Adams High Parent-Teacher Committee (AHPTC), I am writing to you to provide an update on Carolyn's progress as you were not in a position to attend the event on Thursday evening.

Carolyn is a bright, attentive and imaginative young person. As you may be aware, Carolyn moved quickly from basic math and English classes to trigonometry and Honors English within a couple of weeks' time at Adams. She demonstrated an above average intelligence in all of her classes, and I felt she would be better served in more advanced classes. Since adjusting her schedule, I believe that Carolyn is settling in remarkably well. She has a wide vocabulary and excellent writing ability, and it is evident that she is an avid reader of works of all kinds (Carolyn mentioned her father is a published author, which is not hard to believe given her writing skills!). You will receive updates from her other teachers but she is a good addition to our English class and I understand from informal conversations with other teachers that this is the case across the board.

I have encouraged Carolyn to get involved in extracurricular activities, in an effort to round out her applications for colleges.

All in all, Carolyn is a well-rounded and intelligent young lady, and a pleasure to have in class. As stated above, I am only sorry that we did not have the opportunity to meet in person, but I understand from Carolyn that you have a busy work schedule.

Yours sincerely,
Stephanie Simpson

6

The night after Shane asked Carolyn out, the Hot List was updated. The blog had been started four years ago, before we were in high school, and it ranked the ten hottest girls at Adams High. It was anonymous, of course, but everybody speculated about the identity of the blogger—we said it was like "Gossip Girl," only this person seemed to have a more focused interest, and maybe a little less time on his or her hands—and we guessed and guessed and guessed, but nobody could say who it was for sure.

There were rules for the list, and these were up on the site: you had to be at Adams High, registered and in classes, you couldn't nominate yourself, each email address could only get one vote. Pictures of girls were posted and within a twelve-hour period, you had a chance to vote for who you thought was hottest. The blog had a gmail account—adamshighhotlist@gmail.com—so that people could send pictures, or add comments to their votes. The previous year, Blake Wyatt had tried to hack the account, to see what was sent, and who sent what, but gmail's security was too good and, plus, he wasn't that smart.

The blog was updated all the time, but the list was only once a year or so and a bunch of us had subscribed to it as an RSS feed so we could vote and so we wouldn't be the last ones to know what was happening, who was up and who was down. Our freshman year, Brooke had been number one and this was weird, 'cause she wasn't even a senior. Her picture was amazing, professional, sexy but not trashy—she wasn't wearing a top, just covering her breasts with her hands—like some picture of Jennifer Aniston we had seen a few years ago, or like Megan Fox, only not so gross. Her hair covered one of her eyes, and the picture was in sepia—black and white and gray and green, old-fashioned. Every curve on her body was shadowed just right and we wondered if she had had the picture touched up—but this was before the weight gain, and probably when she was still throwing up after every football game, after every meal, so she looked really good. It was probably the real thing. Everybody said it must have been Shane who took it. And that's why people called her a prick tease—she'd do everything except for intercourse, that's what she told Taylor Lyon, who told Lauren Brink, who told the rest of us. Brooke had taken the virginity pledge, after all, and if we knew what was right, we'd do the same.

Gemma Davies was on the list too: she was number four. Her picture was plain, her looking straight into the camera, zoomed into her face, just a collarbone visible. Totally PG compared to Brooke's, clearly cropped from a family candid, or from a school picture. There wasn't anything about Gemma's picture that made you think she cared about the list, and that's probably why she always scored so high. Tiffany Port had placed at number three— she was just wearing her underwear, and she was smiling but her eyes looked scared.

That night, the night after Shane had crossed the cafeteria and asked Carolyn to hang out, we got a message to say there was new content and we got onto the site as soon as we could, as soon as our parents would let us be excused from dinner. We opened up the page and there were fifty pictures for us to vote for. Carolyn's was the only one that was new. Carolyn Lessing. A color photo of her, fully dressed, standing next to her locker, in jeans and an Abercrombie hoodie, laughing. For the first time, we noticed that her eyes were maybe a little too far apart, that she was maybe a little too thin. We put in our votes. We texted each other to make sure everybody had done the same. And we waited for the results.

The next morning, before seven o'clock, we logged on. The site was updated and there was Carolyn Lessing, at number one. The picture was huge, so you had to scroll down for forever to get to second place. And now that was Brooke.

Texts went around. "Brooke Moore has been DUMPED!" and "Brooke Moore #2." Nobody felt that sorry for her, not really. She wasn't nice like Gemma, and it was good for her to have to try to work for things, people said. The following day, she started walking a different way to her classes, and we knew it was so that she wouldn't have to run into Shane. And when we were in Mr. Overton's office, we had to file her request to have her schedule changed so she could have a different lunch period—she even had a note from the doctor, saying she had low blood sugar. Despite all that, she pretended like it hadn't happened, that she didn't know anything about the blog—or maybe she didn't care—but everybody talked about it, everybody knew.

With Shane, with the list, Carolyn was popular. People said she was cool, she was sick, she was beautiful. She made us want to be new, to move to a new town, to start over, completely, with new hair and makeup and new clothes and maybe even a new personality, if you believed that was possible—which we did. You could leave everything you didn't like behind, and everybody too. We realized later it wasn't that easy, that moving would probably be a pain, but she made it look simple and fun and she was protected, we thought, more than anybody else at the school. The cheerleaders were bound to come next, we said, cementing her popularity. And we were right.

After school and after they'd practiced, the cheerleaders sat on the track and talked and laughed and choreographed routines to "Boom Boom Pow" and "Poker Face" and whatever other addictive song they were obsessed with. They played with one another's hair and compared French manicures and the closeness of the shave on their legs and made plans for what they would do on the weekend. From the first day of junior year, Gemma and Brooke didn't do this anymore. They spent more time on their own—just the two of them—away from the rest of the girls. As the days passed, this started to piss off Taylor and Tiffany and the others. But Gemma and Brooke would drive home together and go to Sonic instead of sitting on the track. They separated from the group. Taylor talked loudly about it in study hall. And Tiffany agreed with whatever she said.

"They want to get in with the senior girls." Taylor had her Spanish book open, but on the final chapter in the book. She didn't even try to look busy.

"It's pathetic." Tiffany had her head down, trying to finish her vocab or something but unwilling to let the opportunity to talk to Taylor pass.

"What do we care?" Taylor tossed her hair over her shoulder. Tiffany did the same. "We don't."

"Well, forget them." Taylor said "forget" in a whisper, as if she were saying something else.

"Yeah, forget them." Tiffany took out her lip gloss, offered it to Taylor. We looked back down at our notebooks, kept ourselves to ourselves. We were sitting right behind them, but they didn't seem to know we were there.

"Brooke and Gemma are so over anyway," Taylor said. "Aren't they?"

Tiffany knew this wasn't a question. "Totally over."

Maybe it was because of this, because of Brooke and Gemma's departure, that Taylor was so excited to include Carolyn in everything. But we guessed it was because of Shane, because Carolyn was with a senior. Maybe it would have happened anyway, we couldn't know, but by the end of September, Taylor had asked Carolyn to hang out with them after practice—we saw them sitting on the track, in a circle, Carolyn in the center, talking, smiling, fitting in. She sat with them at lunch too: they even found her another chair and squashed it in at the end of the table. And in between classes, they met one another in the halls, and they walked together, linking arms. Taylor and Tiffany and the rest of the cheerleaders said Carolyn would win "Friendliest" when we did Class Favorites, 'cause that's how much people liked her, that's how cool she really was.

On Fridays in the fall, our school looked like somebody had thrown up all over it: orange and black everywhere, on the walls, on our bodies, on our faces. Pep rally days, that's what Fridays were. And the cheerleaders were in charge of everything, of the color coordination, the structure of the event, the signs throughout the halls. The guys got their chests painted, keeping the same letter every week, spelling out ADAMS HIGH RULES. And their girlfriends volunteered to help paint the letters on or wipe them off.

The first Friday pep rally, Carolyn came to school in blue, not orange and black. At first we said it was 'cause she was conceited, thought she was too cool. But we found out later that she hadn't known, and that Taylor Lyon lent her an orange T-shirt of hers and Tiffany Port a black boyfriend cardigan, just so she wouldn't feel left out. We saw them in the bathroom during lunch. They didn't acknowledge us—we said later it was lame how hard they tried to forget us—and we went into the stalls and we listened to Taylor and Tiffany. Even though we couldn't see them, we could imagine them touching Carolyn on the shoulder, talking to themselves in the mirror, just so they could watch themselves as their faces lit up. This is what we remember them saying:

"What about Blake Wyatt?" That was Taylor. We always knew her voice.

"No way—he's too skinny for her." Tiffany was whispering. And laughing.

"Which one is he?"

"No, Tiff is right. He's not for you."

"Dylan Hall?" Tiffany laughed again.

"Vomit." Taylor made a retching sound.

"Oh, I think I remember him—he almost has a mullet?"

"*Yes.*" They spoke in unison.

And then we weren't sure who spoke next—if it was Taylor, she had lowered her voice so much that we couldn't recognize it. But it still seemed too deep for Tiffany. "Are you sleeping with Shane yet?"

There was a pause. She nodded, or shook her head: we weren't sure.

"He's way better for you," Tiffany said.

"Have you told Brooke yet?"

"She's going to freak out."

Taylor laughed. "Well, that's her fault. Anyway, she knows."

Carolyn almost whispered, "I don't really know her—I'd be afraid to say it to her."

"Oh, don't be afraid of her."

"I thought you guys—y'all—were friends?"

Somebody sighed and then Taylor said, "Oh, we are. She's just—you know, kind of bitchy."

"Shane said that they were never together."

"Yeah, she just liked people to think they were," Tiffany said.

Carolyn spoke again, "Well, I like him."

Taylor laughed. "He's *hot*."

And they all laughed and ran the water and the hand dryer blew. We walked out of the stalls to do the same and watched them leave as they fluffed their hair, putting on lip gloss, still talking as they walked out the door.

"You look great."

"Totally great."

"Thank you for these."

"Can't have you sticking out."

Minutes later, in the gym, Tiffany and Taylor and the other cheerleaders ran onto the stage to "Pump up the Jam," "Groove Is in the Heart"—songs so old that we'd never heard them on the radio, but not old enough for our parents to know them either. Miss Simpson's choice, for sure. The cheerleaders danced—movements sharp and in time—and we sat back and watched, wondering why this wasn't lame, why this was okay: to dance and smile and look like you cared. It was okay if you were a cheerleader, we guessed, but that was the only way. Coach Cox came out—made another lame-o speech—and the football team ran onto the court.

Varsity, then junior varsity, and they were like two versions of the same thing—one a size down, but still broad and big and stronger than what they looked like in class, in their jeans or in their khakis. They wore shoulder pads under their jerseys but there was something else too—they looked larger when they were on the court, when we were all looking their way.

The cheerleaders looked happy and clapped and gave spirit fingers and thumbs-ups—the lamest thing they did, for sure—and toe touches and back handsprings.

We watched Shane watch Carolyn and we were pretty sure we saw him wink. She was lucky. Brooke was on the edge of the court with her pom-poms. She had stopped moving—she was staring at Shane and then back at Carolyn. Gemma turned to her and mouthed something and Brooke flinched and brought her pom-poms back up to her chest. She did a toe touch. But she didn't smile.

Coach Cox came to the microphone, told us about the squad, about the plan to make it to State, about how strong the boys were, how good they were, how they needed every bit of our support. He asked Shane Duggan to come to the microphone. As Shane approached him, people screamed, squealed, shouted, *"Duggs!"*

Shane smiled, took the microphone: "Can y'all bow your heads and pray?" We did as he said. And he began the "Our Father." We watched Carolyn out of the corner of our eyes, seeing if she knew the words—if this was a prayer that Catholics knew too—and her mouth moved along with the words, just a little.

Some parents were there—most of the guys' dads had played years back, and they knew how important all of this was. When the prayer was over, when everybody was whooping and cheering and stomping their feet, we looked over at Mr. Duggan, all tan and red-faced, wearing khaki shorts and a red polo shirt, his beer belly hanging over his belt. His legs were all muscle and toned, but when you looked at his stomach—he looked about seven months' pregnant. And his face was Shane's but not Shane's. We wondered if he still threw the ball around, if he still lifted with Shane, if he still thought he could hold his own on the field. We watched as Mr. Ferris, our trig teacher, walked over to him and, within seconds, Mr. Ferris was all in Mr. Duggan's face, pointing at Shane, looking as if he might actually explode. Mr. Duggan was laughing at first and then he got redder and redder and pushed Mr. Ferris with one hand. Mr. Ferris lunged forward and then Coach Cox got in between them. Mr. Ferris walked away. Coach and Mr. Duggan laughed.

Adams High School
PTA Meeting

September 30, 2010

The meeting was called to order at 7.35 pm, following the Pledge of Allegiance (led by Principal Overton) and the Lord's Prayer (led by Reverend Davies).

There were 37 people in attendance (see attachment), of which 32 were parents of pupils at Adams.

The minutes of the last meeting were adopted, subject to the amendment of the Vice-President's report, which should include reference to the proposed changes to the code of conduct in relation to the school's athletics policy (as proposed by Billy Duggan and seconded by Bonnie Moore). Mr. Ferris's apology to the PTA and the relevant students was noted.

Committee reports:

Tammy Davies (President): Parent involvement in the Homecoming Parade, Game and Dance is going well, with 18 parents actively involved in the preparations. Special thanks to Greg and Trish Hall for offering the use of their farmland for float making. Corsages will be sold on special offer from Celebrations! on 5th Avenue. The theme for the Dance this year is Mardi Gras.

Concerns were raised regarding the suitability of the theme, and the connection between Mardi Gras and alcohol consumption. It was **AGREED** to purchase a breathalyzer for use at the dance, with a view to using this again at Prom.

Special thanks to Coach Cox and the football team for performing so well so far this year.

Melanie Grady (Treasurer): The balance of the PTA fund is $2,317, and the grapefruit and orange sale scheduled for November/December should lead to an additional sum of at least $2,000 being added to the fund. Parents are encouraged to participate in the fund-raiser and sign-up sheets are available from Melanie.

Faculty reports:

Mrs. Matthew (Guidance): Two college fairs have been organized for the second half of the year, with all major Alabama universities sending representatives, along with representatives from a number of universities from out of state.

A proposal was put forward (Abby Lessing) to extend the number of out of state universities in attendance. It was **AGREED**, however, that budgetary restrictions and the overall level of interest in out of state schools meant that this would not be feasible.

Counseling sessions are now being offered to pupils on an "as needs" basis and a service is now offered for parents who wish to come in and talk to the Guidance Counselor in relation to behavior by their children which is of concern. A school assembly on bullying is scheduled for the second half of the year, and a new DVD on same subject is being shown in Health classes across all years.

There was a general discussion regarding the recent suicide attempt at Lincoln High. Principal Overton noted that his report would include items that should address this, but that additional concerns could be forwarded to Mrs. Matthew.

Principal Overton: Attendance at Friday football games is up 15% on last year. New weightlifting equipment was purchased last year thanks to PTA sponsorship, as well as new uniforms for both the football team and cheerleading squad. A proposal to contract additional training sessions with a college coach was agreed and would be implemented in the lead-up to State.

The Alabama State Aptitude test will be administered in October and teachers are preparing students for the test, which has implications in relation to funding levels for 2010–2011. Results from the 2009 test were above average and the PTA thanked Principal Overton and his team for their hard work in this area.

The introduction of a cell phone discipline policy has been proposed and copies of the policy were circulated to those in attendance (and are available on the PTA intranet). Bonnie Moore objected to several points within the policy and it was **AGREED** that further comments/amendments should be forwarded to Bonnie, who will give a formal response from the PTA to the policy. It was **AGREED** that the policy would be put on hold until such submissions were made and considered.

The refurbishment work in the gym and to the exterior of the buildings is now complete, and parents acknowledged the improved appearance of the school. The proposal to build an extension to the Math building is still under consideration by the Superintendent, but it is understood that a response will be made shortly. In the interim, the trailers adjacent to the Math building will be used to deal with the overflow of students/classrooms. General dissatisfaction was noted in relation to this and it was agreed that a complaint would be lodged with the Superintendent regarding the acceptance of new students to Adams.

The next meeting will take place on the last Thursday of October (October 28) at 7.30 pm.

Those present extended their thanks to the Davies family, the rest of the committee and the school faculty for their work thus far this year.

The meeting ended at 9 pm, followed by cake (provided by Tammy Davies) and other refreshments (provided by faculty).

OCTOBER

7

Our town doesn't change much in the seasons—the trees are green and leafy until November, December sometimes. In the old part of town—that's Southwest, where we live, where we go to school—huge oaks line Fifth Avenue.

The fall in Alabama—when it arrives in October—means jeans and long sleeves and corduroy jackets. It means no more flip-flops and it means lots of layers. It means football games and cheer-leading and standing around afterward in the Hardee's parking lot.

Our town is old and our town is new. Southwest and Southeast. Adams High School and Lincoln High. Fifth Avenue curves through the old part of town: the Regal Theater, the Old Court-house, Anne's Antiques, Jimmy Kelly's Jewelers, and dozens of storefronts, empty, abandoned. You can just make out the old creepy clown on the signage for Merrymakers, and a silver balloon is still floating around inside, a full year after the Closing Down sale. Puffs Ice Cream Parlor looks creepy too, we say to one another: a giant yellow ice-cream cone outside the front door, now covered with moss and mildew and mud from the street. We heard somebody might turn it into a frozen yogurt place, or maybe it was gelato, or something weird like that. Puffs was never good, we said to each other. But it had been there forever.

The oaks are everywhere in the old part of town, and once you veer off Fifth Avenue, going farther west, you meet subdivision after subdivision of houses. Brick and plaster and wood. Red and yellow and white. If you keep going, you meet farmland, red clay that sticks to our feet and it gets tracked onto the cream carpets in our remodeled living rooms.

Maybe you go east, though. That's where Carolyn lived. Take Fifth Avenue east, take a sharp turn at the lights opposite the Dollar Movie Theater: you hit the Stripline. We go to the Stripline for Wal-Mart and Lowe's and Winn-Dixie and Sam's. Two lanes on either side, parking lots and retail as far as you can see. They have the Crown Movie Theater—twenty screens—and the country club and a middle school identical to the one in Southwest. Identical. Keep going east and you reach farmland, once again. Southeast is where the new people move, it's where the new houses are. There are no oaks in Southeast—it's all pine. The houses in Southeast are newer, bigger. Uglier too, our parents said. Lincoln is overcrowded—they have trailers for most of their classes now, and they're sending new students to Adams. Our PTA lodged a complaint, but the school board overruled.

We're white in Southwest, mostly. The black people that live in Southwest are doctors and lawyers and teachers. In Southeast, they could be anything. We don't see many black kids at Adams, but we see them when we go to the Stripline, or when we go to football games or when we travel across the county line to buy alcohol.

Adamsville is dry. No liquor stores and no fancy restaurants. Fast food's the thing we have, and we have a lot of it. There's a Taco Bell in Southwest, one in Southeast. The same goes for Sonic, Whataburger, Burger King, McDonald's, Wendy's, Chick-fil-A, Dairy Queen, Pizza Hut, Domino's. Two sit-down restaurants—one in Southwest and one in Southeast. Blue Bistro, in Southwest, is better, of course. We make reservations early to make sure we get tables for Homecoming.

Homecoming comes around in November. That month, we build a float and get ready to watch a parade and attend a football game. We go to a party at some senior's house. But, mostly, we make an official Hot List, one that's older than the blog. We announce the names of the prettiest and most popular girls in school. We select the Homecoming Court.

We had already predicted the four who'd be on the list from our year: Brooke Moore and Gemma Davies, of course, and probably Taylor Lyon and Tiffany Port. And maybe, if she could inch out one of the others, Carolyn Lessing. You weren't allowed to campaign for these things, and the criteria were pretty vague— "the girls who best represent your class and the values you represent." The year before, some senior girl—Heather Hunt, a non-cheerleader—had been voted on, but then we heard she had gotten pregnant and miscarried over the summer, and people said if they'd known that, they never would have voted for her in the first place. "Just 'cause she got lucky and miscarried doesn't mean she should still get to do it," Taylor Lyon told our first period. "And just 'cause I love "16 and Pregnant" doesn't mean I want it on the Homecoming Court." She'd laughed then, and everybody else did too.

Some senior girls put together a petition to get Heather off the court—it did the rounds on Facebook. And then Mr. Overton had brought her into his office, and when she left she was in tears. An announcement went out over the loudspeaker later that day to say that Heather Hunt was being replaced by Kerry Karle, there'd been some kind of miscount. Heather finished the rest of the year from home. People thought she got pregnant again. That's why she left.

The day before the nominations, Lauren Brink watched Brooke push her shoulder into Carolyn in the hall, in between first and second period. She said that Brooke pushed her so hard that Carolyn's books and binders and purse and everything fell to the floor, her papers going everywhere, getting in everyone's way.

People walked around Carolyn and Brooke and they rubbernecked a little bit, but mostly they kept on walking. Lauren stood by her locker and watched and listened. She told us what she heard. What she saw.

Brooke stood over Carolyn as she tried to pick everything up. Tiffany and Taylor came running down the hall—Lauren said it was pathetic, like Carolyn had called 9-1-1 or something—and got down on their knees to help.

Lauren said that Brooke was practically yelling, acting all dramatic, trying to get everybody to stop and look. "Oh *no*. I'm *so sorry*." And then in a whisper, "I told you to watch *out*."

Carolyn, still on the floor, lifted herself up. "What did you say?"

"I said, you should be more careful." Brooke was smiling, but in a mean way, a sarcastic way, her eyes like slits, her lips pressed together, her head tilted to the side. She had practiced this in front of the mirror, probably, to get it just right.

Tiffany and Taylor had moved to the sides, still gathering up loose-leaf paper. Carolyn stood close to Brooke. "Why are you so mean to me?"

"Maybe I just don't want to catch anything from you."

Lauren said Mrs. Matthew was moving slowly down the hall, her eyebrows raised, like she was coming to intervene or to observe or maybe she was just going for a walk. Whatever. Mr. Ferris came from the other end of the hall, squinting, like he was confused.

Carolyn's eyes went wide, and then Lauren said they started to tear up. "Catch something?"

Brooke looked at Taylor and Tiffany and then back at Carolyn. "Everybody knows you have herpes." Brooke said this in a whisper, and then she knocked a three-ring binder out of Carolyn's hand.

"What's going on?" Mrs. Matthew's face was full of concern, worry.

Lauren said Carolyn started to say something—maybe to tell, maybe to pretend nothing had happened—and then Mr. Ferris came from the other end. "What happened, Carolyn? Are you okay?"

"I'm fine," she said quietly, looking at Brooke while she said it.

Brooke looked mad, and then she spoke to Mrs. Matthew. "I was just inviting Carolyn to join our prayer group."

Mrs. Matthew brightened. "Oh, that's super, Brooke. Just super." And she put her hand on Brooke's back.

"Yeah, I was just saying that Carolyn would really benefit from prayer group." Brooke didn't look away from Carolyn as she spoke.

"Is that right? Carolyn, is that right?" Mr. Ferris looked annoyed, Lauren said.

"Yes," Carolyn said, quickly. Tiffany and Taylor nodded.

"All right then." Mr. Ferris looked around at everyone, then at his watch. "The bell is about to ring. Y'all better get to your classes."

Lauren said that Brooke walked with Mrs. Matthew down the hall, sucking up, pretending like she was all nice, all friendly, and that Carolyn stood close to Mr. Ferris, until the bell rang and he turned and walked back down the hall.

8

By now, our days, our weeks: they had established a rhythm. We drove and then sat and then listened and then talked. We ate our lunch and did our homework. We walked the halls and crossed the greens. We sat at our tables and we walked the same way, day in, day out. We said hey to the same people, we ignored the same people, we did everything the same. We complained that life was boring, that everything could be predicted, that things in Adamsville were lame. Looking back, we wouldn't necessarily agree with that. It was nice to know what was coming next.

The day we selected the Homecoming Court was different, something to look forward to. No matter how ridiculous, you couldn't help but wonder what it would be like to hear your own name called out, for someone to pick you. The teachers asked for the nominations in first period and we raised our hands and waited our turns and then called out a name and waited for somebody to second or third it. But even if the day was slightly different, the results were always predictable, always the same. Every once in a while, somebody would try to put a pretty band girl forward—Amanda Morris or Ashley Anderson—but this always ended up the same way. Even though the band had 220 members, they didn't vote for their own. They voted for who should be in the court, who they would most like to be in an alternative life. It wasn't even girls we liked, not at all, and if you were to analyze beauty objectively, they might not even have been the most beautiful. But these girls had something we didn't, and so we put our hands up and voted, ensuring the outcome was always the same.

Carolyn was nominated in our homeroom and so were Tiffany Port and Brooke Moore and Gemma Davies and Taylor Lyon. Seconds after the nominations were recorded, Lauren Brink sent a text to say Carolyn was nominated in her class too.

Coach Cox stared at the ceiling and asked us to put our phones away, or he'd take them. We obeyed. After class, we all told Carolyn congratulations. She smiled and blushed: "Thanks. I don't even know what it means." It means a lot, we told her. It means a lot.

Miss Simpson must have had things to do outside of school, but what they were, none of us knew. She had gone to college out of state and studied literary history and Russian and she talked about teaching English in Japan. She had a chin-length, strawberry-blond bob, and she wore leggings and holiday sweaters and scrunchies and she talked about aerobics and cake-making and we heard she was into online dating. She was another teacher/Adams alum, like Mr. Overton, but she freaked us out more, basically 'cause she was so pathetic. She had lived in New York, she told us, right out of college, in an apartment with a "girlfriend."

The guys called her a dyke and it was humiliating to be praised by her. She called on the girls more than the boys—this was weird— and she offered to spend time after school with those of us that were already making A's.

During teaching, she made eye contact and smiled and she always had lipstick on her teeth, her bra straps fell down and she reached inside her top to pull them up, like, every fifteen minutes. She ate during class, which wasn't allowed. As we filed in, she said hello to each of us individually but tried to vary it: "Hey there!"; "Hiya"; "How you doin' "; "What's up?"; "He-ey!" She was in a weirder mood than usual that day, and we guessed it was because Homecoming made her reflect on her sad-o high school life. We were sure she was a reject back then. We couldn't imagine otherwise.

As we took our seats, she hoisted herself up onto her desk, dangling her legs from the front. She smiled and started unwrapping a PowerBar, drinking a Diet Coke. We were always amazed that she was still overweight, based on what we saw her eat. She probably night-binged, we thought.

We went through the motions in class—some reading, some discussion, some stalling by us so she wouldn't have time to assign more work. And right before the bell rang, she asked Carolyn to stay after. Blake Wyatt was sitting in the front row and he turned around and mouthed, "Trouble." We laughed.

The bell rang and we filed out the door. As we passed Miss Simpson, we looked at her: she had a pile of papers in her hand— our essays from the previous week. As she fanned them, we could recognize our titles, our pen color, our penmanship. We could see they were graded, and we wished she would hand them back.

We looked back at Carolyn and she was fiddling with her phone or something and didn't look up. Alyssa Jennings was Miss Simpson's aide and was using the computer to do up some assignment for the freshman class. She was pulling together YouTube clips from Shakespeare adaptations and mashing them up. She stayed in the room while Miss Simpson talked to Carolyn, and that's how we found out what happened.

"So, I was really quite taken with your essay." Miss Simpson was chewing as she spoke. "Really quite taken."

Carolyn kept her head down and stared at her phone underneath her desk. Alyssa had headphones on, but had turned off the sound.

Carolyn said she was glad she liked it. Miss Simpson picked her teeth with her index finger. No wonder she wasn't married.

"Well, I'm being sarcastic. I think you know that." She paused, picking up the last piece of her PowerBar. She put it in her mouth and talked with her mouth open and Alyssa said she had to look away but she could hear Miss Simpson as she swallowed, taking a swig of her Diet Coke or whatever.

"No, I actually *wasn't* quite taken with it, Carolyn. I really wasn't." She paused again. "You defined yourself as *clear*."

Alyssa said Carolyn's face went red, and then she started laughing, just a little.

Miss Simpson was red now, glaring at Carolyn. "Do you think this is funny?"

Carolyn looked down.

"Well, the point of the assignment was to define yourself as a *color*. Clear isn't really a color, is it?"

"I don't know."

"I think you *do* know. I think you *do* know that clear isn't a color. And I think you know that the point of the assignment was to try to put a finger on what makes you unique. Can you tell me what you value about yourself?"

Miss Simpson let out a breath.

"You know, I hate doing this, but this just has to be done." When Alyssa told us later, we wondered why. "I think you *do* know what color you are. You're just afraid to write it."

She paused. For effect, Alyssa said. Miss Simpson was such a drama queen.

"Isn't that right?" She was angry? Or encouraging? Alyssa couldn't tell.

"I don't know." Carolyn was rolling her eyes around, Alyssa said. She said she thought she looked mad.

"So, I'm going to ask you to redo the assignment."

Carolyn let out a grunt or a protest or a groan—Alyssa wasn't sure what.

Miss Simpson paused. She tucked her hair behind her ears and took a breath. She tried to throw her PowerBar wrapper in the trash can and missed. She exhaled.

"What do you think, Carolyn?"

"I wasn't really sure how to, like, approach the assignment."

We could imagine the room: it was always too hot and it smelled of CK One or some other cheapy drugstore perfume.

"You know, Carolyn, I'm trying to help you. I've been trying to help you since you arrived here. I'm a big fan of yours."

The room could be suffocating, it made it hard to breathe.

She continued, "But, you know, the question is this: are *you* a fan of you?"

Out the window, Taylor Lyon and some senior guys were pushing one another in the courtyard. Carolyn watched them.

Miss Simpson sighed. "You girls. I wish you could see yourselves like I do."

Carolyn kept staring out the window.

She sighed again. "I just want you to think about what color you are."

"Okay," Carolyn said. What a totally lame assignment.

Miss Simpson would be really smiling now, we could imagine that, lipstick on teeth.

Blake Wyatt looked at the window and Alyssa stared back out. He gave Miss Simpson the finger, but she didn't see.

"I think you are so special and unique and distinct, don't you?"
Silence.

"Well, I *do*. And I'd be really grateful if you'd rewrite your essay along those lines, okay?" Miss Simpson waited a moment.
"Okay?"

Carolyn nodded.

"Great," Miss Simpson said. "That's *great*."

Carolyn started to get up, to gather her things.

"Oh, Carolyn?"

She picked up her bag, put it on over her head, across her body.

"How are things going otherwise? You're getting along all right with the other girls?"

Carolyn looked at Alyssa—and Alyssa said she couldn't tell if Carolyn was pissed or amused. Carolyn looked back at Miss Simpson and she nodded.

"I hope so. I think you're very special." Miss Simpson smiled and Carolyn walked out the door.

9

In the cafeteria, trays clanked and crashed and we yelled across
the room and threw apples and roast beef sandwiches when the
teachers weren't looking. Some days we brought our lunches and
some days we bought our lunches and we sat in the same seats day
in, day out. The cafeteria smelled of hot dogs and curly fries and
lasagna and chicken fried steak and gravy. It smelled of disin-
fectant and freshmen just out of PE and girls who have just reapplied their perfume. At Carolyn's school, and on every other
school we'd seen on TV, kids got to go out for lunch, leave campus and go to the mall or a restaurant or a gas station or home.
Carolyn used to go for sushi, that's what she told us, or to Whole
Foods, where she and her friends would get a green juice. "It's
weird you don't get to leave," she would say to us. "Yeah," we would
agree, and we resented her, just a little, for making us feel backward again. Not everything different is better.

A low wall ran around the cafeteria, making a square in the middle, and lunch tables that seated six were arranged on either side, gridlike. Brooke was at a table in the center, Gemma Davies and Andrew Wright sitting with her. The rest of the seats were empty. At our table, we talked about the nominations and how lame it was and how it was weird that Carolyn was nominated in so many classes. We said we thought Brooke was probably still bitching about Carolyn's place on the list and we watched her as she broke off tiny pieces of her sandwich, chewing slowly, hand in front of her face.

We looked at the table where the other cheerleaders sat—Amber and Bridget and Emma and Tiffany and Taylor and Carolyn with Shane. Shane had his arm around Carolyn. When Coach Cox passed their table, Shane dropped it real quick—and Coach Cox smiled. And then we watched Shane's hand grab Carolyn's underneath the table, and he rubbed their hands against her leg. We imagined all the things they talked about: her friends back in New Jersey, maybe, or how Shane was doing in football, or maybe they bitched about their teachers like the rest of us did. We didn't know. At the table, all eyes were on Carolyn, and most of the eyes in the rest of the cafeteria too. We couldn't help it.

At the time, nobody was surprised that Shane was so into her, that the cheerleaders linked arms with her as they walked down the hall, that she was invited to every party those first months, even the ones for only the popular kids. She was just so cool.

Janitor Ken mopped as we ate. He was slow or maybe handicapped or maybe just aloof—some of the guys liked to high-five him when they saw him in the halls, liked to try to get him to talk about how Alabama had played over the weekend, or who he thought was hotter, Miley Cyrus or Taylor Swift. When he answered, they almost always laughed and then repeated back what he'd said and then tried to get him to say it again, only louder, and we weren't sure if they were being nice or making fun of him or what they were doing. It made us feel queasy, want to look away, that much we knew. But then maybe we were the assholes, ignoring him every time we saw him—pretending we couldn't see him or, worse, that we could see right through him. We watched him now and we could have sworn Shane threw something in his direction—a curly fry or something—and it landed on top of Ken's head. And it stayed there as he bent over to pick up an empty milk carton.

Miss Simpson sat at a table with Mr. Ferris and Coach Cox and Mrs. Matthew. We never thought about whether or not they even liked one another, we just laughed at Miss Simpson's and Mrs. Matthew's outfits, nearly crying about their excessive use of scrunchies. That day, we were laughing most at Mrs. Matthew: she was wearing a brown and orange sweater, a giant cornucopia of vegetables embroidered on the center. Nicole said she wasn't sure that Mrs. Matthew was cut out to give us guidance after all, if these were the life choices she was making. "That sweater makes me want to hurl. Extreme motivation to keep me out of trouble."

Lauren's dad gave a lecture once a week about leadership in middle management at Cullman Community College and had told her that he'd seen Mrs. Matthew there, along with Miss Simpson. He thought they were both doing cake-making—Miss Simpson was carrying a box of edible flowers, but Mrs. Matthew was carrying two volumes of Freud. Mr. Brink was intrigued and asked her about it. Psycotherapy, she had said, and Mr. Brink told Lauren and Lauren told us. Psychotherapy. We just thought she was psycho. Every day, we watched her eat a sad-looking salad out of a sad-looking piece of Tupperware. And we looked away.

After we'd eaten, we watched Brooke Moore walk into the bathroom. We waited one, maybe two minutes, and then we went too. We hadn't followed her, not exactly, but we liked to be near Brooke, no matter what people said. She was popular, she was cool—if she liked you, this mattered. Things happened around Brooke, this was a fact. She was there when Blake Wyatt made his first bong, when Dylan Hall scored his first keg, when Alyssa Jennings got so wasted she walked in topless to the 7-Eleven. Brooke was there for all of that stuff, and every other thing that had ever happened in our town. We walked into the bathroom after her and went straight into the stalls. We read the walls, covered with Sharpie marker, bubble letters, hearts, crosses.

Jesus Saves!

Alicia Cooper is a SLUTTY SLUTTERSON.

I get high on ~~LIFE~~ CRYSTAL METH

We heard gagging and coughing. We knew it wasn't one of us; the noise had started before we'd closed the stall doors. And it continued after we'd all flushed, after we'd all come out to wash our hands—always washing them a few seconds longer when with one another, to show that we were clean, but not OCD. We stood in front of the mirror and shared our lip gloss and hair spray and Viva La Juicy perfume. If Brooke had come out, we would have shared our stuff with her, shown her what brands we used, let her tell us if our eye shadow was right for our skin tone. But she was slow today—the gagging and coughing was louder, longer than usual, the splash into the toilet heavier than most days. We didn't say anything to one another, not then, not other days either, but we looked at each other wide-eyed in the mirror until the toilet flushed. And then we went back to what we were doing, looking in the mirror, brushing Bare Escentuals loose powder on our noses, smoothing cream blush on the apples of our cheeks. Brooke emerged from the stall, her face flushed and eyes red. She smiled and we told her congratulations. "No big deal," she said. "No big deal."

Trig was after lunch.

Mr. Ferris didn't greet us as we walked in but we greeted him. He was hot. We looked forward to this class, even if it was crazy hard.

"So I've got a little competition for y'all today." He smiled and, when he did, he had a dimple on the right side of his mouth. It was cute.

He smiled as he looked around. He was easy to please, Mr. Ferris, and when we could please him, we wanted to. He'd been in the military or something, but was teaching now—it was kind of sad. We heard he and Miss Simpson had gone on a date in August or something, which surprised everybody, mostly because she was a total lesbian. Blake Wyatt had seen them at the movie theater once—seeing *X Files 2*—and Nicole Willis had served them nachos and Diet Cokes at the Blue Bistro afterward. Dylan Hall worked at Sonic and said Miss Simpson ordered a large order of fried pickles at 11.45 that same night—comfort eating, he said, and that seemed about right.

Mr. Ferris was the most popular math teacher in the school, though, and if you went to RateMyTeachers.com, you'd see hundreds of comments about him—"Mr. Ferris is super nice and even though he is not easy, the class is pretty fun."—and if you stayed on long enough, you'd see something obscene—about his ass or his tongue or about his stamina—before the moderators came in to clean it up.

He cleared his throat: it was all he had to do to get our

attention. "Homecoming shouldn't be the only thing y'all care about." He looked around and he told us to get up out of our seats. Some of the guys groaned. We did what we were told: we loved to look at him. He was wearing dark khakis and a blue button-down shirt and a red tie. He had gel in his hair, or something, but not too much—enough to make him look like he'd just gotten out of the shower. His face was tan and his nose was just a little sunburned. His eyes were pale blue and when the light hit them they kind of sparkled. Lauren sent a text: "His ass is sooooo fine today."

Dylan Hall stayed in his seat. "I'm not getting up until you tell us what we're doing." He was kidding, we thought, but it annoyed us. We didn't want him to piss off Mr. Ferris.

"I'm going to seat you according to your averages. Report cards are out next week."

He wasn't the only math teacher who did this—Mr. Scott and Mrs. Kuby and Mr. Ford did it too—and it was something that you either loved or hated but everybody said they hated it—you'd look like a total geek otherwise.

We groaned a little. We looked over at Carolyn, her eyes flashing around the room. She had her pinkie finger in her mouth and she was chewing on a nail. She hadn't heard about this.

We stood against the blackboard and we waited for Mr. Ferris to call the names. He started with the lowest averages first. This was like "American Idol," we said later, only stupid and not entertaining.

When Mr. Ferris got to the last five, it was only girls left. We were there, of course, but so was Carolyn. Of course she was. We waited by the blackboard, careful not to lean against it, you didn't want chalk marks on your ass, the imprint of a reciprocal function on your back. Mr. Ferris got slower toward the end—we wondered if he'd even seen "American Idol," or if he'd just picked up this kind of suspense thing—and we took our places one by one. Carolyn was last, highest grade—she had taken trig already at her old school, and she hardly studied at all, or at least that's what she said. When her name was called, her eyes got all wide, she looked like she could explode, and she put her head down and walked to the desk in the far right-hand corner, her hair covering her whole face. We were already seated, but we wanted to jump up and tuck her hair behind her ears, so her eyes could see the way in front of her, so she wouldn't knock over the desks, fall on her face. We wanted her hair out of her face so she could see, but also because it looked like she was showing off: nobody cares how thick and long and shiny your hair is, shut up about it already.

Mr. Ferris smiled. "Homecoming Court *and* highest average in advanced trig. Somebody's having a good day."

10

We practiced every day after school, from 3.30 until 5 P.M. in the Aquadome, a glass globe with the pool inside, the only thing like it in the state. Natural light streamed through the ceiling, and when we did the backstroke, we looked up at the sky, watched the sun, the clouds, flocks of birds. If there weren't any clouds, the sun would shine so bright we had to close our eyes. Our parents said that the Aquadome was the brightest building in Adamsville: they wore their sunglasses while they sat on the bleachers and watched us swim.

We were surprised when Carolyn joined the team—popular girls did cheerleading or soccer or, worst case, track. Swimming was nearly the same as band at Adams, and there weren't any cool kids on the team, had never been. Butterfly was Carolyn's strongest stroke, the same as Nicole Willis. She was a little bit faster than Nicole, we noticed, and her flip turns were amazing. Coach Billy made us get out of the pool and watch her.

"Look at Carolyn's form. The power in her kick comes from her hips, not her knees. That's what you should be doing."

We rolled our eyes.

Coach Billy turned back to us. "Cut it out. Watch."

We were put in the same lane for practices. During drills, when we were hanging on to the walls and resting and watching the clock, Jessica noticed a pattern of incisions on Carolyn's right arm. "Like a cat scratch or something," she told us later. "But deeper and weirder." We tried to get a look later, when we had moved on to the kickboard drills, but she caught us looking at her. She dropped her right arm and she began to tread water. Her head and shoulders stayed completely still, but underneath, her legs were kicking and cycling like crazy. When the clock hit sixty, she pushed off the wall and kicked. She moved so fast but barely made a splash. The marks on her arm were visible then and they looked deep, they looked like they would hurt, sting, ache.

She could swim two laps without taking a breath. Her butterfly was beautiful. When she dove into the water, she barely made a splash, and when she swam breaststroke, her first pull and first kick lasted for almost fifteen yards. She was talented, for sure, and after practice, sometimes we would talk to her a little. Sometimes, we wished she could have been a little bit slower. Now Carolyn was first in the lane and we were used to swimming in the same order. Changes like that sucked, but we liked to watch her swim, liked to watch her glide through the water, never making a splash.

When we were in our caps and in our goggles and in our swimsuits, we all looked the same—boys and girls—maybe some of us a little fatter and some of us skinnier, but, really, we were the same. At meets, our parents would mix us up when they were cheering: they'd call for Lauren when they meant Nicole. And it was the same with us: you'd start talking to someone, thinking it was someone else, and then midway through the conversation, when the goggles were pulled down around her neck, you'd realize you'd gotten it wrong—and your mind raced back to remember what you'd said. When we were younger—five and six—our team was the Mighty Minnows, and then we graduated to Blue Dolphins when we got to middle school. We said that now we were in high school, we must be Whales, and we laughed, just a little, even though it never seemed very funny. Not when we were looking at our stomachs and our breasts, or the guys' muffin tops starting to form over their Speedos. Whales, every last one of us. But when we were in the water, that seemed to disappear. We went fast and long and we turned pink and hot and sweaty under the water, as sweaty as the track team, we'd say, only you just couldn't see it. We'd groan at the drills, the sets of 500s, then 200s, then 100s, then 50s, then 25 sprints. We'd groan and we'd complain and we'd see if we could pull the lane rope on the backstroke to make things easier—we'd do all of this but we knew that when we swam we were alive and we were invisible all at once. And this is how we wanted to be.

The locker room was dark, one fluorescent light flickered in the center, but mostly we changed in shadow. When you walked inside, after an hour and a half in the brightness of the Aquadome, the darkness was almost frightening. Lockers lined the walls, old wooden benches in the center, with carvings and graffiti all over them. This was the part of the Aquadome that was old—one set of doors led to the pool, another to the Adamsville High gym, where the basketball players did their drills. An old-fashioned scale—like the kind in the doctor's office—sat beside the door to the gym. We heard that the cheerleaders weighed themselves every day, that Ms. Powell took down the numbers, threatening to kick them off the squad if they went over 125. People said Brooke Moore had adjusted the scale over the summer, to ensure that she stayed put. We didn't know how that was possible but, still, we believed this was true. We weighed ourselves once or twice a year, more than that was too painful, and we watched the number creep up every time, and we promised that the next year would be different, that we would work to make the numbers smaller, like they were when we were freshmen or, better still, in eighth grade.

Carolyn dressed in the bathroom stall, not out in the open like everybody else. We'd watch her gather her bag and try to walk silently away, but we still saw her. She was the skinniest of all of us, for sure, so we thought it was weird, even though we might have wanted to do it ourselves.

We talked later about the marks on her arm. And maybe we should have asked what was wrong, but we didn't and plus, Carolyn wouldn't have answered anyway. When we were waiting outside for our parents, she was all covered up and we wouldn't want her to think we were looking at her body, so we talked about practice, about how much we hated the butterfly drills, about how pruned our fingers had gotten in the pool. Looking back, we realized these were the only times we really got to speak to Carolyn, and we didn't say anything that mattered, nothing that counted. Our parents eventually arrived and we got in our cars. Carolyn was still standing on the curbside when the last of us left.

She waved. "Bye."

"Bye."

Sometimes, we wished we'd said more.

Carolyn left her messenger bag in the locker room the following Tuesday. It was a blue Jansport one, with CEL monogrammed on the front—we spent a while guessing her middle name.

Lauren said it must be Esther. We laughed.

"Or Evelyn?" Nicole guessed. "That would be kind of cool."

"Eugene," said Jessica, her eyes wide and flashing. We laughed some more.

Nicole said it was probably Elizabeth. And we all agreed. That seemed the most likely.

We stood in a circle around the bag, as if it were a living thing, as if it might bite us or talk to us or walk away. We thought about bringing it to Mr. Overton's office, or texting somebody who might have her number, but we went into the handicapped bathroom stall and opened it up.

Two three-ring binders, new and clean and with handouts inside them from trig and English. The pages were lined up straight against one another—like textbooks or something you'd buy; they were perfect and looked barely used, even though they were full. Her notebooks, one for every class, labeled in her handwriting—handwriting so neat it was kind of scary. We skimmed through these—afraid to say anything out loud in case somebody walked in. We were ready to find her secrets, notes about Shane or other guys or the boyfriend back home. But, instead, we found notes from class. Everything verbatim, exactly what our teachers had said. So mostly we talked about her handwriting. It was like a font—Times New Roman or Arial—just perfect or anal, one or the other. In the front pouch, she had makeup—Lancôme Juicy lip glosses, Maybelline BB cream, a bottle of NARS Body Glow (Lauren told us that these ran from around sixty bucks on the Sephora site). We found tampons. We found a skinny package of meds: Yasmin. We weren't surprised she was on the Pill, but we said we were—somebody said that we should steal them, see how long it would take before she got pregnant. But we put them back where we found them. There were photographs, wallet-size ones, lying loose in the bottom—some of her, old ones, where her hair was shorter, lighter—the lighting looked more professional than the school shots they did at Adams. She was airbrushed, we said. A copy of *The Bell Jar* and *Girl Interrupted* and *A Room of One's Own* and *Glamour* magazine. A Slim-Fast meal replacement bar. Ibuprofen. Marc Jacobs Daisy, half empty. A pack of cigarettes: Newport 100s. Nobody knew she smoked. And gum, five or six packs of gum, all sugar-free. An envelope with her name on it—we opened it—a card. A bear on the front, blue and gray, with a balloon and a speech bubble: "Happy birthday, Daughter." We opened it up and there were two words written on the inside: "Love, Dad."

The door opened and we felt a *whoosh* of air. We piled the things back into the bag and we left the stall, walked out of the locker room, the back way, not looking to see who had walked in, feeling a little afraid. We told one another that it was unlikely that it was Carolyn and unlikelier still that she would have seen us.

We told a few people what we had found: a letter, birth control pills, cigarettes, Slim-Fast. Pictures of herself. Weeks later, we heard this story repeated back to us, about a bunch of girls finding Carolyn Lessing's messenger bag, and about all the stuff they'd found. Only the list had changed and gotten longer. It included Ecstasy, razor blades, copies of *Playgirl*. Maybe somebody else had found her bag. Had found it in a different place, at a different time, with different things inside it. More interesting things, more exciting things. Because what we heard back just wasn't the same.

11

Carolyn's mother had some big job at 3M. She was one of only a few female senior engineers at the plant in New Jersey, and the job in Adamsville was a promotion. Most everybody from the new part of town worked for 3M; there had been articles in the paper about how it had saved Adamsville, how it had made us rich, the town was now "booming." But we didn't notice much change, only that an Abercrombie came to our mall, and a bagel shop had opened, and Banana Republic was going to open soon, along with a Kate Spade store. Three Starbucks had come too. That year, though, around the time that Carolyn moved in, we heard about things closing: we were forced to watch the news in first period, and we heard about the "recession." It didn't matter to us, we said, but our parents looked a little more tired, maybe, and there was a little bit more arguing at home. We heard Shane Duggan's dad lost his job, and Brooke Moore's mom had had to take up hours at

Parisians to supplement Mr. Moore's cut in shifts at Monsanto. Brothers and sisters of kids who had graduated from college moved home, while they waited to get jobs in Birmingham or Nashville or Atlanta. Really, though, nothing had changed. One of the Starbucks eventually closed, but it was stupid to have three anyway. Plus, drinking coffee was for poseurs.

We heard that Carolyn's mother was some sort of genius, and that she was like the guy on "The Apprentice," only a woman, and that she had lived in the North all her life. We heard she was divorced, or separated, and maybe she'd had Carolyn when she was sixteen? Like Lorelai Gilmore. We weren't totally sure.

After we'd found her bag, we tried to be extra nice to Carolyn, tried to find ways to show her we were sweet, friendly, to show that we weren't bitches who snuck around looking through people's stuff. It wasn't as if we thought she knew about it—nothing like that—but we still wanted to make things okay. Looking back, we wondered if we had already started to realize things wouldn't always be so great for her at Adams, that maybe Taylor would end up dropping her too, the same way she'd dropped us. We asked Carolyn to go to Wendy's with us after practice or we told her we thought her flip turns were great or we asked her where she got her bathing suit. In the meantime, Carolyn started talking to us a little more and we learned a little more about her. And a couple of weeks after the thing with the messenger bag, she invited us over to her house after school.

As we drove to the other side of town, we didn't say much to one another, didn't talk about how excited we were to be going to Carolyn's, to have been invited. Tiffany and Taylor had been there during the second week of school, but just to pick Carolyn up to go to the mall. Carolyn had told them honk when they got there, she'd run out, no need for them to come in, but Taylor said she had to go to the bathroom, and then Tiffany did too, so she and Tiffany got to go inside and they used the half bath in the front hall.

Taylor told our study hall that the bathroom was "wicked" and that there were little tea candles and L'Occitane soaps and Tommy Hilfiger hand towels and tons of expensive crap and that was "just in the *bathroom.*" Whatever, we thought. We were the first ones to get invited for, like, an afternoon, with an actual invitation. We weren't sure what it all meant, Carolyn asking us, but we knew it was something. We tried to stay calm but we smiled to ourselves and we turned up the radio and looked out the window.

FOR SALE signs lined the streets, along with wooden signs, red and black for Lincoln High—GO CATS! and LINCOLN NUMBER ONE. On our side of town it was orange and black and bears. This was a new subdivision and every third home was under construction—hollowed-out spaces with trucks in front, nobody inside. Trees were thin and tall, new and spaced apart at even intervals. Our football team had tried to roll four of the houses on D'Evereux Drive last year and had failed, we heard, 'cause the trees were so far apart, and they had so few leaves. We knew that John Maltby lived on this street—he was quarterback for Lincoln—and so did Candace Starrs, head cheerleader. The two of them had dated in the sixth grade, until they realized they were third or fourth cousins. We went to Candace's birthday party in eighth grade—she had invited everybody from church group—and the guys fixed it so that she did Five Minutes of Heaven with John. They were blindfolded and when they came out from the closet, and pulled down the scarves, Candace started to cry. Our mothers made us write thank-you notes for attending, and we had to apologize in the notes too. Only Nicole did that, as far as we knew.

As we drove into the subdivision, we tried to imagine the interiors of the homes—we had been inside some of them with our mothers during open houses over the past few years—but nobody had been inside Carolyn's. Our houses were old, and our parents thought this made them better, but we didn't think so. We had thick, beige carpets in every room, kitchens with crappy oak cabinets and ugly gold lighting fixtures. There were too many rooms in our houses, we thought, after having watched HGTV and seen "open plan" places. Our houses were cluttered and too small and too old and our parents didn't care. We tried not to care, too, but with Carolyn's house, with all the new builds on the other side of town, it was hard not to.

She had a circular driveway, and we parked behind her Honda and a silver Audi: her mother's, we guessed. We rang the doorbell and heard footsteps. Carolyn opened the door and we breathed in the smell of freesia. She let us in and we shifted from side to side to side in the front hall, Carolyn taking our backpacks and putting them on the stairs. The floors were hardwood, and the hall was filled with sunshine—we looked up and saw a skylight. Carolyn smiled. "That was my mother's idea. She had it put in after we bought this place." She led us down the hall, the smell of freesia still strong. We said later that the house was amazing—furniture straight out of Pottery Barn and all eclectic and cool. Containers from the Container Store against the wall and there were framed paintings evenly spaced as we moved through the corridor. We didn't have time to look at them properly, we said later, but we knew that it was all bright and pretty and cool.

Carolyn kept saying they hadn't finished, but we didn't know what she meant. The house was like something out of *Martha Stewart* or *Real Simple* or one of those. The kitchen was at the end of the hall and it was all granite and steel and modern. Pretty jars and pots were stacked on the counters—in a way that looked cluttered but orderly. Like the apartment on "How I Met Your Mother" or something. Carolyn's mom was sitting on a bar stool as we walked in, a newspaper in front of her on the granite counter.

Carolyn's mother insisted we call her Abby. She was pale and didn't wear makeup and her hair was so shiny we said later that we wanted to touch it. She had eyes that were small and green and sparkling. She was pretty, and we talked later about how she was like an old actress from the Independent Film Channel—maybe like Julianne Moore?—or a musician or some alternative person like that. She was skinny and pretty and older for sure, but not old like our parents. She looked a lot like Carolyn, we said later. They really could have been sisters.

All of their food was weird: Abby fixed us a snack of wheaten crackers and hummus and almonds. When Carolyn asked for some chips, Abby made a face. "Chips aren't food," she said and laughed. She was eating an almond in several bites. We sat and we ate and she asked us questions about our classes and Homecoming and she asked Lauren where she got her hair cut. She said that Carolyn needed a trim and asked Lauren how long she let it go between appointments. She asked us about swimming and if it made us hungry and if we ran cross-country. She asked Nicole what kind of grades she got and she asked Jessica if she had a boyfriend. She asked us what our parents did and where we wanted to go to college. We didn't get a chance to answer any of her questions, not really, and before we had finished, she said she was going out and that she'd be back around ten or eleven.

Carolyn let us into her bedroom, down the hall from the kitchen, and it was huge, like a showroom from "Selling Houses." She had gadgets and books everywhere: her own MacBook, one of the old ones that was pink, with a handle. Four, maybe five bookcases and books everywhere. Pictures, dozens of them, some framed and some not framed, but lots with this thin, tanned man. Silver-haired. Like George Clooney, only not hot. When we asked who the man in the pictures *was* she told us he was her dad. She told us he was a writer, a novelist, and that his books were published in lots of different languages. We had never heard of him but we didn't admit it, and Jessica asked if she could borrow one of the books.

"As long as you're really careful."

"Of course." Jessica smiled. Later, we all took turns reading it. A novel, hard to follow, about a man who was studying physics in some New England town—or maybe it was in Europe? We couldn't tell. He was trying to make a breakthrough or something. He had a wife who was leaving him because he was so obsessed with his experiments. But then he had all these other women that he had sex with. The sex in the book was weird—we weren't even sure it was describing sex, only that we kept seeing the words "cock" and "wet" and we knew it had to be something like that. We read later that he was a "literary writer who struggled to find a sympathetic audience." We had never read anything like it. In his biography in the back, it said he lived alone and it didn't mention Carolyn. At a sleepover months later, we got laughing about it—the book, the sex, the bio—and somebody said that she'd probably made him up, and we weren't really sure if it was that funny, but we laughed at the time. It somehow got back to Carolyn, though, that people had been saying this, and we wondered how she could have known. We told each other that it must have come from somewhere else.

A digital scale lay on the floor next to her desk and to its right, up on the wall, was a piece of graph paper, and penciled there were dates and numbers: 10/1: 113.2, 10/2: 113.0, 10/3: 113.7, followed by three exclamation marks, 10/7: 111.0, followed by a smiley face.

Lauren used Carolyn's bathroom. In her shower, she found Kerastase shampoo, Benefit bodywash and on the sink counter were her GHDs, more Lancôme Juicy lip glosses, Marc Jacobs fragrance. Things we begged for but weren't allowed to have, too expensive and too "mature." Lauren looked in the medicine cabinet and she told us later what she saw: an orange pill case, with Carolyn's name and address typed out. Something called Seroquel.

We texted people about this later, to tell them about her house, about what we had seen. We took photos of her bathroom cabinet and the scale and put them up on Instagram, Facebook, wherever. Looking back, it's easy to see how fucked up that was, how irresponsible we'd been, with information and with other people's feelings. But we couldn't have known what was going to happen. We couldn't have known what those things meant or what they were for or why they were there or what she might do. At least, this is what we told ourselves and one another, over and over, for years to come: we couldn't have known.

facebook
(posts deleted and recovered)

Brooke Moore and **Carolyn Lessing** commented on this.

Gemma Davies
What can be found CL's bath room? crack, cloud 9, cristal meth & pepto bismal. GROSS.

10 people like this.

Brooke Moore Cloud 9 = crystal meth

Carolyn Lessing since you've never been to my house u are a liar

Gemma Davies Relayble sourse

Carolyn Lessing u shouldn't believe everything you hear

Gemma Davies look whose talking. Stop spreading rumers about my freind

Carolyn Lessing She spreads rumors about me. I thought we were friends?

Gemma Davies ive lots of freinds

Carolyn Lessing I thought you were nicer than her

Gemma Davies PM me

Carolyn Lessing OK.

12

Adamsville Plaza looks like any other mall you've ever seen, only lamer, and smaller, and with hardly any good stores. Two floors, with a department store on each one. Parisians, the best, on the top, and a Kmart in the bottom. There'd been talk about a Kohl's coming to Adamsville Plaza, but that never happened, so we traveled to Birmingham once a year to get the stuff that we couldn't get here. Every three storefronts lay empty, mannequins dismantled and signs that said, YOUR STORE COULD BE HERE! Spencer's Gifts was doing a going-out-of-business sale, and we heard Payless Shoes might be closing too, which sucked, 'cause they did the dyed-to-match pumps for Homecoming and prom. Every corner had a fountain, and when we were little, we would throw pennies in and make a wish. We wondered what we wished for back then, we couldn't remember, but now we knew what we wanted: for some guy to see us outside of Aeropostale and want our phone number, for Brooke Moore and Gemma Davies to come up to us and ask us to walk around with them, for something, anything, to happen.

On game days, we went to Adamsville Plaza after school, hoping we'd be able to afford something new to wear, that there'd be some kind of clearance at Abercrombie that would put things at a price our allowances could manage. But mostly, we sat around eating Great American Cookie Company cookies while complaining about our thighs. One day in late October, we saw Carolyn there, walking through the food court with Taylor Lyon and Tiffany Port. We waved and said hello, but Taylor and Tiffany ignored us, kept walking straight ahead, their eyes determined not to meet ours—but Carolyn stopped, looked right at us and waved.

"Hey, you guys." She walked over to us, Taylor and Tiffany hesitated a little, but then kept moving ahead, away from Häagen-Dazs and toward Payless.

"Shopping?" Carolyn looked us straight in the eyes. Jessica offered her a piece of cookie and she shook her head.

"We're getting new makeup," Lauren told her, even though we were just walking around, had no money to buy anything.

"It's bonus time at Clinique." Carolyn pointed toward Parisians. "But I think their stuff is gross."

We nodded and wanted to ask her where wasn't gross, where she got her makeup in New Jersey, and if she had to wear makeup at all, her skin was so perfect.

"Bobbi Brown is the best," Carolyn continued. "But they don't have that here. I can't believe there's no Sephora." She sighed.

"We don't have anything here. It's like living in a third world country." Nicole wadded up the bag that our cookies had come in, threw it in the trash can. "You have to go to Birmingham."

"My mom was saying that. About Birmingham. Not the third world." Carolyn kinda laughed and so did we and she put her hand through her hair and we wondered if she used Argan oil or if she'd had it permanently straightened or was it just that silky. "I think we're going next week or something. You guys should totally come."

We smiled. And then we weren't totally sure if she meant it, and if she did, if we could convince our mothers to let us do this. A day of shopping with Carolyn Lessing. Epic.

"Carolyn." We looked around and saw Taylor barking at her from outside Aeropostale. When we looked at her she glanced down at her phone.

Carolyn rolled her eyes. She took her phone out of her pocket, and it was all lit up. Lauren said she saw Shane's name on the screen, along with a picture of him, his hair all sandy and in his eyes, his mouth open as if he were screaming in your face. We imagined Carolyn taking the picture, how close to him she'd have to have been to get that, how relaxed he must have been around her.

"I better take this," she told us and then the phone stopped flashing. She shrugged her shoulders and she smiled and turned to walk toward Taylor and Tiffany, standing with their hands on their hips, pissed off with us for detaining their friend. And then she turned back. "You wanna come shopping with us?"

We looked at one another, wondered what it would be like to shop with Taylor and Tiffany and Carolyn, if they would make fun of our untoned stomachs, our slightly too rounded thighs. If they would laugh at stuff we thought was cute, or worse, tell us stuff was cute that wasn't.

"I think we're about to go home." Jessica said this with her eyes lowered, her hand in front of her mouth, her long brown layers covering half of her face. She sucked at lying.

"Oh, totally. I should go home too . . ." The phone lit up again, with Shane's face. Carolyn put her finger in the air and mouthed, "One sec."

She picked up the phone. "Can I call you right back? I'm shopping with the girls." And then we heard his voice, all muffled, on the other end. She laughed. And then said, "Totally. Call you in a sec."

We said later that we wished they had talked for longer, we wanted to know what he needed from her, what they talked about and if he texted or if they did iChat or what. We wondered if we were part of "the girls" and if she ever talked about us, whether Shane even knew who we were. We talked about how cool she was with him, how it was awesome that she was able to reject his calls, wasn't sitting around waiting for him all day. We wondered if that was why Shane liked her so much, 'cause she was so cool, so laid back.

Carolyn looked at us and smiled. "Sorry." We shook our heads, were quick to say not to worry.

"But you're coming to the big game tonight? And to Skate Night?" She did air quotes around the words "big game" and "Skate Night" and we thought it was funny. People sometimes forgot about that later—how funny she was.

"Uh-huh."

"Cool," she said, walking backward. "And if you're buying foundation, try it on in natural light."

She said this in a nice way, not in the way that Brooke or Taylor would have, with a laugh and then an insinuation that we looked all trashy, too made-up. "I only ever buy foundation after I've looked at it on me in daylight," she continued, almost skipping. "Otherwise, I look like a gypsy." She turned around then and ran toward Taylor and Tiffany. We smiled when she said this, thought it was cool of her to tell us something like that, even if it was only small.

We went to the game. Stood halfway up the bleachers, in front of the fifty-yard line, all in a row, cheering and clapping and stomping our feet and looking around to see who else was there. It didn't matter who we played, not to us, and even though we would say it didn't matter if we won: it did. We didn't understand all the rules in football, not really, but we watched our boys and we watched the scoreboard and we watched the cheerleaders yell and dance and sparkle.

We painted our faces before we went: bear paws on our cheeks and glitter on our lips and orange and black ribbons in our hair. We slipped Absolut into our Gatorade and we snuck sips of beer from cans hidden in the trunks of seniors' cars. We watched the boys play their hearts out, watched Coach Cox scream for them to do better. And we watched Carolyn Lessing come to the bleachers halfway through, smiling and waving and stopping to talk to every other person she passed.

Usually, we won. That year in October, we won every home game we played. The guys were thrilled, the coaches ecstatic, the faculty delighted, our parents beside themselves. We were glad: winning made everything more fun, made everything feel better.

After every home game, we had Skate Night. Organized by the PTA or the coaches or maybe it was just some moneymaking thing from the Adamsville Bowl—it didn't matter to us, not really, 'cause it was something we did. There weren't many of those things, not in Adamsville, and Skate Night was fun, no matter what we said about it out loud. After the game was over, after the team had showered and changed, after we had gathered our banners and reapplied deodorant and put the GHDs through our hair one more time, after the band had locked their instruments away and after our parents had kissed us and told us not to stay out too late, after all that we got into our cars and we drove the four miles across town to Adamsville Bowl, where our school had the place for the night.

We followed Blake Wyatt's minivan into the parking lot, got a space around the back, and as we pulled in, we watched football player after football player hobble across the lot, we watched the cheerleaders run up behind them, grab onto their shoulders, pull themselves onto them, lighter than a backpack, prettier than anything.

We took our ribbons out of our hair, pulled out our mirrors, wiped off our face paint, tried to make the glitter look more subtle. And we remembered what Carolyn Lessing had told us earlier that day, but it was impossible to find natural light in a car at night.

Adamsville Bowl was just off the Stripline but behind it was a mile or two of farmland. When you parked around the back, you could see hay bales and cotton and corn or whatever, and there was hardly any sound—the Bowl was so big it blocked out the noise of the Stripline. Around the front, it was all lights and highway and trucks and cars, the odd ambulance or police car, the occasional lowrider blaring the Black Eyed Peas. We preferred to park around the back. Plus, you could sneak cigarettes there before you went in to skate.

Inside, the lights were dim, a strobe flashed across the rink and we watched as about half of our high school class lined up to rent skates and put them on and gradually made their way to the center of the rink, where people had already started circling, the weirdo skate freaks whipping around at a speed that made us dizzy.

We handed over five dollars to Miss Simpson, who was standing by the rental desk with a cash box and taking our names. She was wearing a sweater with a turkey on it and Jessica took a picture of it with her phone, uploaded it onto Instagram and let the comments start pouring in.

Miss Simpson smiled at us. "You girls look great." She nodded as she spoke. "Just really, really great."

"Thank you," Lauren said, and she tucked her hair behind her ears, ran the other hand over it to make sure it had stayed smooth since we walked from the car.

"New makeup, maybe?" Miss Simpson squinted her eyes, as if she were really trying to figure out what was different.

We nodded and turned and rolled our eyes and wished we could go home and shower and change. What a loser.

We stood in the line for skates and we made jokes about how old and gross Adamsville Bowl was, how lame it was that our parents had had Skate Nights back when they were in school, how embarrassing it was that we'd had birthday parties here back when we were twelve. We laughed and we made fun of the owner, who was the son of the original owner and some kind of low-level alcoholic who was too stupid to realize that a place called Adamsville Bowl should really be a bowling alley, not a skating rink.

We laughed and rolled our eyes and looked around and then we saw Shane and Carolyn come in together, holding hands. People whispered and then people called Shane's name and then Carolyn's: the king and queen had arrived. We looked and then we stared. Shane was anti-PDA, everybody knew this, but he was walking so close to Carolyn, his tanned body all over hers, his size dwarfing her, making her look even skinnier than she already was.

We took our skates—orange and brown and crappy—and we sat on a bench and laced them up, but we didn't take our eyes off Shane and Carolyn. Nobody did.

They sat down on the bench next to us and, up close, we thought Shane was even hotter than he was from far away. His hair was long with little curls on the ends, and when he bent down to take off his shoes, every muscle in his arm showed, he even had definition on his back. Jessica said she could see a little under his shirt and that he had a genuine six-pack, and that his body was completely smooth, like Brad Pitt's or Ryan Gosling's or someone.

Carolyn had her own skates. We watched her slide them

on: low-tops, black with a turquoise stripe along the side, and we asked her where she'd gotten them.

"Some random store in the Village." She smiled as she said this, and she finished tying the aqua blue laces, bow and knot, bow and knot.

We looked down at our rented high-top skates, all brown and abused.

"I did roller derby a little back home," Carolyn said, standing up in her skates now, gliding back and forth as she talked. Shane didn't say anything, but he put his hands around her waist, and we imagined what it would have felt like to have him that close, to have someone so not embarrassed to be near you.

"No way," somebody said. We had seen that Drew Barrymore movie, but we didn't know that this was something girls our age actually did.

"It's no big deal," Carolyn said, and we felt grateful toward her. She never wanted to make people feel bad. "I'd say you guys are much better skaters. I'm such a klutz."

"Doubt it," we told her. Shane looked back at us and mouthed, "Doubt it." It was the first time he'd actually spoken to us, and that was 'cause of Carolyn. Brooke would have never let it happen.

Carolyn said bye and gave a small wave and pushed onto the rink, waving to us and to other people as she began her first lap. Shane trailed behind her and then caught up, grabbing her from behind and nearly knocking her off balance. They laughed.

We looked around. There were already sixty or seventy people there, mostly juniors and seniors, but a few underclassmen too. Guys dressed in jeans and polo shirts that had been found by their mothers in the Birmingham Outlets, girls in Gap miniskirts and opaque tights and skinny sweaters.

On the rink, Carolyn skated like she really knew what she was doing but not like one of those losers who spent every free second doing laps and spins or whatever lame-o tricks they teach you in private lessons. She looked natural, relaxed, like everything was easy. She wore short denim shorts with gray patterned tights underneath, an oversize Ramones sweatshirt, which we heard she had found in the Salvation Army. Under the strobe light, her hair looked so shiny it could have been crystal and the height of the skates made her look like a model, she was that skinny. Her outfit was amazing, everybody said it. To her and to each other. And then there was Shane, in old jeans and a white T-shirt, and under the light he looked even tanner and stronger and better than usual. They were beautiful.

We never saw Brooke and Gemma that night, maybe they didn't come, but that was weird, 'cause they were both really good skaters and they went to almost everything. Andrew Wright came late, wearing distressed black jeans and a nappy gray hoodie that he never pulled down from over his head. He sat on one of the benches and he talked to some of the football players and we thought we saw Miss Simpson trying to talk to him at one stage too. He didn't ever get on the rink. Andrew never did stuff like that, just sat around watching, waiting to meet up with Shane or looking for Gemma or just trying to stay out of the house.

When the slow skate came on, only the couples stayed on the rink, and they would hold hands and, if they thought Miss Simpson had looked the other way, the guys would put their hands under their girlfriends' shirts, the girls would kiss their boyfriends' necks. We watched them, the golden couples, skating to "Love Story" by Taylor Swift and we almost felt sad watching them, most of the time, 'cause it was never us up there: skating, holding hands, prized.

There were only a dozen other couples on the rink at that stage and, of them, Carolyn and Shane were the most beautiful, the most perfect. They looked happy, we thought, like they had been together for years, like they would be together forever.

Jessica took a picture of them, skating close together, arms around each other's waist, and later that night, Jessica sent it to Carolyn.

She replied: "Tnx."

And, minutes later, she changed her profile picture on Facebook. Within twenty-four hours, it had eighty-seven likes.

november

November 1, 2010
Carolyn Lessing
Honors English—Miss Simpson

Romeo and Juliet: contrasts

Question: Please analyze the following section from Shakespeare's *Romeo and Juliet*, outlining the meaning of the piece and also how Shakespeare uses language to express the meaning. You might wish to detail how the piece is relevant today (if at all). In the final section, please outline any areas you would like us to further explore in class.

Romeo and Juliet, III, v
Juliet:
Wilt thou be gone? It is not yet near day.
It was the nightingale, and not the lark,
That pierced the fearful hollow of thine ear.
Nightly she sings on young pomegranate tree.
Believe me, love, it was the nightingale.
Romeo:
It was the lark, the herald of the morn;
No nightingale. Look, love, what envious streaks
Do lace the severing clouds in younger East.
Night's candles are burnt out, and jocund day
Stands tiptoe on the misty mountain tops.
I must be gone and live, or stay and die.
Juliet:
Yon light is not daylight; I know it, I.
It is some meteor that the sun exhales
To be to thee this night a torchbearer

And light thee on thy way to Mantua.
Therefore stay yet. Thou needest not to be gone.
Romeo:
Let me be ta'en, let me be put to death.
I am content, so thou wilt have it so.
I'll say yon grey is not the morning's eye;
This but the pale reflex of Cynthia's brow.
Nor that is not the lark whose notes do beat
The vaulty heaven so high above our heads.
I have more care to stay than will to go.
Come, death, and welcome! Juliet wills it so.
How is't, my soul? Let's talk. It is not day.
Juliet:
It is, is! Hie hence, be gone, away!
It is the lark that sings so out of tune,
Straining harsh discords and unpleasing sharps.
Some say the lark makes sweet division.
This doth not so, for she divideth us.
Some say the lark and loathed toad change eyes.
O, now I would they had changed voices too,
Since arm from arm that voice doth us affray,
Hunting thee hence with hunt's-up to the day.
O, now be gone! More light and light it grows.
Romeo:
More light and light: more dark and dark our woes.

In the above passage from William Shakespeare's *Romeo and Juliet,* the visual contrasts that Shakespeare evokes work to emphasize the contrasting feelings of euphoria and dismay that the title characters will experience throughout the play. While the exchange between the two characters is light-hearted, the use of light and dark, day and night, life and death, all highlight the main conflict of the play.

This passage begins after Romeo and Juliet have spent the night together, and the text shows that Juliet does not want Romeo to leave. She feels full and complete when they are together, and will make up any story to encourage him to stay. Romeo would also like to stay with her, but reminds her of the reality of their situation: "I must be gone and live, or stay and die." Juliet continues to encourage Romeo to stay with her, and is so deeply attached to him that she imagines the world and the heavens are working to keep them together. She explains that the light they see is not the dawn, but "some meteor that the sun exhales."

When Romeo begins to play along, however, Juliet starts to understand their situation more fully. He tells her that he would die for her: "Come, death, and welcome! Juliet wills it so." While it is clear from the tone of the verses, and from the scenes that immediately come before this, that the words are said as a joke, this provides important foreshadowing for the play. When the couple stays together, they are endangering their lives. Juliet realizes this, no matter how she may have pretended earlier: "O, now be gone!" The final line of this piece reinforces the danger that the couple is in again: "More light and light; more dark and dark our woes."

The contrasting images within the text also underline the differences between Romeo and Juliet's families. Everything is one thing or the other, there seems to be no middle ground: "It was the lark, the herald of the morn; No nightingale"; "Yon light is not daylight." Yet the fact that Romeo and Juliet can have such a debate, lighthearted though it is, about the subject, shows how vague and complicated these definitions can sometimes prove to be. They are not as different as they might seem.

Shakespeare dramatizes the feelings that most young couples have: the pressure to date those who are from one's social group, to be accepted, to fit in. Equally, he captures the intensity of our feelings for one another: when we fall in love, we do so fully and it is impossible to feel complete without the other person. While we have had some discussion in class as to whether Romeo is in love with Juliet (as opposed to lust), I would like to have further discussion regarding Juliet's feelings for Romeo, which I regard as true and meaningful, and reflective of how a young woman might feel when falling in love for the first time.

Grade: A-

This is really excellent work, Carolyn. Nice control/grasp of the text and insightful analysis. Very well written and neatly structured. Slightly heavy on quotations, and could use more of your own writing in the next essay. All in all, though, very good. You have a flair for Shakespeare! Keep it up.

13

Every morning, we listened to "The Star-Spangled Banner" and the daily announcements over the loudspeaker. We heard about contests or drug awareness or club achievements or some other issue of the week. Mr. Overton asked us to type them up for him every morning and put everything in point 16 font, so he could read them. We wrote students' names phonetically so he wouldn't mess up, but he always did.

Sometimes, he'd ask students to do an "issue" announcement. On the first of November, Shane Duggan was waiting outside Mr. Overton's office to make a PSA. At nine fifteen, we listened to our quarterback tell us how to behave:

"Technology is changing the way we communicate with each other in lots of great ways. But, sometimes, we forget that what we write can have an impact on other people. We need to treat texts and emails and Facebook updates as we would face-to-face communication—we should never say anything over the Internet we wouldn't want someone to hear in real life. And if we think that somebody is using the Web, their phone or Facebook to bully somebody, then we need to try to stop that. If you get an email, a text or a message on Facebook that's ugly or mean, don't reply to it. Try not to engage. Take a screen shot or make a copy and show it to a teacher or a guidance counselor or to your parents. It's easy to set up filters on your phone or on gmail or on Facebook that will block people from sending more messages or texts, and if you think somebody is trying to bully you, go ahead and set up a filter. But also report things to a trusted adult, whoever that may be. We all need to work together to stop this kind of stuff. Online or in person, if somebody is hurting you or trying to hurt you, there are things you can do to make this stop."

Another girl from Lincoln High had threatened to commit suicide over Facebook a week before. The *Adamsville Daily* and the six o'clock news said she did it because some kids had sent her mean and stupid texts. All of our parents were going crazy about it and some journalists had been in town from New York and D.C. to do a story. It made us laugh how seriously everybody took this— they were so fucking clueless. And the girl was still alive.

Shane smiled when we passed him in the halls later and we told him good job. Shane was always called on to do things like this, even when we were in elementary school. He had been selected to represent Adams at the Lincoln Race Integration Seminar three years ago, and he was the Alabama Leader of Tomorrow. He was good-looking and his voice was almost like a radio presenter's. Ryan Seacrest. Only taller. And hotter.

The Homecoming Court was announced over the loudspeaker that same afternoon. In our year, it was Brooke and Gemma and Taylor and Carolyn. We listened and we texted congratulations and for the next few days we would give hugs to the girls who got in and give hugs to the girls who did not. Behind their backs, we would talk about how lame it was. We would talk about how they would ride on a float and walk into the center of the field during half-time and they would wear a formal dress to the semi-formal dance. They would have their photographs in a special section of the yearbook. They would be in the paper. They would wear crowns and tacky corsages and every year the dresses got more and more ridiculous, long and sequined, like Miss America or *My Big Fat Gypsy Wedding*. Adamsville was like a fucking time warp, we said. We made fun of the dresses but inside them the girls were always beautiful. They were special.

The night the court was announced Brooke posted on her Facebook wall: "Swim team is full of ugly dykes." Two people liked this. One of them was hidden and the other was Gemma Davies.

And, then, Taylor called up Carolyn and told her that she should call Brooke and tell her off for being a bitch, that that comment was directed at her. But Carolyn didn't do that, not as far as we knew.

We had to share the locker room with the cheerleaders on a Friday—something to do with the pep rally schedule, we never fully understood—and we hated this, mostly because their bodies were tanned and perfect and they had Victoria's Secret underwear and their skin wasn't all messed up by chlorine, and when they gave you a compliment you weren't sure if you should say thanks or contradict them. Brooke and Gemma were always the loudest—and the Friday after the nominations, Brooke was really loud. Taylor and Tiffany changed quick and got out of there before we'd even gotten out of the showers. We wished they'd taken more time, that they'd stuck around.

When Carolyn went into the stall to change, the way she'd been doing since September, Brooke put out her arm, hand against the locker opposite her. She put her leg up on the changing bench. It looked like it would be uncomfortable to stand that way, but she made it look really casual, and Carolyn couldn't get through. Carolyn turned around, to go the other way, only Gemma was sitting on the other side, legs stretched out in front of her, pressed against the lockers. Jessica Grady was changing on the other side: Carolyn couldn't really get through, not without somebody moving, not without it being really fucking awkward. Carolyn stopped. She asked to pass. We kept changing, and we listened to Brooke and Gemma. They were smiling as they spoke.

"Um, Carolyn? Why do you change back there?"

"Is it because you're a *lez*-bian?"

"You can't be trusted around us? Right?"

"Or is it 'cause you're so hot?"

"Are you worried we're all dykes?"

"Is that what people in New York—sorry, New *Jersey*—do?"

"We don't think you're that sexy, Carolyn."

"But maybe she's a *dyke* and wants us all to be dykes too." Brooke put down her hand. Carolyn looked around at us.

We looked away and we combed our hair and tried not to look like we thought it was mean or funny or even that we were listening at all.

Brooke laughed. Carolyn looked toward Gemma.

"What?" Gemma asked. "God. Can't you take a joke?"

After we changed, a few of us were waiting outside for our parents to pick us up. Carolyn was waiting too.

"I'm not a lesbian."

"We didn't say that."

We looked at each other.

Lauren spoke first. "Did you say that?"

"No," we answered, not quite in unison.

"See? Nobody said that."

"Anyway, people were, like, kidding."

"You need to learn to take a joke."

We stood still. It was dark and it was getting cold, our hair was still wet. We could hear the football players practicing in the field, grunting and yelling and doing drills.

Carolyn stared at us. "Anyway. I'm not. In case you cared."

We didn't know what to say.

A couple days later, Adam Simmons got written up for smoking in the parking lot and he was waiting in Mr. Overton's office for his punishment when Carolyn came in. Brooke walked in the door a few minutes later. He said he was surprised to see both of them, he figured they were getting some kind of award or something, only they looked too pissed off for that. Carolyn's skin was blotchy and she had eye makeup on one eye but not the other. Like a "before and after" picture, he said. Brooke sat with her arms crossed and kept rolling her eyes. At what, Adam didn't know. He told us he tried to talk to Brooke—he didn't really know Carolyn.

"S'up, Brooke."

She ignored him, he told us, and he thought that was kind of bitchy and he said he was about to tell her he regretted voting for her for the Homecoming Court but then she spoke.

"Hey." She looked at Carolyn, looked at him and rolled her eyes. "What are you here for?"

"Usual." He pressed his thumb to his pointer finger, brought them up to his lips, squinting his eyes. "You?"

"For some bullshit reason." And as she said this, she glared at Carolyn, who stared at her hands. Adam watched Carolyn as she pushed her sleeves up and he told us he could see these dark marks all up and down her forearms—and he said she was digging into them with her fingernails, so that one of them started to bleed. And then Miss Simpson came out of Mr. Overton's office.

"Would you two ladies join me in here? Mr. Overton's asked me to attend this meeting."

Adam said he was tempted to push his ear against the door but he got a text from his brother telling him about a party at Cullman Community over the weekend. And he got distracted. Guys sucked at these kinds of things.

Later, we heard that it was about the thing in the locker room: either Miss Simpson overheard the conversation, or it was reported to her—nobody was totally clear—but it wasn't one of us that said anything, not as far as we knew. If it had been one of us, we would have included Gemma—she said some stuff too—but she never got called to the office. She was too good.

Later, when the school was under investigation, Mr. Overton talked a lot about this meeting; he wanted people to know that it had taken place, that they, the faculty, cared. The school administration couldn't punish the girls for just talking to each other, but the reports later said that the "language used in the discussion caused concern" and that "the faculty were eager to see the dispute resolved." They went on and on about this meeting in the end, but Adam said they were in there ten or fifteen minutes, tops.

At the time, we couldn't believe they paid so much attention to it—this kind of shit happened every day—and some people said it was just because of Carolyn and her being new and needy. Reporters asked us later if we still thought the meeting was unnecessary. "Yes," we told them. "What difference did it make anyway?" This was rhetorical. We were never sure they understood that.

14

Our church doesn't look like churches on TV. The building—or the complex—was meant to be a Lowe's with an adjoining office space and a gym. Lowe's had gotten a bigger site, though, farther down the Stripline, and our church had been given the building by the city. That meant that the nice church in the old part of town could be renovated or something, so we all went to the same one. And it was big enough to accommodate people from other counties and the parish's new website let the service stream directly from the church—Reverend Davies wore a microphone on a headband, like an aerobics instructor. Our church was global, Reverend Davies said.

Our church was big but the parking lot was bigger. When you pulled in from the Stripline, the church was a tiny dot, a speck in the distance. If you got there early, you'd see lines and lines and lines, mapping out the parking spaces, white and yellow crosses

on the gray cement. But if you got there late, or even a few minutes before preaching started, you saw a sea of cars. In the
summer—actually, for most of the year—the mirrors caught
the sun and you'd cover your eyes or you'd be pushed off the road.
The cars swayed in the heat, and the tar on the pavement was
liquid paint, and you'd be afraid your car could be swallowed up
by it, quicksand mixed with tar. As you pulled farther into the
parking lot, the church got bigger—if you weren't from here,
you'd reckon it was a Wal-Mart or a Kmart or a Winn-Dixie or a
warehouse or something. But it was our church. And even if you
weren't Baptist, you ended up coming here for something or
other—on Sundays and Wednesdays we were all believers.

We always stayed outside in the parking lot as long as we could—
watching to see who we could see, trying to stand near the guys
we liked, talking about what we'd done the night before. Inside,
it was still a warehouse, and it didn't matter how much stuff they
put on the altar, how many tapestries they hung: it was a warehouse. It smelled of cars and candles, and it was theater in the
round, with the altar and the lectern in the center, pews all around
them, white and plastic and bolted to the ground. The morbidly
obese people had to sit in the back, in chairs that had been do-
nated by the Ruby Tuesday's across the Stripline. There were one
hundred twenty-four pews, each one holding five to ten people,
depending on how fat they were. That's what we had counted, and
on Christmas, people still had to stand.

We went every Sunday and every Wednesday. It was part of us,
something we never debated, never questioned. We never minded
it, if we were honest, not really. Church was something to do, a
place to see people, a chance to dress up. Later, when we went to
college, we would miss this. We would go to church on campus,
of course we still did that, but it was never quite the same. It felt
different, colder, stranger. We missed the safety of our own
church, the familiarity of the service, the closeness we felt with

one another. We even missed the smell—on a Sunday, you could smell coffee, mixed with the perfume and cologne of the young, the old and the very old.

The church was bright. The lights were dimmed on Christmas morning, and sometimes when we first came in, but eventually they went on full blast, and when you looked up, you could count hundreds of lights, most of them directed toward the pulpit, giving Reverend Davies a spotlight, a glow. There were lights coming up from the floor too, blue ones, and we heard that the lighting technician from the Regal Theater had been kept on a retainer to ensure that the lighting for services was to a high standard.

When they first moved, Carolyn and her mother didn't come to church—they were Catholic or something—but after a few weeks, and when Carolyn and Shane had started hanging out, and after Reverend Davies had ground them down, Carolyn and Abby made the odd appearance. They didn't get there early, they didn't sing or shake hands, they didn't hang around afterward. They closed their eyes a lot and some people complained that they shouldn't be there, if they weren't believers, if they hadn't been saved. But nobody stopped them, and they came more regularly over time and then not at all. You'd think with so many people, we wouldn't notice if they were there or not. But we did. Especially with Carolyn.

One Sunday in November—close to when Carolyn had been put on the Homecoming Court—we had a special youth service, something that Dave Dillon, our Youth Action Leader or YAL—had come up with to get us more involved. We'd do the readings, a senior would give the sermon—something Reverend Davies had prepared, he wouldn't trust us that far, and they'd change up the music—play some cheesy ballad that had been on the radio four years ago that could vaguely be made to be about Jesus—and bring in some Cullman Community reject to play guitar while somebody sang along. It was lame, we knew this, only we planned it for months, held auditions, our parents taped it, we cared about it a little too much.

We got to the church early that day in November, and we remembered seeing Brooke and Gemma talking when we came in, near the altar, Brooke's face a little blotchy, Gemma's hand outstretched and stroking her hair.

"You just need to ignore her." Gemma's voice was in a whisper, but the altar was so heavily miked, we could hear them, just a little.

"I know, I know." Brooke's head was turned away from us now and we stayed far back, not wanting to look like we were spying, but wanting to hear what we could hear.

"She needs to be put in her place, you know?" Gemma's voice went even lower. "She's a slut is what she is."

Brooke, or maybe it was Gemma, let out a cough, and the microphone squealed. They turned their heads. We walked up the aisle, waving at them as we got closer.

We took our seats near the front—we'd be taking the first collection—and we sat and we waited as the church filled up; mothers and fathers and cousins and second cousins and neighbors and teachers and coaches and everybody we knew, or had ever known, filed into our church and shook our hands and gave us hugs and kisses and we hugged and kissed them back, because that's what we did in Adamsville, that's what we did in church.

Carolyn and her mother were there, sitting on the side near the front, maybe three or four rows back. We could make out their faces, could recognize Carolyn's outfit from the Anthropologie catalog we had seen in her bedroom weeks before. Both of them—Carolyn and her mom—their hair was still wet, their faces almost dewy, like they'd just been for a swim. Maybe they had. We wondered what it would be like to have hair so perfect you could do that—just let it air-dry, skin so immaculate you only needed mascara and lip gloss, a body so toned even a white, oversize sundress could make you look perfectly proportioned. We tried not to stare.

Music filled the auditorium and we rose to our feet, and Reverend Davies walked down the aisle, shaking hands, giving hugs, salutes, kisses. A group of freshmen guys and girls followed him in, wearing purple T-shirts that said, CROSS—"Christians Reaching Out in Selfless Service." Shane Duggan walked a few paces behind them, in a novelty football jersey that read, DOING IT FOR JESUS on the front. As he walked further to the front, we read the back: "John 3:16." Some parents started clapping as he walked through—Coach Cox gave him a fist pump, Shane gave one back.

Somebody told us later that when Shane walked down the aisle, he gave Carolyn a wink. Somebody else said the wink looked like it was directed at Abby. People laughed at that, and we heard from other people that Carolyn had actually blown Shane a kiss. But we hadn't seen any of this, not from where we were standing.

We joined hands as the service began, and we looked around us, clocking what people were wearing, making notes to ourselves. We sized ourselves up, pulled cardigans around our shoulders as we felt the air-conditioning stream down on us. We prayed.

About halfway through the service, Reverend Davies invited Shane to come up to the altar, handed him a roving microphone so that he could "say a few words." As Shane climbed out of the front row, making his way across the purple-shirted freshmen, a spotlight came up and followed him to the altar. If you took a picture of him, he would have had a halo.

He cleared his throat, the sound boomed through the auditorium, and Shane began to speak: "I'm real humbled to be here, to speak to y'all, to represent all my friends, all us students at Adams." His face had started to redden; we thought that his hands were shaking.

"You read a lot these days about how things are for teenagers, how hard it is for kids to fit in, to make friends, and to do all that while staying away from temptation, keeping clean of sin. In other towns in America, this is really tough. Folks don't know each other, the church isn't something that matters—in Moulton, just a few towns over, they're not even allowed to pray before football games. They can't think about Christ before they take the field, can't talk to Jesus and feel His love, the love that gives them the strength to play, to be the best that a person can be.

"That's why we're blessed here in Adamsville. We share values, a love of Christ, we know that He is our savior and that everything we do should be in praise of Him. We know that drinking, sex, drugs—all of that gets in the way of being close to Him. We have parents and friends who love Jesus as much as we do, who help us keep on track."

We listened to him speak, and we thought of Shane at Blake Wyatt's house over the summer, doing keg stands, making out with Brooke in Wyatt's pool.

"When somebody offers you a drink at a party—when somebody says, 'One beer can't hurt'—you should think about Jesus for a moment, ask in your heart if this is what He would want you to do with your body, your body which is a gift from Him."

We looked at Reverend Davies, seated behind Shane, reading along on a sheet of paper, smiling, pleased.

"In Ecclesiastes, the Bible gives us warning about desires of the eyes: 'Rejoice, O young man, in your youth, and let your heart cheer you in the days of your youth; walk in the ways of your heart, and the sight of your eyes; but know that for all these God will bring you into judgment.

"We are faced with temptation every weekend, at every party, every dance we attend. But the Lord wants us to replace these sins with prayer, with spiritual discipline. Scripture gives us guidance: 'See if there is any offensive way in me, and lead me in the way everlasting.' " Shane looked up, toward the ceiling, then shifted his weight, moved himself out of the spotlight, rubbed his eyes.

We looked at Brooke and Gemma, sitting close to each other, Gemma whispering into Brooke's ear.

Reverend Davies got up, came to Shane's side. "Thank you, Shane."

"Thank you, Reverend." And then Shane looked straight into the congregation. "Go, Bears. Hope to see y'all this weekend." He put his head down, walked back to his seat. Reverend Davies raised his arms and we got to our feet. The service continued.

After we did the collection, Gemma and Brooke did a duet; some random community-college guy played guitar. It was Faith Hill's "Breathe," only they had changed the words—"Caught up in the prayer/God, I know you're there/Jesus, isn't that the way that love's supposed to be/I can hear you breathe." We laughed about this later, the lameness of the lyrics, the nasal sound of their voices, the guy fumbling on the guitar, but people posted on Facebook how good they sounded, how cool they were, how the two of them should go out for "X Factor" the next time it came to Birmingham.

After church, we went to the country club for lunch. Mashed potatoes, macaroni and cheese, fried okra, fried chicken, fried green tomatoes, green beans, buttermilk biscuits, all laid out in a buffet in the main clubhouse. We couldn't wear jeans in the club, or tennis shoes. We looked like a J Crew catalog when we were there, we'd say, only fatter. The club used to be white only, our parents would tell us, but there were some black members now, if only a few. All the staff were black, though, and on the weekends they were mostly our age. They served us food from the buffet.

Carolyn came with Taylor, and maybe because Tiffany and all those weren't there, they hung out with us. Later, everybody disagreed about when this happened—whether it was before Homecoming or after or what—but it must have been before, that's what we said, 'cause the air was still just a little warm, and Carolyn was still smiling, she was still speaking up, laughing. And people still wanted to be near her.

After we'd gotten our food she said it was weird that all the servers were black and asked us if it made us uncomfortable. We told her that we hadn't really thought about it, and that was true, mostly. We said later that we thought she was faking. It was easy to be the way she was if you weren't from here. Things are more complicated when you're in it.

The parents stayed together at the tables, and we took our food in Styrofoam containers and went out to the golf course to eat. The guys smoked, if they were sure we were out of view of the clubhouse, and we would take drags in turns, if we were in the mood. It was still warm that day in the fall; the heat from summer lingered longer than usual that year and the humidity made it worse— and we sat in a sandpit because we said this would keep us cool, but we felt sweat on the backs of our necks all the same.

If you looked to your right, you could see the rest of the course, and trees and the pool and tennis courts and more trees. To your left, trees and then a clearing, and through it, the Stripline, with traffic blurring by. You could just make out the Wal-Mart sign, open twenty-four hours. On the golf course, though, you could barely hear the traffic, and on a Sunday evening, with the course closed at five, you could just hear crickets and see fireflies. When we were little, we used to try to catch them in our hands, always forgetting to bring jars from home. We would hold them for a second, but then they would tickle, and we'd have to open our hands, letting them fly away. Andrew Wright could catch anything when we were little—but once, he'd gotten too excited and smashed a firefly in his palms. We thought he'd been stung by a bee—he screamed, tears in his eyes—but there was no mark or bite, just the wings of the bug on his hands. We stopped doing that a few years ago, when we got older. And in a couple of years, when we'd finished high school, we'd have to sit inside with our parents, like our older brothers and sisters and cousins did. But not for now.

That day, Carolyn dared us to go swimming in the pool, even though it was only open in the summer and we didn't have our bathing suits. We thought she was joking, and we stayed on the green as she ran through the parking lot and then jumped the fence into the pool. We looked at each other and realized she was for real. We thought we'd hear a splash or something, but we didn't. So we ran to be near her and we looked through the wire fence. Just chaise longues, folded over; big blue and white umbrellas, down; an orange and green beach towel lay on the ground near the baby pool—*Little Mermaid* or something—and we guessed it had been there since the summer, molding and fading; a pair of white Keds were thrown at the side, next to a pair of crusty cream athletic socks probably there since the last decade. We were about to turn and walk away, when we heard the diving board bounce, creaking and dry. Carolyn on the edge of it—the high dive—the one we were allowed to dive off only after we could swim a length without stopping to rest at the side. She wasn't smiling or looking at us, she was just bouncing on the edge in her bare feet. She put her hands in the air, as if she might dive, and one of the guys called her to stop. She looked up—eyes empty and wide. She didn't say anything and then she smiled and took off her shirt, took off her skirt, threw them onto the concrete by the lifeguard stand. We could see those marks on her arms, and some on her stomach—maybe they were just scars? We stared at her, just bouncing on the edge. And then she dove: she barely made a splash, and she was in the water, head wet, diving down and touching the drain, staying underwater for what seemed like forever. We didn't know how she'd get home, or what we'd say to our parents or what we'd do if any of the staff walked by. We watched her swim, though, underneath the water, her tiny hips and the muscles in her shoulders, her spindly legs, knobby knees and elbows, her hair streaming out behind her, like a tail. She could go on and on without taking a breath and when she did come up for air, she didn't look our way or even seem to know we were watching.

None of us said anything at all. We didn't yell and the guys didn't say anything gross. We stood still and we watched. And we thought about getting in with her, thought about taking off our shirts and skirts—wasn't your underwear and bra just like a bathing suit anyway? But it was easier to watch, we decided.

Nobody got any pictures of that day, of us on the lawn, of her in the water, in her bra like a mermaid, but we said later we were happy that we didn't. People would never have forgotten it, never let her live it down. We let her get away with it, gave her a free pass, and we just sat and watched and we took pictures in our minds and didn't text or talk about it until months and months later. Her body was tiny, she was perfect and she was unafraid.

Years later, we would remember this and we were all a little hazy on the details, and what one of us was sure of contradicted something someone else was sure of. So we patched things together like a quilt, somebody's memory stitched onto somebody else's until it made something large and something real, something that couldn't be torn apart. It was important for us to have this—a shared truth—and we never shared it except with one another, and it wasn't so clear why.

Andrew Wright was with us that day. We wondered why he wasn't with Gemma—they had been joined at the hip since school started, making out under the bleachers, in the parking lot, outside study hall, during first period. They were together wherever we looked. But Andrew Wright was alone that day, and we wondered if Gemma would have minded—if she knew—her boyfriend staring at the new girl as she took off half her clothes and got into the pool. Looking back, we wondered if that's when his whole thing for Carolyn started. We guessed it might have been earlier—thinking of him at the balloon festival, looking so tense and alone—and then others thought it might have been much later, and that she had pursued him. In any case, we remembered a lot about Carolyn from that day, and we also remembered Andrew's face. Maybe because of everything with his mom, or maybe because he'd always been a little afraid of the water, his eyes were glued to Carolyn in that pool, his mouth hanging open. If we had wanted to make fun of him about it, we could have. But we didn't. And we were glad of that because, in the end, words hurt Andrew. People said sticks and stones and all that. But not with Andrew.

facebook

Dave Dillon

"The LORD is my strength and my song, and he has become my salvation; this is my God, and I will praise him, my father's God, and I will exalt him."

Brooke Moore and 12 other people like this.

Gemma Davies "People who conceal their sins will not prosper, but if they confess and turn from them, they will receive mercy." What's your Bible quote for today?

Brooke Moore "When you follow the desires of your sinful nature, the results are very clear: sexual immorality, impurity, lustful pleasures, idolatry, sorcery, hostility, quarreling, jealousy, outbursts of anger, selfish ambition, dissension, division, envy, drunkenness, wild parties, and other sins like these. Let me tell you again, as I have before, that anyone living that sort of life will not inherit the Kingdom of God."

Dave Dillon Good one, Brooke! Great to see you at service!

Gemma Davies "So put to death the sinful, earthly things lurking within you. Have nothing to do with sexual immorality, lust and evil desires. Don't be greedy, for a greedy person is an idolater, worshipping the things of the world. Because of these sins, the anger of God is coming."

Dave Dillon Right on, Gemma! Your dad would be proud!

Gemma Davies Thank you Dave. Can me and Brook meet with you? We now that some kids where skinny dipping (after service) and we are conserned. ☹

Dave Dillon Thanks, Gemma. I'll give you a call.

15

We made the Homecoming float at the Halls' farm. We came up with ideas after school and the committee wrote them up and we were assigned tasks and we worked from five in the evening until ten or midnight or whenever we were done. We slipped vodka into Red Bull and some of the girls acted drunk and some of the guys smoked behind the barn. We painted and we sang and we drank. We stood together and tried to flirt or tried to ignore one another. This is what we did.

The Halls' wasn't a working farm. Dylan's dad's dad had worked it, but when he died, Dylan's dad didn't keep it up; he had gone to UAB Business School and owned three Sonics—two in Adamsville and one in Cullman. Dylan was in the Future Farmers of America Club all the same, and his dad was the parent leader. We weren't sure why. They did tours of the farm sometimes—for some of the county summer camps—and they kept horses and we sometimes saw Dylan riding. The farm was huge—you could put two of our high schools in it, Dylan's dad said, and we all loved to be there, and we loved to imagine that it was still a working farm, that Dylan and his family lived off the land, milked cows, gathered hay. But Dylan's dad brought us Sonic fried pickles at regular intervals during the night, and we remembered what was what. Still, though, there was so much room, and we could build incredible floats—mess up and start again—and we could go places to hide and talk or make out. Whatever we wanted. We loved this time of year.

It was evening when we arrived, the light fading in the sky, but the barn was illuminated with Christmas lights. We worked inside but looked out at the farmland as we sorted out the plywood, the papier-mâché, the spray paint, the glitter. The Halls' dogs—two golden retrievers, probably eight or nine years old—ran across the fields hiding behind bales of hay, barking every time a car arrived down the long gravel driveway. The Halls' house was lit up in the distance—at least half a mile from the barn—yellow, with white shutters and a wraparound porch. All the lights were on inside, and we imagined Mrs. Hall and Dylan's younger brothers inside, Mrs. Hall making dinner and the boys gathered around the television, watching some cartoon before they ate, before their bedtime routine began. A tire swing hung from a large oak next to the four-car garage, a jungle gym and a slide just behind it. The Halls were lucky to have so much space, we said to one another, though we'd never seen Dylan or his brothers out in the yard.

As we worked, we watched as Brooke Moore laughed, rolling her head back and drinking a Red Bull. She was talking to Gemma, but most of the barn was watching her, that's the way it used to be with Brooke. She was in charge of the lettering—the cheerleaders always did perfect bubble letters, from years of practice for pep rally signs and banners for the buses, the front of the school. Brooke held a paintbrush in one hand, her Coke in another. We couldn't tell if she was drunk or just really happy—we could hear her laughing from the other side of the barn.

Carolyn arrived about an hour after us and, as she walked in, as she moved out of the darkness of the field, we could just make out Shane walking behind her. And that's when we looked back at Brooke and saw her face kind of change—not looking angry, really, but nervous or annoyed or uptight or something. She stared at Carolyn—wearing old sweatpants and a mismatched hoodie, still looking pretty, still looking perfect. Brooke took her phone out of her pocket and she typed something. She walked out of the barn and got into her car. A door slammed.

The headlights on Brooke's car went on and the light filled the barn: People yelled for her to turn them off, put their hands to their faces. Carolyn kept looking straight ahead and her face was lit up—her eyes were clear and glistening, her skin was so pale the light practically bounced off it. She was staring into the light and she didn't blink. The car reversed and the barn went dim.

Carolyn stood close to Shane and she didn't say much, or not much that we could hear. She had gone quieter since the thing after swim practice, quieter with us and maybe quieter with everybody, and we didn't know what to do to make it right, to bring her back out of her shell.

She worked on the same piece of the float as Shane did—the theme was Mardi Gras and while he cut pieces of timber for the frame, she painted a jazz musician on a flat piece of wood that would be mounted to the front of Mr. Overton's vintage Ford Mustang. Her painting was detailed, the saxophone looked like it was in 3D and, later, we talked about how good she was. How she could paint without a pattern or a stencil, on her own. How she didn't worry about messing up or people not liking it or just getting it wrong. We wondered if she cared deep down, but somehow we figured she didn't. We wondered what she thought about a lot of the time, but we never got around to asking her. She did everything

right, as far as we could see, and everybody was aware of it, probably Brooke most especially. Looking back, we admitted we could
imagine it was all kind of hard for Brooke. But at the time, we
thought she was a selfish bitch.

We stayed working until midnight in the weeks leading up to
Homecoming—we talked about how we'd never get it done, how
we were way behind, but we knew we would finish, because we
always did, even in middle school. We worried that this year's
wouldn't be as good as last year's, that the standard was dropping.
We weren't the most artistic class—the year above us was—but we
were the hardest-working, we were told, and the most commit-
ted to the parade. Carolyn changed that for us that year, she was
put in charge of all the artistic parts—and she constructed the plan
for the whole float. Looking back, maybe it wasn't so great for
her that she was so talented. When you're new, and when you're a
girl, it's not so good to be good at something. Better to be average, to be barely visible, to make yourself scarce. Carolyn never
did that, though, never blended in.

We built a bonfire after we'd finished making the float—this
was tradition too, and Mr. and Mrs. Hall helped us find stuff that
would burn well. They took logs from the barn—they'd had to get
rid of some oaks when the Wal-Mart bought a part of their land—
and lined them around the fire so we could sit and watch.

The fire started out small—a little flame in the center of the
circle—and within five, ten minutes, after Mr. Hall had loaded up
more kerosene and more branches and newspaper, it was huge and
high and blue and red and black and smoke. We had to sit back
and away so we wouldn't be blinded and so it wouldn't burn our
faces. We sat all around it, in pairs and in threes and in fours.
Shane and Carolyn were directly across from us, and through the
fire, through the blue and the red, you could see them making
out—his hand sliding up her shirt, her hands in her lap.

Mrs. Hall gave us stuff to make s'mores and sparklers to light.

The fire got too big and our marshmallows caught fire and went black, too black to eat—only Dylan would take them, and he loaded up a sheet of graham crackers with twenty fried marshmallows.

We liked the sparklers best. Once they were lit, we'd walk away from the fire, away from our seats and into the darkest parts of the field. We'd swirl them around and try to make words with them—our names, if we could, and the guys would do curse words, like they would with their calculators, and then we'd make shapes—hearts, stars, flowers—then just lines and circles, like an Etch A Sketch. Mr. and Mrs. Hall told us to be careful, and we kind of laughed at this, thinking nothing could go wrong, and we watched Blake Wyatt put around twenty unlit sparklers into the front of his pants, mouthing to us that we could use them later. While we played with fire, Shane and Carolyn stayed on the log, making out. Once Brooke was gone we guessed they didn't care who saw them. We would look back, and we could see their faces, through the orange and the smoke, and we wondered what it was like to be her, to be wanted so badly, to be accepted so easily.

We stayed away from the fire, long after our sparklers had gone out, just standing, talking, flirting. When Dylan went into the house to get more food, Blake Wyatt said we should go follow him and call 900 numbers—Mr. Hall did it all the time, he said, so nobody would know. We thought this was funny, and he tried to get a bunch of us to go in with him, but we didn't—so he didn't—and we stood around for as long as we could stand it.

We looked back again at Carolyn and Shane. Now Shane was gone—she was sitting on the log on her own, everybody had moved away, the smoke was too much. But Carolyn stayed there, had her phone in her lap, was looking at the screen and then looking into the fire and then back to the screen and then back to the fire again and again—we didn't understand how it didn't kill her eyes. Blake called out her name, but she didn't seem to hear. And then we thought she was coming over to us. But she just walked toward the fire—like, really, really close—so close we thought she might walk right in.

"What the fuck is she doing?"

"Leave her alone."

"Should somebody go over there?"

"Let her do what she wants."

"She's just waiting for Shane."

"Duggan's left."

"He's just in his car."

"Should we go over there?"

"Leave them alone."

"She's just looking at it."

"She's just waiting for Duggan."

"But what the fuck is she doing?"

She stood completely still—and then she swayed a little, back and forth—and she put her hands out in front of her. It looked like she was touching the fire, but she couldn't have been. She would've had third-degree burns.

Andrew was with us and he started to walk away, walk toward her, we didn't know why. Blake called her name again and then— only then—Carolyn looked up. She locked eyes with Andrew, or at least that's what we thought, and she stepped back, crossing her arms in front of her chest. She turned her back and walked toward where the cars were parked. By the time Andrew got to the fire, she was already gone—the lights of Shane's car were on, she had gotten into the passenger seat and they were driving away.

Adamsville Daily News

HOMECOMING 2010—A.H.S. Students Bring Bourbon Street to Fifth Avenue

NOVEMBER 17, 2010

On Monday evening, Adams High School students put the final touches on their Homecoming floats in advance of Friday's parade. Working with the theme of Mardi Gras, Friday's parade promises to provide Adamsville residents with a taste of Bourbon Street through our historic downtown. Local businesses have underlined the importance of the annual parade in involving local business and attracting trade.

Adamsville Hardware Store owner Brent Moore says of the parade: "Although the parade only runs for a few hours, all of the businesses in the downtown area benefit from increased foot traffic. Additionally, the students continue to buy materials for their floats from our independent stores. While it must be tempting for them to shop at the new, large-scale stores such as Wal-Mart and Lowe's, we are grateful to the students for investing locally and in ensuring that certain traditions are maintained."

The parade will also feature the 2010 Homecoming Court, which is comprised of four young ladies from each class of the high school. The 2010 court is of:

Freshmen	**Sophomores**
Jessica White	Kayla King
Ashley Moore	Brittany Baker
Brittany Clark	Amber Cook
Amanda Lewis	Danielle Gray

Juniors

Gemma Davies

Carolyn Lessing

Brooke Moore

Taylor Lyon

Seniors

Heather Watson

Jasmine Smith

Sarah Barnes

Emily Simmons

Heather Watson, a senior and daughter of Henry and Judy Watson of Branch Brook Road, told us she was thrilled about the inclusion on the court. "This is my fourth year to do it and being a senior and all it's great to have one last great Homecoming memory." Heather has been accepted through early admission to the University of Alabama and plans to study sociology and also pursue a teaching degree.

Sophomore Kayla King (daughter of John and Marjorie King of Oak Ridge View) was last year's winner of the Miss Teen Tennessee Valley Authority Beauty Pageant and says she hopes she won't be as nervous being part of the court as she was when participating in last year's pageant. "Even though I practiced so much with my pageant coach, I was still really nervous before the show. I walked around my house in heels for months to get ready!" Kayla is also a member of the Junior Varsity Cheerleading squad. Her older sister Kristina is a freshman at Auburn University and a former captain of the Adams High Varsity Cheerleading Squad.

Junior Carolyn Lessing (daughter of Abby Lessing of D'Evereux Drive) moved to Adamsville recently from New Jersey and made the honor roll during her first semester. Her hobbies include swimming and art, and Carolyn told the *Daily News* that she is "excited" to be part of the court and that she had a key role in making the junior class's float for the parade.

We can't wait to see it!

The parade begins on Friday at 2:15 pm from Adamsville Hardware Store on Fifth Avenue. Families are advised to arrive early to find suitable parking.

16

The Homecoming Dance was an Occasion. It came after the parade in town, after dinner out, after the game at our field. The game was planned to be against a team we could beat for sure, and the band did a special set, one they practiced all summer long. The whole student body drove downtown to watch the parade. So did the middle school kids, so did our teachers, so did our parents. We wore school colors: every shade of orange you could find, and black jeans and black ribbons in our hair. We wore face paint— bear paws or AHS on our cheeks and glitter on our eyes. The jocks wore their football jerseys, the cheerleaders wore their uniforms, the band wore their marching gear. The Homecoming Court wore their dresses, sequins and sparkles and heels they couldn't walk in.

They let us out of school early and we arrived downtown at two o'clock. Everywhere was already mobbed: balloons and kids and moms and dads and flags and posters. Even from inside the car, you could hear the chanting, the band warming up, the cheerleaders doing their cheers. People held their phones in the air and took pictures and flashes went off at every corner. The traffic lights were all flashing orange. Adamsville stopped everything for Homecoming.

We found a spot to watch from outside Stewart's Coffee Shop on Fifth Avenue, away from the kids and the parents and close to the seniors and some of the kids from Cullman Community. We liked where we stood but it stank of bacon and grease and fries. We took pictures of each other, tied our jackets around our waists, pulled our hair back and got ready. Andrew Wright and Shane Duggan stood in front of us, with the rest of the varsity team. They barely moved. At two fifteen, or around then, we could hear the band approaching, the drumbeat, the clack of their sticks, the stamping of feet. We stood and we watched. The band was always first.

We watched them turn the corner. 220 members, and the flag corps. They walked in small and uniform steps and they were in even rows. When they filed onto Fifth Avenue, they started their routine, or their set, or whatever it was they called it: some were marching in place, while the rows behind weaved in and out and in and out. From where we watched, we could make out a few faces, but it was hard. Hard to distinguish our friends from the others, who was white, who was black, who was skinny, who was fat, who was male, who was female. The set lasted nearly ten minutes, with excerpts from songs they played in full at half-time at the games: "When the Saints Go Marching In," "Summertime," "Adams High Fight Song," "Amazing Grace." It took a few moments to recognize the songs—we were close to the drums and that made the melody hard to make out. But when we did, we sang along, just a little. We saw families across the street sway and little girls twirl around, dancing. The music was perfect, perfectly timed, perfectly pitched, and we said that they were like robots, only that wasn't true at all: they were coming together and moving in time, and we loved the brass and the drums and the flutes and the sound of the sticks against each other. One person's feet on the ground made no sound but 220 made a beat, and we wanted to make a beat too, with our feet on the pavement, but we didn't—we held our breath and listened. We felt goose bumps on our arms, and we brushed them off, pulled on our jackets from around our waists.

The band marched on, the music still audible, the set repeated as they moved to Shop Street, turning onto Fourth Avenue. Minutes later, we saw the floats: Bourbon Street, a Chinese dragon, comedy and tragedy masks, a river scene. Kinda cool, kinda impressive, each papier-mâché and homemade and strange, but each amazing. 'Cause we'd done them ourselves.

And then the court. We watched the seniors, they always came first: beautiful, perfect, older. And then the junior court turned the corner: four girls in Mr. Overton's vintage Mustang. They waved, Brooke and Gemma sitting close to each other, Carolyn and Taylor behind them, just as close. Carolyn was perched near the edge, looked like she could fall off. People screamed and clapped. The parents took pictures.

Brooke wore a bright red dress, Gemma's was aqua blue, with white flowers on the back, Taylor's was purple and gold—all three in sequins, all over. Carolyn's dress was black and long and looked like silk—no sequins, no sparkle—and it hung a little too big on her body. She had worn the dress to something else back in New Jersey, we heard—to some formal event her school held on a yacht. We thought this was incredible and exotic, but we didn't think it was right. You bought something new to wear if you were on the Homecoming Court. You went to Special Moments on the Stripline and tried on every dress that you could, you got dyed-to-match shoes, you had your hair done. We thought she looked different and beautiful, but some people said she looked weird, like she wasn't even trying.

Before we met her, before we saw her, before Taylor Lyon's mother had done their window treatments and the photos of Carolyn Lessing had started flying around, we had imagined something else: New Jersey was "Jersey Shore," "Real Housewives of New Jersey," that kind of crap. We had imagined a girl who spent her free time on a tanning bed, applying acrylic nails with diamante, getting drunk and throwing up outside a hot tub. We hadn't known that New Jersey was bigger than that—not really—and Carolyn was from this other place. It was half-Manhattan, half–boarding school, all money and gloss and grooming. Things were understated there; she applied her makeup in natural light and wore the barest minimum. She shopped at Vineyard Vines and had four North Face jackets and a Burberry scarf. We hadn't even known this stuff was in, that these were the things we should be wearing, but when Carolyn showed us her pictures of her friends back in New Jersey, or when we pored over her pictures on Facebook, we saw how cool they all looked, how clueless and out of touch we were in Adamsville. In the beginning, we did a lot to try to look like her, and she did little to look like us. Later, things changed around a bit, but never that much. She knew things we didn't, things we didn't even know we should know.

She had been to places in Europe, we heard, to Paris, to London, to Venice, to Berlin. She learned early on that Shane Duggan didn't even have a passport and Carolyn had gone all wide-eyed about that, and then had laughed, thinking he was kidding. But he wasn't, and there were lots of us like Shane.

We looked at Carolyn now, sitting in the back of the Mustang, and somebody called her name and we thought we heard somebody boo. She looked out of place there, too plain or too dark or too city or something. That was the way they did things where she came from: barely there makeup, clothes that are simple but expensive, an expression that says you are pretty but don't care. We understood that now, and she was the prettiest, by far, but people said it wasn't fair for her to be there. She was new and she was hanging out with somebody else's boyfriend. The car seemed to hardly move, and Brooke and Gemma and Taylor waved and waved, they smiled and laughed. Carolyn sat still. She held tight to the side of the car—if the car moved too fast, or took a turn, she'd fall right off. But we doubted she would.

Jason Nelson grabbed Andrew Wright's phone during the parade: in his pictures, there were thirty-two of Carolyn and Shane—mostly Carolyn. People laughed, talked about how pathetic he was, and people threatened to tell Shane, or worse, Gemma. But people still felt sorry for Andrew, and the phone was returned. Nobody said anything. At least not for a while.

For the dance, we dressed up. We wore semi-formal dresses and the guys wore khakis and ties. After the parade we ran to the hairdressers for a blow-out or an updo and to the nail salon for a manicure and pedicure. We wore stockings and heels. We shaved our legs. Just in case.

We were buzzed by the time we got to school. In the gym, our parents were all there, sitting in the bleachers, waiting for us to come out.

We had our pictures taken in the art room and we waited just outside, against our lockers. The water fountains where the baseball players congregated, the broken pay phone where the stoners hid during study hall, the trophy case where the faculty stood at the start of every day: everything was different when we arrived there in the evening, dressed up. The loose-leaf paper gathered round the garbage cans, the hall passes dropped on the floor, the papier-mâché human skeletons constructed during biology—all cleared away. The lighting was different, of course, but the air was different too—it was dry and clean, no chlorine, no water vapor from the pool, no trace of PE sweat.

We inched closer to the art room and we lingered at the door, looking in to see who we could see. The backdrop, airbrushed and pastel, comedy and tragedy masks that looked almost identical. The words MARDI GRAS forming an arch over our heads, a Bourbon Street sign and a park bench to our left. It didn't look like New Orleans but we didn't really care, we just hoped it wouldn't clash with our dresses.

While we waited for our turns, we remembered what we'd read in *Glamour*—place a hand on your hip, jut your shoulder forward, stick your chin out and press your tongue against the roof of your mouth. These things helped us look thinner and they usually worked, so long as nobody could tell what we were doing.

After we'd had our pictures taken, we waited for one another at the side, rolling our eyes, fanning our faces. And then we linked arms and headed to the bathroom, to do shots before Lead-Out.

In the bathroom, we drank Absolut mixed with Gatorade, and then shared our Lancôme Juicies and deodorant and Mentos. We laughed and talked about how we hoped our pictures weren't all lame, and we promised to exchange wallet-size ones when they were printed. We heard coughing in one of the stalls, then gagging, then a heavy splash and then a flush. We looked at one another in the mirror, Jessica mouthed "OMG," and the stall opened. Carolyn's eyes were red and bloodshot, her mascara had run down her left cheek, her foundation all blotchy and uneven. Her hair was still smooth and shiny, and her black dress wasn't crumpled, and from the neck down, she still looked like she did in the parade. We made room so she could wash her hands and Nicole was the first to speak. "Um, are you, like, okay?"

Carolyn looked back at us in the mirror and she smiled, real big, inhaling deep through her nose. "What?" She held herself against the sink. She looked like she could fall over. "I'm fine. Just nervous." She sneezed. "Nervous, I guess."

"I love your dress." Jessica said this, but she'd been ragging on it all afternoon.

"I like yours. I like all of yours." Carolyn looked at each of us, through the mirror, and she said it like she really meant it and it made us smile, just a little.

She rubbed her hands for what seemed like hours. "You'll ruin your nail polish," Lauren told her. Carolyn laughed. "Oh, yeah. I forgot about that." She got some toilet paper from the stall, wiped her hands dry, waved to us in the mirror, and she left.

"Is she, like, bulimic?" Lauren sucked in her cheeks as she looked in the mirror.

"She said she was nervous," Nicole said. "God. Give her a break."

"Whatever. I'm just saying, she's really skinny."

"She's *nervous*."

"And I'm saying she's *skinny. God.*"

"She *is* really skinny," Jessica said. "Lucky bitch."

We walked out, moments later, and Andrew Wright was standing outside, looking down the hall, holding Carolyn's black Kate Spade bag, Carolyn nowhere to be seen. Shane emerged from the men's room, punched him on the shoulder and grabbed the bag from Andrew's hands. Shane laughed and Andrew blushed. We texted the others, to tell them what we had seen.

In the hall outside the gym with or without dates, we were organized into alphabetical order—the guy's name, not the girl's—and got out of it as soon as the teachers were out of sight. We wanted to talk to one another and fix ourselves up and calm ourselves down. We moved slowly and then quickly and rolled our eyes at the teachers as they moved us back into line. We held onto each other's arms to keep from stumbling after the vodka and the rum and the champagne that we had found in the limo. We ate more Mentos so nobody would know that we'd been drinking and that the guys had been smoking. We complained about our heels and our stomachs and our eye makeup—we watched Taylor and Tiffany laugh and hold their compacts for each other and spray perfume into the space in front of them, almost blinding the kids ahead of them in line. Some of us wished we hadn't worn strapless—our boobs couldn't hold them up—and some of us wished we'd gone long instead of cocktail, so that we could wear flats and nobody would know.

Carolyn was near the front of the line—with Shane—and we could see the back of her hair from where we were standing. She wore it down—nobody else did this—and when she moved her head, her hair swooshed and fell: she was a Moroccan Oil commercial. She was so thin. When she put her arm in the air, you could see her shoulder caps—she was like a puppet, one of the freaky ones from *Pinocchio*, just sockets and bones and white, white skin. She wore flats—how had we not noticed this before?—and Shane held his hand around her waist. His hand, his arm, his body—they made her look even smaller. They were like Disney characters, out of proportion: him giant and strapping, her tiny and wide-eyed.

Inside the gym, Miss Simpson stood to the side, in front of the proscenium arch, at a podium, a list of names in front of her. She called Shane's name and then Carolyn's. And then they disappeared through the doors. The applause echoed through the gym, into the halls: the loudest so far.

"She's pretty."

"She's okay."

"Her dress looks old."

"That's vintage."

"What a slut."

"Total whore."

"Shut up."

"Be nice."

"Total fucking slutty whore."

We came out in pairs afterward, into a spotlight, just for a second, as our names were called and our parents and teachers clapped. Sometimes people yelled. For a second, we thought we were famous, that the whole of the world was there, in our gym, watching us, photographing us, preserving us forever. We were young and hopeful and beautiful and fearless, for just a few seconds, and it made us smile, until we heard the murmuring behind us, and we moved to the side of the gym and took our phones and our mirrors and our lip glosses out of our purses, and we checked to make sure everything was in place. We texted one another as soon as we could:

You looked GREAT ☺
She is such a WHORE.
He's a douche
Don't be so meeeeaannnnnnn!
I heart your dress . . .
Um? Your flowers??? What happened
This is soooooooooooo lame ass
I hate her guts

Andrew Wright and Gemma Davies were the last to go through, our other golden couple. We watched him more than her: he barely smiled, his khakis were a few centimeters too short, his tie wasn't tied quite right. He pulled Gemma across the stage—they moved faster than anybody else—and then Lead-Out was over. The dance began.

Glitter everywhere, confetti on the floor. The girls' restroom reeked of Jimmy Beam and cranberry juice and Dr Pepper and Estée Lauder White Linen. Taylor and Tiffany had been drinking premixed margaritas since the parade and we thought that explained why they were being so friendly, why their eyes were so watery, almost glassy.

We danced and the cheerleaders were always ridiculously good. Even when they were joking; they looked professional and they hardly sweated. The DJ played songs we knew and we sang along: "Single Ladies," "Paper Planes," "Love Lockdown," "All Summer Long," "Sweet Home Alabama." Slow songs came along every three and we left the floor, sat in the bleachers; our dates only wanted to be friends. We watched the couples rock back and forth, back and forth.

Shane and Carolyn stood far away from everybody else and they danced slow, even to the fast songs. She looked like she was on a string when she moved—like a floating dancer, held up with invisible pulleys, like Peter Pan in the middle school play. She had done ballet or something, we guessed, or maybe being that skinny made you more graceful. She didn't sweat or go red—not like she did in the bathroom—and her skin stayed white and when the light hit it, she sparkled. She didn't talk to anybody except for Shane and nobody talked to her—even though, at that stage, we still wanted to. She was beautiful and she was perfect. Our corsages were fake overgrown mums with tacky streamers that fell to the floor, with plastic bears sticking out of them. The bigger, the longer: the better. This was the way it had been for our parents, the way it was for us, would be for our own children. But Carolyn's corsage was small, a mum the size of her fist, and we knew that she must have told Shane to get it that way, no way would he have done that on his own. People liked her for that, we thought, for telling Shane what to do, for doing something cooler, smaller, different. It was only a corsage.

Brooke Moore never turned up at the dance. It was the first time a girl on the Homecoming Court hadn't been there. Like, ever. People said she stayed at home watching *The Notebook*, over and over, and other people said she was masturbating, watching Channing Tatum in *Step Up*. Some people said she laid on her bed and read out scripture, and other people said she made a voodoo doll of Carolyn. We weren't sure, couldn't know, but we did know that she wasn't there, and that it didn't seem like anybody missed her. Not really.

We went to Waffle House after the dance, at around midnight, to talk about what had happened, to stay together as long as we could, to take advantage of our later curfews. We ordered silver dollar pancakes, and chocolate chip ones, and the guys got bacon and eggs too, and everybody drank coffee so we wouldn't seem drunk when we got home. We spilled maple syrup on the floor and the waitresses and the farmers stared at us, looking like they wanted to tell us off, tell us to go to hell. The whole school was there by 1 A.M. Carolyn and Shane weren't there, of course, but everybody else was.

"I bet she's blowing him."

"She's pretty."

"A whore."

"He wouldn't go there."

"Oh yeah, he would."

"She was wasted."

"You're a douche."

"You're a whore."

"Shut up."

"She's hot."

"A dyke."

"Be nice."

"Poor Brooke."

"Brooke's a bitch."

"Shut *up*."

"No, you."

After we'd eaten and paid and sat around for forever, we got up to leave. Our hair had come undone, the guys had taken off their ties, we had asked the limos to go home. We walked along the Stripline, and then through the farmland, and back over to the old part of town, carrying our heels in our hands. Our stockings got stained with red clay, the bottom of the guys' pants were ruined, and some people stopped in the hay bales and made out for a little while, before running to catch up with the others, stopping at the 7-Eleven to get Slurpies and gum and Krispy Kremes.

A bunch of black kids sat in the parking lot of the 7-Eleven, on top of an old Renault. Three guys and two girls—we didn't see them at first, not until Blake knocked over a can of Sprite on the hood of the car. One of the black guys leaped to his feet and Blake stood still, laughing. One of the girls slid down the front of the car and put her arm on the guy's shoulder. "Leave it."

We piled into the store and Blake followed, still laughing. We looked back—it was easier to see them once we were inside—they were getting in their car and leaving. We heard later that it was Alicia Cooper and her boyfriend and his cousins—they were from another county. It was hard to see, we couldn't tell who was who. If we'd known it was her, we'd said, we would have said hello.

We left the store and kept walking. We took pictures of one another and deleted most of them—we looked gross—and Blake played Rihanna on his iPod as we ran through the Halls' farmland, heading toward our subdivisions. The sky was just starting to get light—a lighter orange than the red clay—and the guys put their jackets around all of us, so we wouldn't get cold. Some of the guys smoked, and somebody had some weed; we took turns taking a hit. We kept running and stopping and running and stopping and we stood around a lot, waiting to go again. It took three or four hours for us to get home.

Brooke's house was on our way—two story, red brick, lights out.

We stopped for a second outside of it and Jason called out her name, laughing. Blake punched him on the shoulder. We told them to calm down and shut up and we started to leave. And somebody—nobody can remember who—noticed the Moores' mailbox. We looked back at it and we all saw it: Carolyn's tiny mum tied to the mailbox's red flag. Somebody took a picture—and then somebody put it up on Facebook early that morning, with a caption: "RIP Brooke Moore. Carolyn Lessing lives."

adams hot list

A word about the Homecoming dance: Taylor Lyon rocked in Michael Kors, her best dress ever, as far as this blogger is concerned. Brooke Moore looked ever so polished in her sequined floor length, but was (OBV!) let down by her candid camera appearance later that night. Rumor has it some Cullman Community boys (former Black Bears, no less) found her throwing up outside her car by the Winn-Dixie and took turns posing with her naked bod. Check out Twitter now (#SloppyMoore) before all the pics are taken down!

And what of Carolyn Lessing, our favorite boyfriend stealer from the Jersey Shore? Her black vintage Calvin Klein was, of course, to die for, but her bony arms are a little on the sickly side, no? And this in via my email (don't forget to send all your juicy stories to adamshighhotlist@gmail.com!): Care Bear Lessing was seen in the bathroom doing lines of coke before dragging Duggy Duggs in there for some anal action. You heard it here first, folks!

Internal memo
Richard Overton to all faculty

November 30, 2010
Dear colleagues,

As you know, the Adams High varsity football team has had a very successful season, and is currently undefeated. The team will travel to Montgomery next week to compete for the state championship. If Adams were to take State, it would be the first time since 1983 for the team to hold this title.

With this in mind, we would ask for increased support and encouragement for the team from faculty members. As you know, the season is a short one, and it is important that the team is able to devote itself fully to the challenge ahead. Following conversations with Coach Cox, I would ask that midterms involving team members be rescheduled to early January in order to avoid any conflict for the players. Equally, if any disciplinary issues are to arise, I should be the first port of call in dealing with these. I do not anticipate that there should be any such problems, but Coach Cox and I thought it was important to reiterate this policy in the lead-up to State.

Thanking you in advance for your cooperation,

Richard Overton

DECEMBER

17

We knew that Carolyn and Shane had had sex. They'd done it at least once, probably twice. The first time—the time we weren't sure about—was in the men's restroom in the west wing of Cullman Community College. The second time, it happened in his car—in the parking lot at the Crown Movie Theater off the Stripline. Blake Wyatt worked the box office and, a week after the Homecoming Dance, he sold them tickets to see *Unstoppable*. When the movie theater closed, and Blake locked up, he saw Shane's Explorer parked a couple of spaces away from his minivan. Shane had token tags: IMAJOCK. Somebody once tried to paint over the *J* to make it funnier, and you could still see the spray paint.

Blake said he could hear the engine, cab light was on, windows open a crack, something like Eminem playing, and he thought the jeep was shaking from the bass. He said from far away, all he could see was Shane and he wondered where Carolyn had gone and what the fuck Shane was doing. As he got closer he could see Carolyn's hair. He said he was going to knock on the window and scare them, only when he got closer, when he got a better look through the fogged-up windows, he could see Shane's belt on the dashboard, Carolyn's jeans draped over the steering wheel, her bra hanging from the back of the passenger seat. Skin everywhere, Shane's tanned all over, Carolyn's so white it was almost blue. Blake stood still, he told us, and he watched Carolyn's head go down, below the driver's seat window. Shane's left hand followed her head and his right hand held onto the steering wheel and his body rose up and fell and rose and fell and shook, and then he laid his head back, against the window. Blake couldn't see Shane's face, he was behind him, and after a minute or two, Carolyn came into view again, and Shane held her body and then pressed his on hers, pushing her against the passenger seat door.

Blake moved to the side, got himself out of the light, and he took out his iPhone and started to record. The image was grainy and he was too far away, but at twenty-two seconds, he was able to zoom in—you could see Shane's back as he pushed himself against Carolyn, fast and slow and fast again. He had a Confederate flag tattooed across his left shoulder blade and it moved as he pushed forward and pulled away. You could see Carolyn's mouth, her hair covered her face, and you couldn't tell if she was smiling or frowning or laughing or what.

At one minute and twenty-seven seconds, you could hear music and we thought it was Chemical Brothers or some Eurotrash crap like that, not Shane's kind of music at all. Shane leaned back and then Carolyn was on top of him and her skin was shining and white and, in one part, you could see dark marks on her breasts and her arms. Later, we would pause there—at two minutes twenty-four seconds—and try to enlarge the image, to see what we could see.

We couldn't tell if the car was shaking or if it was Blake's hands—the image jumped and you could hear him breathing as he filmed. At three minutes in—or just before that—you could see Carolyn's ass. She was tiny, and her shoulder blades looked like they could hurt you, cut you. Shane's arms were bigger than her waist and he was grabbing her so tight he looked like he could throw her out the window if he had wanted to.

That night, Blake posted the clip on Facebook. And it went Adamsville-viral in a couple of days, and people did voice-overs for Shane and Carolyn—some of them were funny, some were creepy. Somebody tried to do a mash-up with the video and *Titanic*—that scene in the car?—and it went up on YouTube, but was taken down the same day. They all were. But we circulated it on Facebook and the comment threads got longer and longer. We wanted to tell her to be careful, that she could talk to us, that she should stay away from Shane, from Brooke. But we didn't tell her anything. We just watched the clip, again and again, and we tried to figure out what it was we saw. Later, it would be evidence in court and they would show seconds of it on the nightly news.

The next Monday at school we did sexuality in health class. When Coach Cox put up the picture of the vagina, two guys yelled out Carolyn's name.

That same day, while we worked in the office, Blake and Shane were waiting to see Mr. Overton. He called them in, and as he ushered them into the office he patted Shane on the back and asked him if he was gonna take State. Shane grinned. Shane and Blake came out just minutes later, then Coach Cox knocked on Mr. Overton's door. As Mr. Overton called him in, we heard one of them say, "Boys will be boys." We weren't sure which one said this, or what exactly it meant, but Blake and Shane weren't written up, in any case. It was a week till we played Montgomery at State.

We got two days off school in December so we could travel to Montgomery for the game. Everybody went; the school hired buses, block-booked hotel rooms. Everything. We all went—only Carolyn didn't—and we won 45–35. There was a parade in town the Saturday after everybody got back. Shane, Andrew, all of them—they were heroes.

It wasn't long after State that Shane stopped driving Carolyn to school. He and Brooke started holding hands in the halls. We didn't know if Shane even told Carolyn he was done with her—we imagined he had. Maybe he was embarrassed about the video, maybe he just missed Brooke. She'd lost the weight she'd put on over the summer and then some. In any case, Shane was meeting Brooke at her locker, bringing her to school. She wore his jersey and his school ring. In English class, Brooke complained that it was cold and put on Shane's letter jacket. It drowned her.

The week after State—Carolyn came into school with no mascara, no foundation, no lip gloss, no hoodie. She wore a turtleneck—some Land's End thing your mother would force on you for Christmas. Her face was pale and blotchy and we said it was like "Stars without makeup!" from *Us Weekly*: "Stars—they're just like us!" We laughed, only she still looked pretty—maybe prettier, even. And in homeroom, she looked out the window and didn't blink and her eyes looked like they were deep inside her skull, resting on the back of her head, asleep. She stared out the window, long and hard. But she was staring at nothing. The blinds were down.

In trig, we heard a voice over the intercom: "Carolyn Lessing to the front office." She'd been called to the guidance counselor before, and we'd lost track of how many times. She picked up her books and headed out the door. A band kid put his foot out—on purpose, we weren't sure—and she tripped and fell. Her books slid across the classroom and some of the girls laughed, only a little. As she grabbed for her notebooks, her sleeves were pushed up. We could see those marks again, purple and black. She could see us looking and pushed her sleeves down, and she gathered her things and got up to leave. As she walked out the door, we could hear Mrs. Matthew's voice.

"I hear that you're having a little boy trouble."

Minutes—no seconds—after that, a text went round: "Shane and Carolyn are SO OVER." Before fifth period, everybody knew.

Nothing happened for a few days. We thought that things were over, that the drama was finished. Carolyn had had a chance on the Homecoming Court, a chance with Shane—that was all over now. We thought everybody had moved on. We saw her eating lunch alone. And then couldn't find her in the cafeteria at all. We heard she was eating her lunch in the bathroom and that's why we were there that day in December, the week before Christmas break. We wanted to bring her back into the cafeteria, back into the school. We thought she might like us. And we wanted to be near her. It doesn't matter what people said at the time—people wanted to know her.

When we got into the bathroom, there was no one there. We heard a voice outside, near the door. It was a girl's, the tone coarse. And we could just barely hear another girl, with a voice that was thinner. Carolyn's, for sure. Every word she said sounded like a foreign language and you had to hold your breath to hear her.

The door opened and the louder voice was almost shouting now. We hurried into the stalls. We didn't know what else to do.

"Why are you doing this?"

We held our breath.

"Running around with other people's boyfriends?"

"I'm not."

"You are."

The water was turned on.

"You're a whore and a slut and the only reason guys even talk to you is 'cause you're a 'ho."

The water piling up faster, the drain blocked?

"You don't even know me."

"I don't have to know you. I'm just saying what everybody already says about you behind your back."

Water was hitting the floor. Splashing out, the faucet running hard.

"I know all the stuff you say about me. I've read it all already."

"Well, now I'm saying it to your face."

Faucet turned off.

"You're a bitch."

A slap. A ring hit the wall. The hand dryer whirring.

The bell rang. A flood of air. The sounds of the hallway filled the room.

We came out of the stalls and we talked about what we had heard. It wasn't right and it wasn't fair, but we were happy and relieved and excited it wasn't us. Later, we talked about how we could have said something—could have told a teacher or our parents, or flushed the toilet or coughed or cleared our throats. But we didn't do anything. And we didn't say anything. It wasn't our business. Not really.

Alyssa Jennings's mother was a nurse in the Adamsville Public Hospital and admitted Carolyn that night. Mrs. Jennings told Alyssa, said she was to tell no one. But she did tell a few people and, eventually, we all knew. Alyssa would tell us later that she felt guilty about that, that she shouldn't have said anything, but how could she know? The following year, Alyssa was nicknamed "Perez": she was a gossip, people said, she had a big mouth, didn't know when to shut up. She transferred halfway through our senior year.

Something about pills. Carolyn had taken a "shit load," according to Blake Wyatt. She vomited in the waiting room, we heard, and had soiled herself in the ambulance. People will do anything to get attention, they said. We heard she ordered them off the Internet and took them with Ecstasy that she'd gotten in New York. The papers said later that she was on a prescription for depression. But that wasn't what people talked about, and nobody seemed to believe that was true. Months afterward, we remembered what Jessica Grady had seen in her bathroom. We wished we had said something, had told an adult. But we didn't, and people kept talking.

Shane came into school the day after and nobody asked him about it. He wore his football jersey, orange and black, and his eyes were bright and clear. He gave a presentation in chemistry—we each had an element, he had strontium. He was five minutes in before he asked to be excused. Mrs. White let him, and you could hear him gagging in the halls. When the bell rang, the janitor was cleaning up vomit off the floor.

We realized later he had cared. We realized later he thought he'd done it. That he'd fucked it up. That it was his fault. It was weird, though. When Carolyn came back to school after Christmas, he ignored her. We watched him pass her in the halls and he wouldn't lift his head. He stared at the floor or, sometimes, he just turned and walked the other way. We wondered what would have happened if he had just kept doing that—just looking the other way.

18

Christmas time in Adamsville meant lights. It meant lights on the fast-food restaurants, around the pig outside Dairy Queen, on the edges of the Winn-Dixie, wrapped on the flagpoles in front of school, lining the telephone poles in and out of town. Farmers put lights on the hay bales, they put tinsel on their electric fences, they put wreaths around their scarecrows. And the houses had lights too: the cheaper the subdivision, the brighter and bigger the lights. Coming down Azalea Avenue, you could be blinded by the flashing white and blue and red and green. Going into a trailer park was a safety hazard.

And with the lights came objects and figurines, and with that, every subdivision had a theme: candy canes or reindeer or Christmas trees or snowmen or Santa Claus and his sleigh or wrapped-up presents with bows. Manger scenes at every corner—outside the churches, the schools, the Wal-Mart, the Taco Bell. Jesus and

Mary and Joseph in plastic and in straw and in papier-mâché, in the mall, in the cafeteria, in the middle of the Halls' farm. And the slogans outside the churches:

JESUS IS LORD—HE IS THE REASON FOR THE SEASON.
DON'T FORGET THE CHRIST IN CHRISTMAS.
THE TOMB IS EMPTY. NO BONES ABOUT IT.
DON'T LOSE FAITH. MOSES, TOO, WAS ONCE A BASKET CASE.

We dreamed of snow. We saw white blankets covering the fields along the Stripline, white pillows over the Stripline Baptist and country club, thick and clean powder dusting the bike paths and parking lots. In our dreams, the town was quiet, small gold lights glittering from the flagpoles and telephone lines. We saw the white ground glowing in the moonlight, cars parked, not moving, the town silent, waiting. No red clay, no signs for the pep rally, no Burger King wrappers on the side of the road. Just white, as far as we could see.

When it did snow, the little it did, the white powder turned orange from the ground, the snow on the roads went dark gray and black from the cars. It was sludge and messy and disgusting and it was cleared away over days, sometimes weeks. It was never as white as our dreams. We remembered some of the pictures in Carolyn's house: Central Park in the snow, the tree at Rockefeller Center, a photograph of her in ski boots outside a redbrick building—her school, we guessed—topped with a layer of white. None of us had ever been to New York or New Jersey or wherever, and some of us had never been out of the state or let alone to the North. Sometimes, we thought, it was better not to know any better. We laughed about this, only sometimes this wasn't that funny, sometimes it wasn't funny at all.

That Christmas, we were greedy to know everything about Carolyn's life, about her places, her people, her food. At the time, it seemed a little sad that she had had to leave her old life behind. Looking back, it hurts to think about it.

In the weeks before Christmas, when we weren't studying for midterms, or writing our Christmas lists, our conversations revolved around Carolyn: what had happened with Brooke and Gemma, with the clip, with Shane, with the pills, the hospital. We loved her and hated her and followed her, in person and online. We texted one another about her hair—if it had any frizz, if it had a nice wave—and about her hands—if they were red and calloused, if they were white and smooth. She changed from day to day and we watched her, but at a distance, where we were safe.

At school, things went back to normal, kind of. People were still talking about Carolyn, for sure, but there were other things going on too: the choir did a Christmas show, the Drama Society put on *A Christmas Carol*, the Audio Visual Club did a screening of *Miracle on 34th Street*, the marching band did an assembly where they played nondenominational Christmas songs: anything Christian, really. The cheerleaders had red and green Christmas-themed uniforms that made them look like sexy reindeer and the teachers wore Santa hats and Christmas sweaters. We gave one another gifts or, if we didn't know somebody that well, we at least gave them a candy cane. Or a red or green York Peppermint Patty.

The last Friday before Christmas break, after our midterms were over and the class parties were done, we cruised around downtown and looked at the lights. And then we went to the mall and stood around the food court, pretending to buy our Christmas gifts, but really, trying to see what everybody was doing.

Muzak blared out at every level. The mall was freezing: they had the air on full blast always, even when it was cold outside. We wore our puffa coats indoors, no point in taking them off.

"It's to make us buy sweaters."

"It helps you burn calories."

"You're always cold."

" 'Cause you're too skinny."

"Am not."

"Are too."

"I'm fat."

"Oh, please."

The mall was all lit up—Christmas trees in every wing, red and green and blue and white lights lining the escalators, the elevators. At the center of it all, on the ground floor, underneath the food court, we could see Santa's Workshop. It looked the same as the Easter Bunny's Rabbit Hole, we said, and the Santa was wearing a beard that was too long and too white. We stared at him and the workshop and then we saw Blake Wyatt and Dylan Hall and Jason Nelson on his break from Abercrombie. They looked over at the Santa, looked at one another and one of them—we couldn't tell who—yelled out, *"Perv."* We were pretty sure that the guy playing Santa was Gemma Davies's first or second cousin and we were afraid to laugh, just in case.

We sat outside Sbarro's and ordered cheese pizza and we took off the cheese and blotted it with our napkins. We would eat frozen yogurt later, topped with Oreos and Reese's Peanut Butter Cups and M&Ms. We tore our pizza into pieces and ate one mouthful at a time, careful not to look hungry. Somebody got a text: "Carolyn L in the mall with HER MOTHER."

And then we saw her—with some girl, drinking lemonades in front of the Chick-fil-A. They were talking—the other girl was laughing—both so small. They moved a little bit closer to us and we could see that Carolyn's eyes were black with eyeliner and the girl she was with: it was her mother. Abby. It was the first time we had seen Carolyn since the thing in the hospital. We didn't know if we should talk to her or what. Wouldn't want to make her feel awkward.

"She looks good."

"The same, really."

"Well, that's good."

"Don't stare."

"I'm not."

She must not have seen us, because she didn't wave or come over. She was carrying a bag from Abercrombie, and a small one from Parisians. "Retail therapy," Lauren said. We watched them walk around the food court, Carolyn's shoulders slumped, hair covering her face. They walked around and then they stood still and then they walked away, toward the elevator. They didn't end up eating any food, at least not that we could see, and we wondered if Carolyn was still in recovery and whether or not she felt better or if she would be coming back to swim team. She looked skinnier than before and maybe we were jealous that she could keep on losing weight, and we wondered what it would be like to be so sick or so sad or mad or whatever it was she was, to be sick enough not to want to eat. It would be nice to be free of that, we thought.

As they walked away we admired the way her boyfriend cardigan fell off her shoulders, the way her distressed jeans hung from her hips—she was a human coat hanger, and we imagined fifty Carolyns hanging in our closets, draping every piece of fabric perfectly.

We saw Brooke Moore and Gemma Davies walk into Abercrombie later, and we followed them, wanting to know what they were doing, what they were buying, who they were meeting. Lauren had seen Andrew Wright and Gemma Davies in Olive Garden the night before, the two of them sitting across from each other, tapping their phones and picking at a plate of fried cheese. She said that they didn't even look at each other, not for the whole meal, that they acted like they didn't know each other or care about each other, like they "were some kind of old couple about to get a divorce or something." Lauren said she guessed they were breaking up and we wondered if that were true, and we kind of wished it would be, for a reason we didn't quite know.

In the store, we tried on distressed skinny jeans and long-sleeve waffle tees in gray and blue. Nicole's jeans were too tight and she refused to go up to a size four. We told her that clothes just ran small. We started to try on tops when we heard voices. Brooke's and Gemma's, we were sure. They'd gone into the room next to us, talking and swapping clothes.

"I need an extra, extra small. This is too big."

"Yeah, it's huge on you."

"Will it shrink in the wash?"

"Yeah, yeah."

We held our breath.

"I hate my abs."

"I hate my shoulders."

"I ate too many curly fries."

"I drank too much over the weekend."

A phone beeped. One of theirs. Not ours.

A groan.

"I hate that Yankee slut."

"I hate her weird accent."

"She thinks she's so fucking hot."

"You think?"

"What are you saying? Don't you?"

"Yeah, yeah."

"What?"

"It's just weird what happened with the hospital. The pills."

"She's a drama queen. My mother has a friend who was a friend works in admissions in the hospital and she said it wasn't even a big deal."

"I just wonder what she takes the pills for."

"For being a slut?"

They laughed.

"You're so mean."

"Well, she's a whore." And they laughed again.

"Shut up." And then, in a whisper: "She could be in here."

We waited until they left and then we went to the counter and paid for our tops. As the cash register jangled, the store's alarm went off, and we looked in the mirror at the counter, and we could see Brooke and Gemma walking fast out of the store, heading toward the food court. The woman ringing us up rolled her eyes and ran to the front of the store. She ran past Jason Nelson, who was folding sweaters by the entrance. He didn't look up and we watched her stick her head out the front, turning from side to side. She flipped a switch and the noise stopped. She looked at Jason. She rolled her eyes again. And she came back to the counter to ring us up.

When we went back to school after break, Brooke and Gemma were wearing their pale blue cashmere sweaters, formfitting, with long, long sleeves that stretched to the end of their fingertips. One hundred twenty-two dollars each. We remembered 'cause we had thought about buying them ourselves.

JANUARY

19

Nobody was that surprised when Andrew and Carolyn started hooking up. Or at least that's what everybody said. That thing at the Homecoming parade had been weird—all the pictures in his phone?—and even though people didn't say this was why they thought the hook-up was logical, we all knew that's what people meant. Andrew would go for anything that moved, he wasn't picky like Shane. Plus, we'd all seen him following Shane and Carolyn around at parties, at the Homecoming Dance, or wherever, so people said either Andrew had a thing for Carolyn, or he really was a faggot for Shane.

We weren't totally sure when it started for real—like girlfriend-boyfriend stuff—but we'd seen them together after swimming: standing outside the art room, where Carolyn had started going after practice, staying until the janitors kicked her out. Dylan Hall worked for the AV club and he was next door. He told people that

Carolyn and Andrew were making out in the supply closet every Tuesday and Thursday—he had seen Andrew go in too many times for it to be anything else. Plus, he'd gotten Janitor Ken to confirm things. We weren't sure that this meant much, but Dylan said it did.

Taylor told Tiffany, and Tiffany told Gemma during PE the first week back from Christmas break. We were doing the President's Physical Fitness Test and while we stood around waiting to do our chin-ups—the part we dreaded the most—we overheard them.

"I just thought you'd want to know."

"Thanks."

"Well, that's what people are saying, is all."

"I can't believe her."

"I know. She's a 'ho."

"I swear, if she comes fucking close to me I'll fucking kill her."

"Somebody should tell her to fucking back off from other people's boyfriends."

"Shouldn't she still be in the hospital?"

"She should be told to go the fuck home."

"I can't fucking believe her. I thought she was nice."

"Well, now you know."

"Yeah."

"Total slut."

Ms. Powell stood by the high bars with a clipboard and she was taking notes and keeping time—if you couldn't do a chin-up you just had to hang there as long as you could—but she looked up from her stopwatch and stared straight at Gemma and Tiffany. We could only see the side of Gemma's face: her cheek was a deep pink.

"I'm going to have to write you girls up for language if you don't quit."

"Yes, ma'am."

Later that night, on Facebook, Gemma changed her relationship status to single. She posted on her wall: "CL is a skinny Yankee slut." Sixteen people liked that, including Shane Duggan and Brooke Moore. And Taylor Lyon. Nobody posted a comment.

People said it was a little shady that Carolyn had been with Andrew when he was probably still with Gemma, and the fact that she'd been with Shane right before—that was really shady. If she'd just been with one of them, we said, it might not have been so bad, people might have still thought she was okay. But two of them, right in a row, that seemed different, changed everything. It was harder to see her side.

The dates were never really established, though, that's what we talked about later: nobody knew if she'd stolen anyone from anybody. And Andrew and Shane stayed quiet and nobody ever blamed them. It was just between us girls.

Andrew explained later that he was just trying to be there for her, he was just to listen, to help her fit in. He felt sorry for Carolyn after the thing with the hospital and after all the crap with Shane. We stopped seeing Carolyn with Taylor and Tiffany and all them after cheerleading practice, didn't see them linking arms in the courtyard. We saw Taylor brush by Carolyn in the halls: she either didn't notice her or wasn't speaking to her. We assumed it was the former. Over Christmas break, Taylor was seen with Gemma in Sonic on the weekends and, when we got back to school, Taylor was hanging out with her at the water fountain before the first bell rang. We guessed things were back to normal.

Andrew never dumped Gemma, never actually broke up with her, not as far as we knew: he just stopped calling her, stopped meeting her after school. Maybe he thought the thing on Facebook meant they were over, maybe they were never as serious as we thought. In any case, Christmas break was good for that kind of thing—you didn't see people for a while and if you wanted to, you could ignore someone, or at least phase them out. It sucked but it happened.

Gemma, like all the other girls in our class, was already

thinking about college. Sororities, mostly. "If you're a junior, and you have a senior boyfriend, you're, like, automatically a Tri Delt or a Phi Mu." She would tell people this at lunch, or in the halls or in the parking lot after church. And we'd squint our eyes a little, unsure if this were really true, not exactly sure how this could matter. And then she'd continue: "I mean, as long as you're together the next year. Then you can go to the frat parties on the weekends and you meet all the girls and you're, like, an automatic in." She'd smile, satisfied with herself that she'd satisfied us. And then she'd finish up, her eyes bright and excited: "Andrew's undecided between Auburn and Alabama." We thought she was kind of deranged.

She got carried away, people said later, was too caught up in the future to see what was right in front of her nose. That Andrew Wright had a major thing for Carolyn Lessing. Now Gemma Davies's reputation was tarnished, she'd been dumped by a senior and it didn't look like she'd be going to any frat parties at Auburn in the fall. And, for that reason, and maybe because she actually liked Andrew at least a little, she was pissed.

In January, Carolyn was working on a major art project—a series of paintings and prints—and that was the official story for why she was in the art room every night until late. Andrew probably wasn't meant to be there, but maybe because he was such a good student, people turned a blind eye. Or maybe Mr. Ferris just had a soft spot for Carolyn. We didn't know.

Mr. Ferris taught art along with trig, and he told everybody how talented Carolyn was, that he thought there was some connection between her skills as an artist and her aptitude for math. "She became extremely focused during the second semester," he told people later. "And we put up the work in the halls as kind of a treat—a reward. I thought it would be nice for her to have an exhibition." And then he would sigh. "I'm not sure if it was wise, in retrospect."

The exhibition went up in the halls of the new English building—there were thirteen pieces and there was even a photograph of Carolyn with an "artist's statement" at the entrance. Like a real museum or a gallery. At first, people were really impressed with the work—they were half-paintings and half-collages and really cool, up close and far away. They were made with maps and magazine and newspaper clippings and all sorts of things that had been painted over and enhanced and enlarged. Some of them had photographs in them—and if you looked closely enough, you could see her eyes in a couple of them. They were weird but cool. We didn't know anything about art, not really, but they weren't anything we thought we could ever make. People said it was a little conceited—some people even said she had forced Mr. Ferris to put them up—but they were still really good, no matter what you thought of her.

The colors were pretty much the same in all of them: lots of red and blue and purple. And lots of white. Most of them were shapes, squares and circles and parallelograms and triangles, but all mixed up and layered on top of one another. Over the shapes, she'd pasted the clippings and they were painted over again and again, and in her little description she said she used nail polish and Wite-Out to make those stick. There were pictures of models' bodies, and Barbie dolls and captions like "10 Ways to Make Him . . ." and she'd cut off the end, we guessed 'cause it was too dirty for school. On some of the canvases, underneath the models and the lines from *Cosmopolitan,* she pasted pages from textbooks or dictionaries: long words with definitions. We weren't sure we understood them—the clippings or the definitions or the paintings. But we knew they were good, even if we didn't know why.

The work was up for a week—toward the end of January—before one of them was slashed, a big gaping hole in the center of the canvas. Somebody took a staple gun to the three that had the photographs of her eyes. And somebody wrote "WHORE" in red Sharpie over one of the plainer prints. And the photograph of Carolyn was completely mangled—we never saw that one for ourselves, but the paper said somebody had put "something phallic" right next to her face. Mr. Ferris took the whole exhibition down within the day. Nobody ever got caught.

20

Nicole Willis had a pool in her backyard and her dad had just installed some kind of heater, which meant they could have pool parties twelve months a year. The Saturday after our first week back after break, Nicole's parents went to Moulton for some work thing of her dad's. So she had a party at her house and Carolyn was there.

Nicole told us to get there early. We pre-gamed before people arrived: some Jell-O shots and purple Kool-Aid made with water and Smirnoff. People arrived in twos and threes and fours and then in gangs of more than we could count. We stayed in the kitchen, mostly, sipping and laughing and watching and waiting for the cool people to arrive.

Gemma and Brooke came with Taylor Lyon and Tiffany Port. As they walked out of the kitchen and onto the porch, Jessica turned to us: "Look! The whole gang is back together again." And we laughed. We followed them out there later, and they stood around, sharing one cigarette between the four of them, looking bored then happy then bored again. They talked really low and they looked over at Carolyn and we couldn't hear what they said, but we guessed, and Jessica acted out a dialogue and we laughed. Shane walked over to them every ten minutes or so, to put his arm around Brooke, kiss her on the cheek or the shoulder. She would whisper into his ear and she would laugh. Then he'd look around.

We'd seen them all at church earlier—a youth group meeting to prepare for our next youth service—and Gemma had picked out the psalm she was going to read—something about enemies and not shouting in triumph over them—and Brooke begged Dave Dillon to let her read that Corinthians one about love and being patient and everything. Taylor and Tiffany had picked out a song they wanted to sing—Alan Jackson's "A Woman's Love"— but with Jesus instead.

Carolyn stood close to Andrew and, at first, nobody really noticed if she was drinking or not. She was wearing some old tank top and it was white and thin, like something your dad would wear. People would say later that her clothes were amazing and vintage— she was a hipster, boho, original. But at that time, people had started to say she was a freak: freaky clothes, freaky stare. Even band kids were making fun of her.

As it got later, Brooke kept calling Andrew over to them. He pretended like he couldn't hear her. This encouraged her, we guessed, or annoyed her, because she kept calling his name, every three or four minutes. He put his arm around Carolyn and moved them away. Then Brooke and Gemma and Taylor and Tiffany, and sometimes Shane, they'd move over closer again. It would get on anybody's nerves. Andrew looked freaked. Carolyn smiled.

Later, we wondered if it was because of Brooke and them that Carolyn started to drink so much as the night went on, that she started to pour everything back so fast. She drank shots and bottles of High Life and she went inside and she played flip cup and was terrible. She swayed a lot and she looked like she might cry. Later on, she told jokes, we heard, and was doing impressions of Miss Simpson and Mr. Overton. "She could do the accent perfect."

"Yeah, she was good at that."

When somebody asked her about the exhibition, she rolled her eyes and said she didn't care. "I'm no stranger to controversy." She laughed. And people should have thought this made her a good sport. Instead they called her pathetic.

People got in the pool when it was late—the girls in their bras and panties, the guys in their boxers. We stayed on the deck. Andrew Wright sat on the steps in the shallow end, Carolyn right below him, both of them stripped down. The pool lights lit up the water—you could see the moisturizer swirling off the girls' legs, the hair gel gathering at the surface. People splashed and played Marco Polo and the boys did cannonballs, and we tried not to get our hair wet.

"Marco."

"Polo."

"Fish Out of Water?"

A splash. Swimming hard now. Laughter. Yelling. Brad Paisley playing. Lights flashing as a body swam past the pool's lights.

"MARCO!!!"

"POLO!!!!"

"Fish Out of Water?"

"No!"

They were playing and laughing and pushing. Blake Wyatt did a flip and nearly cracked his skull. Tiffany Port got pushed in, wearing a peach T-shirt and no bra. The girls screamed every time they were splashed, the guys tried to make waves with an inflatable alligator. They were having fun. And they were all so busy splashing and swimming that they almost didn't notice Carolyn, her head between Andrew's legs, his eyes closed, mouth open. We almost didn't either.

We looked over to Shane. He was standing with Adam Simmons and Dylan Hall, head-butting each other or something. Brooke walked over to him and pointed to the pool. His face went blank and then he laughed. He went inside, like, two minutes later. We heard he left shortly after that. We only thought about how he might have felt about the whole thing later. We guessed it must have pissed him off. Shane was so good-looking, so popular, so certain, you never thought that he could get jealous or pissy. When we asked him about it in school on Monday, he told us: "She can do whatever the hell she wants." And we believed him at first. But not in the end.

People talked about the thing in the pool for weeks, and it went round and round on Facebook; we texted each other updates about what had happened. A few photos went up on Instagram, all hazy and hipster, and people tagged Carolyn and then Andrew, but the pictures there were all PG. People had to make up the rest. At first it was just a blow job, then it was full-on sex, and then that she took it from behind later that night. This seemed unlikely, we all agreed, but Tiffany and Taylor and all of the other cheerleaders whispered it was true, and people believed them. "Andrew is so sweet," people said. "Sweeter than Shane." And then: "Poor Gemma." But we had seen Gemma making out with Jason Nelson a couple weeks earlier, outside the mall, after he had gotten off his shift at Abercrombie. We hadn't told anybody—nobody wanted to hear bad things about her—and it might have changed things, we thought, if people knew. But we didn't say anything, and neither did Andrew, even though we found out later he must have known. And the chatter got louder and louder and the texts came more and more often. She should really have quit while she was ahead. Carolyn, that is.

While I had hoped to conduct this interview in person, my father's trip to Adamsville was cancelled at the last minute. As I had already prepared the questions, I thought it would be better to carry on with my original interviewee.

January 29, 2011
Carolyn Lessing
Honors English—Miss Simpson

Catcher in the Rye—Interview about high school life

I know that it often seems as though adults forget that they were once teenagers, attended high school and had experiences similar to what you are going through today. Now is your opportunity to lead an adult (this can be a parent, grandparent, aunt, uncle, family friend) down memory lane and see what high school was like "back in the day."

Your assignment is to interview one such person and write a narrative account about what you learned. Ideally, the interview should be conducted in person.

Once you have completed the interview process you will then write a narrative about that person, which will include the following:

1. Why you chose to interview this particular person.
2. A physical description of the person you interviewed.
3. A description of the setting of the interview.
4. Detailed examples of what life was like for your interviewee in high school.
5. An account of what the interviewee thought of *Catcher in the Rye*.
6. Actual quotes from the person you interviewed (at least 3).
7. A final paragraph that includes a *reflection* of what you learned from doing the interview and how, if at all, this relates to *Catcher in the Rye*.

For this assignment, I interviewed my father (Jerome Hadden), whom I spoke to over Skype. I interviewed my dad to find out what high school was like for him and whether or not *Catcher in the Rye* was a book that he read and whether it was important to him. Additionally, I sought to find out if high school was different for him than it is for me. I chose my father because he is the adult I find the easiest to relate to and the adult I have learned the most from, particularly in terms of politics and culture, over the past years.

My father's apartment is in Brooklyn, and he lives in a diverse and vibrant neighborhood, in a studio apartment above an Indian restaurant. Even when I am Skyping my father, I feel that I can smell the scents of curry wafting from his apartment through my computer. The apartment is small and cozy, and is all one room, with a separate bathroom. When I'm in the apartment, I'm struck by how little space one really actually needs and how excessively large our home is in Alabama. My father keeps his life very simple, which is important to his writing, and he does not have a television. Before he and my mother divorced, we lived in a large house all together, but Dad prefers a smaller place now that he's on his own.

I interviewed my father on a Thursday evening, at around 8 pm my time, 9 pm his time. He sat in a vintage leather armchair with his computer in front of him. Dad was wearing a blue t-shirt and his favorite corduroy blazer, which he has had since I was little. My dad is 50 years old and has thick, silver hair and dark, bushy eyebrows. He wears reading glasses most of the time, and is skinny and not very tall. As we chatted, I could see a large bookcase behind him, and the shelves were bent because his books are so heavy and there are so many of them. I interviewed Dad from my bedroom, at my desk, and I was wearing my purple fleece onesie. While I interviewed Dad, I drank a Diet Coke and Dad sipped a glass of red wine. Even though I could see him on the screen and talk to him, I felt really far away from his life in New York. Alabama is a million miles away from my old life.

My father was in high school from 1974–1978. He went to a public high school in Newburgh, New York. Dad was a strong athlete and was on the golf team, the swim team and the baseball team. Sports were a very important part of school life in Newburgh, as were academics. Even though he enjoyed school, he says that teachers were generally much stricter then than they are now, and that kids were not encouraged to be individuals. "We memorized huge amounts of material and were never expected or encouraged to be creative or write things like essays. Tests were very formulaic. If you grew your hair too long, or if you wore something too outlandish, you would be punished or even suspended."

Dad said that he wore bell-bottoms and a blazer when he wanted to dress up, and that during his senior year, he tried to emulate the look of John Travolta in *Saturday Night Fever.* Later, he emailed me some pictures of him and his date before his senior prom. He wore a burgundy velour blazer, burgundy bow tie and burgundy bell-bottoms, along with a pale blue shirt with a wide collar and a pair of white boots. His date wore a long blue check dress and a pair of blue platform boots. He said that dancing was important and that he and his friends would practice before prom so that they could show off their "moves." He and his friends were allowed to drink when they were 18 years old (as opposed to 21 for us) and he also said that smoking pot was fairly common. He said he didn't know anybody who did any other drugs at that time, and that most of his friends were pretty "tame."

Dad said that he feels my generation has more freedom than his did, and more self-confidence. Now, when we go to school, teachers are more concerned with students being happy and being well-rounded, whereas his teachers were more concerned with what colleges the kids would get into. When Dad told his teachers that he wanted to be a writer, they told him to get a teaching degree because being a novelist was not a real "profession." He says that nowadays teachers seem to encourage students to pursue their dreams. I'm not sure that this is really the case, but I'm not sure if that's the point of this assignment either.

Unsurprisingly, Dad's favorite subject in school was English (the same as me) and his teacher, Mrs. Healey, had very good taste in books and led interesting and exciting discussions about the things that they read. "We often read books that were unusual, or that you wouldn't expect to read in school," he said. "And Mrs. Healey allowed us to write reports on anything that we were interested in, including mysteries and comic books." Dad told me that this was the first time he had been encouraged to read for pleasure and that that stayed with him for life.

Catcher in the Rye was an important book for Dad and his class. Dad said, "It was one of the first books that we read in school that everybody responded to. Probably because it was about a young person and told from his point of view and in his voice, and many of us related to Holden Caulfield." Dad explained to me that the book seemed very relevant to him at that time because he thought most adults were "phonies" and he wanted to be authentic. Dad also went to New York City a lot with his family, so he recognized a lot of the places named. This was exciting for him and their class took a field trip to the Natural History Museum as part of their course work for the novel.

My dad pointed out that he has read *Catcher in the Rye* many times since high school and that every time he reads it, he sees something new, which he thinks "is a sign of a very good novel."

The first time he read it, he thought it was about being "authentic" and not being a "phony." When Dad read the novel in college he thought it was mostly about sex and coming of age. When he read it a few years ago, he said he realized it was mainly a book about grief, and Holden coming to terms with the death of his brother.

Overall, *Catcher in the Rye* was a very important book to my father and to his classmates. High school was different in many ways when he was a teenager, and it seems as if kids our age have more freedom than he and his friends did. That being said, it also seems like kids back then had closer relationships with their parents and extended families. Dad said he really related to the book and that it was really different and it shocked a lot of people. I have to say that I didn't find it shocking at all and I doubt any of my friends would.

When my father and I finished our conversation, at around 9:30 pm that evening, Dad suggested that we go to the Natural History Museum the next time I visited, where he took me when I was seven years old. I could not help but feel that I would have the same experience as Holden if we ever made it there again: struck by how everything at the Museum had remained the same, while my father and I have changed tremendously in the meantime.

Grade: A

While I am disappointed (mostly for you!) that you could not conduct the interview in person, this is a strong piece and I'm impressed with the level of observation of both your father's surroundings and the text itself. I would have liked slightly more context as to why you chose your father, but I understand the limitations of the word count and think this is another very good essay. I would strongly encourage you to consider taking creative writing next year as an elective, particularly since you have shown a strong aptitude and interest in poetry.

FEBRUARY

21

Brooke hated Carolyn. We knew that much. In Spanish class, she talked loudly about Carolyn's crappy clothes and her probable STDs and her annoying accent. She did the same in English class, which was awkward, we said, 'cause Carolyn was actually there. In the halls, Brooke would walk into Carolyn as she tried to pass. Deliberately, it had to be. In the cafeteria, she would laugh in Carolyn's face and then stop abruptly. And Shane went along with it all, maybe even made it worse. The reasons for Brooke's behavior were pretty obvious—she was jealous, felt threatened, all the usuals. As for Shane, he was just trying to support his girlfriend, we guessed. And he was probably pissed Carolyn was so into Andrew after everything. Shane had, in fact, seen her first. He had called dibs.

Carolyn didn't react, not that we could tell, but it would have been impossible not to let it bother you. Now that Taylor and Tiffany weren't her friends, she walked through the halls on her own, mostly, if Andrew wasn't there.

Gemma moped around school at first, didn't say much about Carolyn out loud. We thought she might take things a little better. But Brooke brought her around in the end, and Gemma did her own little things: she moved if Carolyn sat anywhere near her, stopped talking if Carolyn got within ten feet. She talked about how she hated the sound of Yankee accents. In church, when Carolyn and her mom shook Reverend Davies's hand, Gemma stood next to her dad, staring at her feet, never looking up. She never said anything directly to Carolyn, not in the beginning, but she made her feelings clear. Brooke did most of the yelling, but Gemma was effective too. She was just a little quieter.

In English, Miss Simpson put Carolyn into a group with Gemma and Brooke, to critique one another's interviews about *Catcher in the Rye*. We thought this was a stupid idea—it was pathetic how badly Miss Simpson wanted everybody to get along—and we watched the three of them while we were supposed to be reviewing our work. Brooke and Gemma moved their desks so that they faced each other, Carolyn's coming into theirs at a perpendicular angle. Brooke and Gemma locked eyes with each other and Carolyn kept her eyes on her paper. We heard Miss Simpson talk to them.

"How are my favorite girls getting along?" She put her Diet Coke on Carolyn's desk.

"Fine, thanks, Miss Simpson." Gemma was always so polite to adults, even when she was being a bitch. She probably knew she had no right to be in Honors English. Only there 'cause Mrs. Davies had complained and made a scene.

"Do you understand the assignment?" Miss Simpson was hovering, she always did.

"Yes, ma'am." Brooke smiled up at her. "We were just telling Carolyn how good hers is."

Carolyn looked up. We thought she might have rolled her eyes.

"Well, she *is* the daughter of a famous writer." Miss Simpson ran her hand over Carolyn's hair. Lesbian.

"Oh, that's *right,*" Brooke said, smiling. Carolyn reddened. "Didn't he write some book about girls who like to get raped? Or was it incest?"

Miss Simpson stepped back. "What?"

Gemma nodded. "Yeah. My dad says it was banned in, like, twenty states."

"That's not true." Carolyn spoke loudly. Like the words came from her gut.

"Right, well . . ." Miss Simpson crinkled her forehead.

"Miss Simpson?" Brooke had turned around. "I think that Dylan needs you."

Dylan Hall winked at Brooke. Put his hand in the air.

Miss Simpson pivoted. "Oh, right." She started to walk away. "Okay, then, well, keep going, girls."

As Miss Simpson walked over to Dylan's desk, at the other side of the classroom, Brooke picked up the Diet Coke on Carolyn's desk and poured it in Carolyn's lap.

"Whoops," Brooke said. Gemma laughed.

Carolyn stood up, knocking her desk over with her. "Oh my God." Coke streamed off her top, onto the floor. Her shirt clung to her stomach.

Dylan Hall laughed. "Carolyn has an outtie." He put his hand over his mouth, cracking up.

Tears filled Carolyn's eyes, and she looked up, trying to blink them back.

Miss Simpson walked toward her. "Oh . . ."

Carolyn ran out the door, slamming it behind her. Miss Simpson's eyes rested on Gemma, then Brooke.

Brooke looked straight back at her. "What? It was an accident." And she smiled.

There were things we would always remember about that year: Homecoming, of course, and swimming practice and the story about the hospital. But there were other things too, things that one of us would remember but the others wouldn't, and we would try to cobble everything together, to make it fit, to make sense of it all. We remembered the texts, and the Facebook feeds and the time in the bathroom. Remembered Brooke telling Carolyn she had herpes. Somebody remembered that Carolyn's tires had been slashed—and another remembered her house getting rolled. Somebody remembered her with a cut on her lip—other people said that was the herpes. Somebody remembered that her hair got thinner as the year went by, and somebody else remembered her shaving an eyebrow off, and singeing her eyelashes with a lighter. We didn't keep journals and we didn't write things down: we thought we would remember it all, and that the memories would be safe in our heads. But our minds do funny things sometimes, and we only realized this later: they mix things up and switch things around, and sometimes what we dreamed about eventually happened, and what really happened ended up in our dreams. An official record eventually formed, though, in the news, on TV, on a thousand blogs across the world. We weren't the authors of those stories but, in the end, what right did we really have to object to them? We hadn't written things down, or even said them out loud, when it mattered, when it could have changed the course of events. We were part of history but we sat and watched. Like a movie. Only worse.

Miss Simpson probably knew the most, out of anybody. Our

five-hundred-word themes, our responses to critical reading, our prayers in her room, our behavior in class, at chaperoned events. And then there was Mrs. Matthew, who called Carolyn to the office maybe once a week. Mr. Ferris watched the whole thing closely too, although we didn't really notice him at the time. His observations to the newspapers weren't that insightful, but they did reveal that he'd been watching us, much more than we ever would have known. In the end, he knew the least, we thought, but he seemed to care the most.

We grew up too fast, that's what they told us. We moved too quickly. Had too much sex, took too many drugs, drank too much. They didn't have a clue, we said, but we looked around and wondered if what they said was true. We knew everything about everyone, and it was hard to outrun our childhoods, hard to do enough stuff to make people forget about the time you peed your pants in second grade, the time you cried when your mother forgot to pack your lunch, the time you puked at the end of PE. We did what we could. We tried to make people forget. But with Andrew Wright, that was always hard.

Andrew was afraid of the dark. It started when he was four or five, but kept on into his teens, and when church youth group went to Six Flags, or whitewater rafting or any other event where we had to stay overnight in a motel, Andrew's fear would become a discussion point. He carried a night-light with him—shaped like Woodstock from Peanuts—and we heard that even with that plugged in, he still insisted that a bathroom or hall light remain on for the whole night. When he was twelve and we were eleven, on a trip to Nashville for a chorus concert, Blake Wyatt and Shane Duggan had stolen the night-light out of his backpack and threw it around the school bus for an hour. Andrew's face was a mixture of distress and irritation, and he tried to intercept the thing as it flew across the rows. He was so tall, even then, and it was weird how he couldn't quite seem to catch it—his arms were as long as some of the guys' whole bodies. Our teacher Mrs. Thompson had fallen asleep in the front, and so it wasn't until we arrived at the Holiday Inn that she realized that something was going on. Andrew was crying—just a little—and she asked him to explain the problem. He said nothing and pushed past her, out of the bus. Later that night, he called his parents to pick him up—he didn't even stay over. Stories circulated over the years that he still kept the night-light, and he always got a single room for overnight games. People laughed about it a little but after his mother died, things changed. It wasn't mentioned. When things got serious with Carolyn, though, a rumor went around that he could only have sex in daylight—he was the opposite of a vampire, people said, and we laughed.

We heard that Andrew had cried openly the year before, in English class. We had written essays about that weird poem, the one about the wheelbarrow and the rain and the chickens, and when Carolyn's locker was cleared out at the end of the year, one of her notebooks was filled with William Carlos Williams's work. She had copied out the wheelbarrow poem at least a dozen times, and Andrew's handwriting was all over the margins. Saying what, we weren't sure. The news made a lot out of this—the poem—but we never really understood what they meant. It was weird.

Andrew loved Carolyn. That much was clear. When they started hanging out, he met her after each of her classes: You would see him running from the English building, through the math building and into science, and back again, just to make sure she didn't walk for two minutes on her own. They held hands. If you walked behind them, you couldn't help but stare at his knuckles, red and calloused, intertwined with her pale, bony fingers. His hands would be white from the pressure of holding onto hers, and she folded her body into his. They looked like they fit.

At that time, we felt softer toward her—a little envious, maybe—wondering why we hadn't noticed how hot Andrew was, how strong and smooth his arms looked underneath his polo shirts, how the freckles around his nose were like little stars, how his eyelashes were longer than ours with falsies. We hadn't noticed any of this, not really, until he started walking the halls with Carolyn, whispering in her ears, smiling only when he was with her. We wondered what it was that she had that we didn't—what she had that could make him run through the buildings, make him write notes, make him hang around after swim practice, waiting on her to finish, so he could drive her home.

Andrew hadn't looked right that year—all that stuff with his mom—and he still didn't look right, didn't look like the boy we had known from the elementary school playground, from church, with the fireflies at the country club. But when he was walking with Carolyn, when he was holding her hand, holding it so tight he must have been cutting off her circulation, he looked happy. Well, maybe not happy so much as okay. He looked *okay*.

Later, when the school year was all over, we thought it was unfair that he was lumped in with all of them, that he was considered part of the same pack. He had been friends with Shane, that was true, but his time with Carolyn was different—it seemed so real. We wondered afterward what would have happened if she had dated him first, if she hadn't gotten caught up with Shane and with Brooke—would it all have been different? Probably not, we told one another, probably not.

Carolyn started to gain a little weight—we saw it first in her face: it looked rounder and her eyes looked brighter and all of a sudden she had a chest, something people had made fun of before. She looked better, if we were honest, a little more human, less like a Skipper doll. We were secretly pleased this had happened too—maybe it would keep going up and up, and she would get chubby and then actually fat. We liked that she wasn't as perfect as we thought. Lauren Brink tried to find her jeans in her locker during swim practice—to see if she still had a twenty-two-inch waist—but once we'd gotten into the locker and we found the jeans, the numbers were all worn out on the tags, we couldn't make them out.

We heard that Carolyn and Andrew skipped lunch in the cafeteria every day, and every day instead they went to a different place: some of the fast-food places we had in Adamsville that Carolyn had never been to, that were specific to the South. She had never had a Hardee's biscuit, had never had Whataburger, had never had gravy that was actually gray. Andrew thought this was hilarious, in a cute way, and everybody would see them around town, eating, reading, holding hands. Carolyn showed him stuff too: she gave Andrew music, music he had never heard before, or stuff that he had heard but not really *heard* heard. She lent him books too: philosophy, poetry, experimental fiction. She inhaled fried pickles and stuffed potato skins, and Andrew inhaled the Beats, Nietzsche, Sylvia Plath. They were caught making out in the AV room, in the dressing room next to the auditorium, in Janitor Ken's closet. All PG, all over-the-clothes stuff, that's what we heard. Andrew was still mourning his mom's death—that was the official line for no sex—but people said he was afraid of all of her STDs. In court, later, it was never established that they had slept together. People talked about that blow job in Nicole's pool, but we were all too drunk to confirm anything. And nobody even knew if that counted as sex anyway.

(Transcript of guidance counseling session between Carolyn Lessing and Carole Matthew. Tape is not dated, and appears to be a continuation of an earlier conversation, but the session took place sometime in the second half of the 2010–2011 academic year.)

Transcript

Mrs. Matthew: You're close with your father?

Carolyn: What?

Mrs. Matthew: You mentioned calling your father. That seems important to you.

Carolyn: Yes—why, is that unusual or something? God.

Mrs. Matthew: How are things at home?

Carolyn: This is moving around a lot.

Mrs. Matthew: Excuse me?

Carolyn: You just seem to be hopping from one subject to the next. Like, really, really quickly.

Mrs. Matthew: I'm just trying to hit on something you feel comfortable talking about.

Carolyn: Because there's nothing wrong with me.

Mrs. Matthew: Nobody's saying there is.

Carolyn: But I'm the one who's seeing you.

Mrs. Matthew: Yes.

Carolyn: Not Brooke. Or Gemma. Or any of the others.

Mrs. Matthew: Well, I can't talk about other students.

Carolyn: Doctor-patient confidentiality? I get it.

Mrs. Matthew: Something like that.

Carolyn: Only you're not a doctor.

Mrs. Matthew: Pardon me?

Carolyn: (laughing) It's just you're not actually a doctor. Or a psychologist. I'm not even sure they should be letting you do this.

Mrs. Matthew (clearing throat): No, I'm not a psychiatrist. Or a psychologist. I'm just here to help.

Carolyn: Right.

Mrs. Matthew: There's no need to be rude, Carolyn.

Carolyn: Ma'am?

Mrs. Matthew: You know what I mean. I just want to give you a hand. Okay?

Carolyn: Okay.

Mrs. Matthew: Yes.

(Pause. 42 seconds.)

Carolyn: Is it for, like, insurance purposes?

Mrs. Matthew: What?

Carolyn: Do you have to do this? You have to interview me? To get, like, covered by your insurance, in case I do something crazy at school?

Mrs. Matthew: What? No.

Carolyn: Like, after the thing that happened before Christmas? You might be, like, legally *required* to ask me questions.

Mrs. Matthew: Carolyn, we're getting off subject.

(Water is poured.)

Now, can you tell me how things are at home?

Carolyn: Fine.

Mrs. Matthew: You and your mother getting along?

Carolyn: Yeah, fine.

Mrs. Matthew: Could you be more specific?

Carolyn: Um. I don't know. Like, I like the new house. It's bigger than our last one.

Mrs. Matthew: And that's good?

Carolyn: Yeah, of course it is.

Mrs. Matthew: And do you feel you can talk to your mother.

Carolyn: (laughs) No.

Mrs. Matthew: You seem very sure about that.

Carolyn (still laughing): It's just—well, she's just busy.

Mrs. Matthew: With work?

Carolyn: Yeah, with work. And with extracurricular activities.

Mrs. Matthew: What do you mean by that?

Carolyn: Oh, you know, like her exercise stuff. And she's got some friends now.

Mrs. Matthew: So she goes out a lot?

Carolyn: Everything's relative, I guess.

Mrs. Matthew: So you're on your own a lot?

Carolyn: Not, like, a lot.

Mrs. Matthew: But a few nights a week?

Carolyn: Yeah. Maybe three or four?

Mrs. Matthew: Mmmmm.

Carolyn: But that's fine, you know?

Mrs. Matthew: So you prefer that?

Carolyn: I guess.

Mrs. Matthew: What can you do in the house that you can't do when your mother is there?

(Pause. 15 seconds.)

Carolyn: When I have the house to myself, I can, like, open up all the windows, you know? And change the air in the house. My mother never does that, you know? And you're meant to do it, like, at least once a day. Even in winter . . . It's, like, with that stupid air conditioner she forgets that it's just recycling the same air in the house, and it gets, like, all stale and it starts to smell or something and it's just like—like, I feel sick to my stomach. And if she's ordered Indian food or something earlier in the week—then the whole place stinks like we live in an apartment over some Indian take-out place or something.

Mrs. Matthew: What else do you do on your own?

Carolyn: I don't know. (Pause. 10 seconds.) I listen to music, I guess. And I can turn it up real loud. In New Jersey? That's what my best friend and I used to do after school. We'd download whatever we wanted—like even old stuff, sometimes—and then we'd put it on the iPod and into the deck and then we'd like sing and scream along and stuff. Nobody likes good music here.

(Water is poured.)

Carolyn: And my dad used to buy me loads of music, you know? Like, even classical music, which I don't really like, but I liked it when he played it.

Mrs. Matthew: And why is that?

(Pause. 12 seconds.)

Carolyn: He'd close his eyes, as soon as it came on. And he would describe the movements to me— like, what was happening in the song and what it meant—or what he thought it meant—and his face would go all soft and he'd have his eyes closed and he'd look like he was almost asleep and he'd ask me to sit with him, in his armchair, and sometimes I hated that, 'cause I'm not five anymore, you know? But when I sat with him, I could feel his heartbeat—at first really fast, or faster than mine—but when I sat really still and close, then his would slow a little, and maybe mine sped up? Or something. But I would put my head against his chest and my fingers on my throat and after a movement of Bach or two, they'd be the same. Our heartbeats, I mean. And I couldn't believe that could happen.

(Coughing. Water is poured.)

Mrs. Matthew: Do you miss doing that?

Carolyn: I'm too old for it. It's kind of weird now.

Mrs. Matthew: How so?

Carolyn: I'm almost 16, that's all. I'm too old for that—people would think there was something wrong with me if I still did that.

Mrs. Matthew: But you miss it?

Carolyn: I don't know. I guess. Not really.

Mrs. Matthew: Would your dad still like it if you'd do that?

Carolyn: When I see him, yeah, like, I guess.
But I told him I'm too old for that.

Mrs. Matthew: And how does he respond to this?

Carolyn: I'm sorry I brought this up, you know?
It's not a big deal.

ENDS.

MARCH

22

In March, right before we got spring break—the pipes in the science building burst and we had to evacuate. We thought it would mean we would get to go home—there had to be a rule against holding students in a building that didn't have functioning toilets—but they just made us go to the library for the afternoon, to "work quietly" and to study for our midterms. We groaned but we were happy all the same—it meant we could sit where we wanted and even if we couldn't talk, we could text and look around and not have to listen to Miss Simpson or Coach Cox for the rest of the day.

In the library, twenty-five Macs lined the walls, and during study hall or free periods, we could surf the Net. The blocks and filters that the librarians had put up were super-easy to take down and we put them back up again after our time was up—it was funny the lengths the librarians would go to keep us away from porn and sex offenders and skeevy chat rooms. We weren't interested in that stuff anyway—we just wanted to go onto Facebook and Google questions—a weird rash, irregular periods, how to lose ten pounds, average age girls lost their virginity—stuff like that.

When we got there, Brooke and Gemma were at the Macs in the far right corner, near the poetry section, where nobody ever hung around. The rest of the computers were taken too—the band geeks had filed in, in a swarm, with their instruments packed up behind them. We took our seats at the round tables in the center. We watched the Goths to our right paint their fingernails with Wite-Out, we watched the freshmen boys to our left unpack paperback copies of *Lord of the Rings*. We situated ourselves so we could watch the computers, so we could see what Brooke and Gemma were doing. We kept two seats open for them at our table— not like they'd sit with us, but still. Just in case.

The librarians shushed us and told us that Mr. Overton would be in later to make sure we were behaving and we rolled our eyes. Brooke and Gemma laughed and they were told to be quiet. They laughed again two minutes later and they were told they had their first warning. They were quiet after that, except for the sound of Brooke chewing her gum and popping her bubbles. She could make a bubble so big it would cover her face. (Guys said this meant she was good with her tongue.)

We were doing our trig homework, or those were the books that we had out, but really we were texting and trying to figure out what people were going to do on the weekend. We looked up at Brooke and Gemma every few minutes—we looked at them as much as we could get away with, as often as we could without them thinking we were lesbian stalkers.

Andrew and Carolyn walked in after the fifth-period bell rang—they'd been in the science building before that, they had biology together. When the two of them walked in, we thought we heard Brooke say "whore" or something like that, but we weren't really sure. One of the Goths laughed, which we thought was weird, since they hated all the cheerleaders' guts, and one of the freshmen losers sitting behind us told his table that Carolyn had had sex with six different guys since she'd moved here, and that she was probably carrying an STD. Andrew and Carolyn walked to a table in front of us—near the periodicals—and as they sat down, one of the Goths told them the table was reserved and Carolyn started to get up to move before Andrew said, "Fuck you," and they sat down. Somebody threw a piece of paper—like a giant spitball—and just missed Carolyn's head. Whether they'd done it on purpose wasn't clear—and we couldn't tell who it even came from but the whole line of computer users were laughing now, backs shaking as they clicked away. Mrs. Kelly, the head librarian, was in her office. The librarians never paid attention to anything, we said later, they just wanted to get through the day and go home to their cats or their DVRed "Grey's Anatomy" or whatever sad hobby they pursued when they weren't in our school.

Andrew took out his books before Carolyn did—she just sat there—and after seven or eight minutes had passed, she put her head on the table and went to sleep or just lay there with her eyes closed, we didn't know. Andrew sat and read and took notes and he didn't look around. He was focused. We heard later that Andrew nearly flunked all of his classes that semester—that when he was dating Carolyn he was on the verge of failing everything except PE and driver's ed, where he was the teacher's aide. Looking back, it's hard to imagine what he was doing, what he was working on so hard, but he didn't look up, didn't look around, didn't lift his head.

A ring tone—the iPhone default one—came from Carolyn's bag. It rang for twenty or thirty seconds and we watched Andrew put his hand through Carolyn's hair, trying to wake her up. She lifted her head, just barely, and picked up her bag and took out her phone and stopped the ringing and we watched her face as she looked at the screen, her mouth moving, her eyes starting to fill up, her cheeks burning red. She threw the phone on the table and Andrew picked it up. He lifted his head and half stood up and looked around, until steadying his stare on Gemma and Brooke, who were looking right at him. They weren't laughing now, but they looked happy, pleased, proud. Like they always did.

Carolyn stood up and put her messenger bag across her body. She turned and Andrew pulled her back. He whispered something in her ear. We tried to look down at our books, but we couldn't—not really. He pulled her in close and her whole body started to slacken, soften. She put her hand through his hair—he was still seated and he pulled her like he was going to kiss her or tie her to the seat, but he didn't. He let her go. She walked out and only then did Mrs. Kelly emerge from her office—to try to stop her, probably. But Carolyn was too fast and as she left we watched Brooke and Gemma wave, mouthing, "Bah-bye."

That same night, somebody posted a search history on the Hot List blog and said it belonged to Brooke Moore. She'd left all her cookies open after we'd left the library, and somebody did a screen shot and saved it. The usual things: "Lose 10 pounds in a week" and "cheap Coach purses" and, the most embarrassing, her own name. Way down the list, there were other things, the things that we remembered most clearly, that became the major points of discussion: "cum in your ass pregnant?" and "teeth in way blow job" and "make boyfriend jealous." It was up for an hour when she put out a mass message, on text and Facebook and in person to anybody she saw: "Some Yankee bitch was on that computer before me. You can guess who that slut was."

We didn't think that it could be true—Carolyn had gotten there late and left early; it wasn't her kind of thing. But nobody confirmed that Carolyn did any of that, and we never found out what was on Carolyn's phone that day. At the time, we didn't think much of it, not really. Everybody got spam or shitty messages from people they didn't like. There were things you just had to live with. Things you just had to get over. Now, we think it might have been better if we'd told her that it wasn't that weird, that she shouldn't freak out or think she was some kind of social leper just 'cause of a couple of texts from some jealous bitches. Or we could have told her to stop hanging out with people's ex-boyfriends, to try to keep a low profile. But we didn't do any of those things. We were busy with our own stuff and, plus, there were things she just should have known.

The following week, after the plumbing had been fixed, we sat in trig, trying hard to stay awake, trying hard not to look out the window, fighting the urge to take out our phones and text one another, check Facebook. We looked ahead at Mr. Ferris as he told us about sine, cosine and tangent. He made us write the Pythagorean theorem hundreds of times, as if this would make sense of it: "The sum of the areas of the two squares on the legs equals the area of the square on the hypotenuse: can you tell me what's important about this theorem?"

Carolyn knew the answer, everybody knew this, but she never raised her hand or called out in class. Mr. Ferris searched our eyes for the answer, but nobody would make eye contact with him. We bit our cuticles and looked at our desks or out the window or just stared at his ears.

He looked around and then smiled. "Bueller, Bueller?"

It was hard, even though he was nice. It was hard to maybe be wrong. "Anybody? No?"

Coughing. A phone vibrated. Another went off—Soulja Boy's "Crank Dat" as the ring tone. Mr. Ferris laughed—he was the only teacher in school who let us leave our phones on in class, let us keep them, and so we never touched them while we were in trig. Reverse psychology probably, but we didn't care.

"Right. Well—it's a statement about both area and about length. It's both geometry and algebra."

He looked pleased. We didn't understand why. He asked us to draw unit circles using our compasses, on graph paper.

He spoke while we drew: "Let a line through the origin, making an angle of θ with the positive half of the x-axis, intersect the unit circle."

He waited. He started to write on the board.

"Okay, ready? The x- and y-coordinates of this point of intersection are equal to cos θ and sin θ, respectively. Can you write this in?"

He took out his big chalk compass thing and drew his circle on the board. The wooden handle scraped against it, just for a moment, just long enough to make a screech, and the classroom erupted in squeals.

"Sorry, sorry." He laughed a little. "Okay. We've got it here. The triangle in the drawing enforces the formula. The radius is equal to the hypotenuse and has length 1, so we have sin $\theta = y/1$ and cos $\theta = x/1$." He paused for a moment, looked at us. Worried, like he'd lost us at the side of the road.

He cleared his throat. "Sorry. Getting excited. Can somebody explain to me, as simply as possible, what a unit circle is and why it's so important for us? Jessica?"

She reddened, hesitated and then spat out her words. "A unit circle has a radius of one. It's a circle with a radius of one."

He smiled. "That's right, uh-huh. And why is that good for us?"

"Because it's so easy?" Jessica kind of laughed when she said it, looked around, and other people were laughing too. She continued, less nervous, her voice firmer, less shaky. "It's simple, I mean. The circle is. It means we can look at lots of different kinds of angles and triangles and lengths and understand things. Or try to understand things. It's good to play around with when you're trying to learn. There's an app for it, you know? The unit circle, I mean."

"Is that right?" Mr. Ferris smiled. "Good, good. That's great."

We continued to fill in the angles, mark in the functions, measure the radians. Using a compass and a ruler, the circle could almost come out looking like the picture in the book and this was something we liked. It was math and drawing, but with less of a chance to get it wrong.

"Keep working, okay? You can just keep working on these until the end of class."

He walked around the room, curving in and out of our desks, and we concentrated hard and long, rotating around our circles, trying to make our writing look like the type in the pictures. Mechanical pencils, graph paper, erasers shaped like fruit or hearts or soda bottles: we liked our supplies. Graphic paper was like a magic-eye poster—if you looked at it too long, you would see shapes coming toward you, from beneath your notebook, from beneath your desk. It took such concentration, what we were doing, and Jason Nelson always stuck his tongue out of one side of his mouth, Jessica Grady wrapped her legs around the legs of her chair, Lauren Brink sometimes hummed show tunes to herself, until somebody would throw a spitball at her and tell her to shut up.

We were so absorbed, so involved, that when Mr. Ferris inhaled and called out, "Jesus. What the fuck?" Jessica Grady actually screamed.

We looked up. He was standing over Carolyn's desk, in the far corner. She was looking up at him, eyes empty and wide, but we could only see the back of his head. Her graph paper was dotted with red and pink splotches, and there was more red on the floor around her desk. She held her compass in her right hand and its point was pressing deep into the flesh of her left arm.

Mr. Ferris pulled it out of her hand and as he did, she let out a gasp—but she held her arm still, the rest of her body shaking. A deep, straight line, with blood running out of it at uneven intervals. Blood was still flowing, and it looked watery and thin, not like the blood in movies and TV. We wondered what was wrong with her. Anemia, somebody said later.

"Somebody get the nurse." Jason and Adam got up together and ran down the hall.

Nobody spoke and we waited for Mr. Ferris to tell us to get back to work or to stop staring or to say anything at all, but he didn't speak. He put his hand on Carolyn's left hand, and with the other took off his tie—dark, dark purple, with flowers on it, that you could only see if you looked really close. He struggled with it—why didn't he use both hands?—and shook his head and breathed really hard as he finally pulled it off. He wrapped the tie around her left arm—she didn't fight back. She kept the same look the whole time—just straight at Mr. Ferris, straight into his eyes, never looking over at us, hardly blinking. Her skin went gray, grayer than anything we'd ever seen before, and her body was flopped into the chair—she looked like a helium balloon that had started to deflate—but her eyes stayed fixed, staring. The back of Mr. Ferris's head shook and shook: "What the fuck, what the fuck . . ."

Mrs. Matthew came into the classroom with Jason and Adam— they said they couldn't find the nurse—and Mr. Ferris pulled Carolyn to her feet—she was lighter than his messenger bag, we guessed—and he left the room with Mrs. Matthew. He didn't tell us what to work on while he was gone, he didn't even put anybody in charge. But as he left the room, we could see his face—he was crying.

People said later that he cried because he was in love with her. They said she had cut herself in class, in broad daylight, in plain view, to get him to pay attention to her. None of this turned out to be true, or provable, but it went round and round and round, until Mr. Overton suspended Mr. Ferris on suspicion of inappropriate conduct. His picture was on the front of the paper. Blake told us he heard from the guys that worked at the movie theater during the day that Mr. Ferris spent every afternoon there, watching every movie showing, and if nothing new opened, he began again and watched them all over. He worked in alphabetical order.

People were surprised he didn't move. He wasn't from Adamsville, so what difference did it make? But he stayed around, and you might even see him at a football game or a basketball game, wearing jeans, no tie. He let his facial hair grow out, but it was kind of thin and patchy, and he started to lose his tan. Even people who had said the suspension was ridiculous, that all the stuff about him and Carolyn had been made up—even those people wished he hadn't turned up at all those games. Get a life, already. And stop being such a skeez.

But all that was later, and he probably wasn't the only one, the only teacher to fall apart. At the time, we never thought about it from their point of view; this was all part of the job. We didn't feel sorry for them, not really, and we didn't think too much about Carolyn, either. We thought it was fucked up, that she took things a little far, but it was the kind of thing we all wanted to do, we thought. If only we had the guts.

Transcript

Carolyn: Is this going to take long? I have a
trig test.

Mrs. Matthew: It's going to take as long as it
needs to take, sweetheart. And I've already
spoken to Mr. Ferris, and you're excused from the
test, and from the rest of your classes for the
rest of the day.

Carolyn: Wow.

Mrs. Matthew: Why do you say "wow"?

Carolyn: You guys must think this is pretty
serious. Whatever this is.

Mrs. Matthew: People are concerned about you,
sweetheart—

Carolyn: Carolyn.

Mrs. Matthew: Excuse me?

Carolyn: My name is Carolyn.

Mrs. Matthew: Yes. Of course. The fact is we're
concerned about you.

Carolyn: Who's "we"?

Mrs. Matthew: Well, the faculty. Your teachers.
Your peers. Your—

Carolyn: (laughing) *Wow.*

Mrs. Matthew: This surprises you?

Carolyn: (still laughing) It really, really does. Wow.

Mrs. Matthew: Well, people are concerned for you, Carolyn. You have friends here, you know.

Carolyn: Oh yeah?

Mrs. Matthew: Yes. *Yes.*

(Pause. 1 minute, 45 seconds.)

Mrs. Matthew: Would you like some tissues?

Carolyn: No, thank you.

Mrs. Matthew: Well, they're here if you need them.

Carolyn: Thank you.

Mrs. Matthew: (pause) Can you tell me how you got the mark on your chest, Carolyn?

Carolyn: What? Oh—I told the nurse already. My mother had a friend over and he smoked a cigar and it fell on me.

Mrs. Matthew: It fell on you?

Carolyn: Yes, it fell on me.

Mrs. Matthew: How exactly did this happen?

Carolyn: I explained it. Already.

Mrs. Matthew: Right.

Carolyn: It was an accident.

Mrs. Matthew: Because if anybody was trying to hurt you, Carolyn—

Carolyn: No.

Mrs. Matthew: We are legally obliged to ask these questions, Carolyn.

Carolyn: Yeah, I get it. And I've answered them.

Mrs. Matthew: Okay. We might come back to this.

(Pause. 1 minute, 17 seconds.)

Mrs. Matthew: Now, can you tell me about the marks on your arms?

Carolyn: I don't know what you mean.

Mrs. Matthew: The incisions on your arms?

Carolyn: Is this actually meant to be therapy?

Mrs. Matthew: I just want to get a few things straight before we begin—

Carolyn: Because I actually *have* a therapist, you know? And he gives me advice and drugs and—

Mrs. Matthew: Your therapist gives you drugs?

Carolyn: Yes, like, prescription medication.

Mrs. Matthew: Right—would you mind writing those down for me on this sheet of paper? And then we can move on to talk about some other things.

(Pause. 3 minutes, 2 seconds.)

Mrs. Matthew: Thank you, Carolyn. That's really very helpful.

Carolyn: Okay.

Mrs. Matthew: I heard you and Brooke Moore had some kind of altercation last semester? In the locker room?

Carolyn: That was dealt with.

Mrs. Matthew: How so?

Carolyn: We had to talk to Mr. Overton and Miss Simpson. We got ISS [In-School Suspension].

Mrs. Matthew: I see. And have you had any other incidents like that one since? That perhaps weren't reported?

Carolyn: Yes.

Mrs. Matthew: With Brooke Moore?

Carolyn: Yes. And with other girls. (Pause. 32 seconds.) But I don't really care.

Mrs. Matthew: You don't?

Carolyn: No. I just wish if they didn't like me they would leave me alone.

Mrs. Matthew: Leave you alone?

Carolyn: Like, stop making fun of me. Harassing me.

Mrs. Matthew: Harrassing you? Like bullying?

Carolyn: I don't know what it's called. But they're mean. They're horrible. And I try to be nice, but it doesn't matter.

Mrs. Matthew: And what about the boys?

Carolyn: A few of them hate me too. But mostly they're nicer than the girls.

Mrs. Matthew: I think it might be a good idea for you to cultivate a few more female friendships.

Carolyn: I had those.

Mrs. Matthew: Yes?

Carolyn: And now I don't anymore. That's what I'm explaining.

Mrs. Matthew: Tell me this: Did you ever have close girlfriends, Carolyn?

Carolyn: Me? Yeah, of course. Not tons, but yeah, I guess.

(Pause. 42 seconds.) When I was little, like four or maybe five—five, I guess, 'cause I had started school—my dad took me and Sara Stewart to the circus—Sara was my best friend and lived only one street away—and I remember loving the acrobats, you know? The ones that do the trapeze act? And there was one that could hold herself up—like pull herself up into a handstand by just using one hand—I can't describe it, not really, but Sara and I were, like, "This is incredible." And we held hands during the whole show—it was like three hours or something insane like that. When it was over, my dad bought us balloon animals—like, we watched the clown make them for us? And Sara's was a flower and mine was a heart. When we stopped for gas on the way home, Sara lost hers and she cried and cried and cried—my dad's face got all red in the front seat and he yelled at her or something. I can remember seeing his eyes in the rearview mirror—

and I was all panicked, like, shut up, shut up—but she wouldn't stop, so I gave her my heart, and she stopped, like, immediately. But, after that, Sara wasn't allowed to come to our house anymore. (Pause. 40 seconds.) Can I have a tissue? . . . I don't know why I told that story. It's so stupid. God, what a freak, right? What was that about?

ENDS.

APRIL

23

Brooke keyed Carolyn's car. That's what we heard. After the thing in the library—after Brooke's search history had been passed around on Facebook, and after it was clear that Andrew was ignoring Gemma for Carolyn—that's when Brooke got serious. It must have happened during sixth period—this was confirmed later—'cause a bunch of people had been out in the parking lot right before the bell rang and Brooke had a free period then, and Gemma had a hall pass and we knew she'd helped her do it.

Carolyn's was a red Honda Accord from 2004, used but it looked good, and she got it for her birthday, which we heard was on April Fool's Day or something. Her car was always clean and she had an Obama bumper sticker on the back and a Radiohead one too. Her windows were tinted but you could just make out a stack of library books in the passenger seat side.

It isn't easy to key somebody's car—not as easy as you'd

think—and Brooke used her keys first, and then Gemma went over the marks just seconds later. And then they went around the car again. It looked like they'd tried to write something too, to make some kind of message. You could barely make out an L and a T—but the S and the U, were harder to read. Doing letters that curved was a lot more difficult and they hadn't had the time to make it look right.

Miss Simpson caught them. She was getting a Diet Coke out of the cooler she kept in the back of her Volkswagen Beetle, and she saw them crouched two rows of cars ahead of her, keys in hand. She called to them and they looked up, stunned and embarrassed and then trying to look casual. Miss Simpson smiled, closed her trunk and walked over to them.

At first they pretended like they'd found it that way—that they were just texting Carolyn to tell her what had happened—wasn't it awful? Miss Simpson hauled them into Mr. Overton's office, and they had to wait for twenty minutes for him to come out and see them. They got ISS for it—but Brooke's mom complained and it was dropped; the school didn't have any proof.

When Carolyn came out to her car after school she cried: we saw it happen. Andrew was with her and put his arm around her and told her not to freak out. When Shane came outside, we watched Andrew walk over to him.

"You better tell your girlfriend to back off." Andrew looked pissed. Angrier than we'd ever seen him.

"I don't know what you're talking about." Shane kinda laughed. We didn't know why.

"Like hell."

"What the fuck? Why do you even care?" Shane was still smiling.

Andrew glared. "Just tell Brooke to back the fuck off."

"You're really losing it, Drew." And Shane laughed again.

"Fuck you." Andrew was loud now. His fists were clenched.

Shane stopped smiling. "Oh yeah? I shouldn't even be talkin' to you."

"Why's that?"

"You think I didn't see the way you looked at her when I was with her?"

Andrew turned white. "Fuck you."

"I hope she's worth it, Drew."

"Fuck you."

"Yeah, you said that." Shane turned to walk away. And then he turned back, got right in Andrew's face. "She's fuckin' crazy, man. I'm telling you now."

They were standing so close and there were loads of us around them and some band kid called out *"Fight!"* Coach Cox started to walk over from the gym. Andrew and Shane looked his way, and Shane stepped back. We watched Andrew and Carolyn get into her car and as the parking lot cleared out, they just sat there, inside her car. And through the tinted windows, we could just barely see her head down on the steering wheel, her hair covering her face, Andrew's arm around her shoulder.

The marks on her body grew hard to ignore. As the weather became warmer, she couldn't wear long sleeves anymore, they would make people suspicious or else they would tease her and, plus, it was really, really hot. People talked.

At swim practice, the marks looked scary. And they were gross. Coach Billy took her aside after practice and we could overhear him talking to her, if we kept our heads just under the high dive.

"Can you swim with that rash?"

"What?"

"The rash on your chest and your arms?"

A rash, for Christ's sake. He was unbelievable.

"Um, oh, yes. Like, yeah."

"Because it looks sore?"

"Yeah? Oh, it's not. It just stings, just a little."

"Well, the chlorine will be good for it. Will help keep it clean."

"Oh, good."

"Are you feeling okay?"

A giggle from the fifth lane. Coach Billy turned and looked down at us, Carolyn still facing the bleachers, facing away, her arms crossed. She wore two bathing suits—like all of us—a normal one and a drag suit, keeps you faster at meets. But her drag suit looked cool, ripped just so, and it was faded teal and black and blue.

Coach Billy knelt in front of us: "Do ten fifties on the clock, starting at the sixty. Five seconds rest in between each."

We pulled up to the side and pulled our goggles down, tucked our hair into our caps and pulled our feet up—we couldn't watch them anymore, we had to watch the clock, and it became hard to hear once the second hand hit the sixty, and we kicked and pulled down the lane. During the rests, we talked.

"Maybe she quit."

"Maybe he made her."

"Maybe it's just really gross that she has those open wounds in the pool?"

"Maybe that's not allowed."

"Maybe she's finally pregnant."

"Maybe she'll just do anything to get attention."

"Maybe she's a psycho."

"Maybe she's pathetic."

"Maybe."

"Yeah, maybe."

Carolyn sat on the bleachers while we did our fifties, wrapped in a paper-thin towel that almost covered her body. She looked cold. Sometime during our drills, she left the bleachers, disappeared.

After practice, we hauled ourselves out of the pool and jumped up and down, trying to get the water out of our ears. As we shook our heads, we noticed Carolyn's iPhone, in its sequined purple case, sitting on the bleachers, next to a puddle she had left. We knew we shouldn't have picked it up, or if we picked it up we shouldn't have been rooting around, but we couldn't help it, it was too hard not to, and she hadn't even locked her screen. No passwords, nothing. She wanted us to see it, we said.

We scanned through her messages and that's when we saw all of the texts from Shane and from Brooke and from Gemma. Maybe twenty or thirty of them. One from Shane: "Leave me alone, whore." One from Brooke: "Die bitch." One from Gemma: "Dirty SKANK. Your a bitch." There were so many of them and they were all different versions of the same thing—it made our stomachs flop and turn and we wanted the phone out of our hands as soon as we could, and when Coach Billy started to walk toward us, we locked the screen and handed it over: "Carolyn left her phone."

We wished we'd had time to scroll back, back to the beginning, to see what she had said to provoke, but we didn't. We said that we were happy Coach Billy had it—then he'd look through and he'd do something about it, try to put an end to all of that. It was one thing to bitch behind somebody's back, and maybe it was kind of okay to be posting crap on Facebook or the Hot List. But this was different, we said. It was really fucking mean.

facebook

Taylor Lyon, **Gemma Davies**, **Shane Duggan** and 3 other people commented on this.

Brooke Moore

Its so pathetic when people have been treated like really really well and they act like their all victimized.

35 people like this.

Taylor Lyon I hate how she wears the same nasty ass hoodie like 24/7

Brooke Moore looks like anorexic roadkill

Tiffany Port nobody asked her to make a sex tape

Dylan Hall nobody wants to look at her bony ass in Duggs window.

Shane Duggan I was so drunk. Didn't know I was hooking up with a slut.

Taylor Lyon She didn't even take those pills

Tiffany Port whole story was fake

Taylor Lyon She was caught stealing from Abercrombie after Christmas.

Gemma Davies No WAY. The dikes on swim teem say shes a cutter

Tiffany Port how COOL. ;)

Brooke Moore If I hear one more person say that they feel sorry for that PATHETIC DRAMA QUEEN, i'm going over to her Pottery Barn house on D'Evereux Drive to cut her myself.

Gemma Davies Carolyn Lessing is a fake, a boyfriend stealer and a slut. Let her cut herself f she wants to.

Brooke Moore Let her slit her wrists for all I care.

24

Andrew had already asked Carolyn to prom. He didn't do it in one of those big public ways, the way a lot of the guys did it, writing out the letters in shaving cream in a front lawn, organizing a boat trip along the river, writing a song—stuff that was probably all ripped off from *Laguna Beach* and *My Super Sweet 16* or whatever, but stuff we still fantasized about. Miss Simpson told us our expectations had been "warped" by television and the Internet and that we should really not "invest so much" in the event. We knew what this was code for: she had never been to her prom, the fat lesbian.

Three days after Andrew asked Carolyn to prom, the clip with her and Shane—that one in the car—was posted again on YouTube. Nobody recognized the poster's username and, at the time, people said that Carolyn posted it herself. Later, when the police were investigating, we heard that it was posted from the office at the

Stripline Baptist Church. Shane posted the video to Andrew's Facebook page, and Andrew took it down twenty minutes later, and we heard he was freaking out. Maybe he hadn't seen it before—though we didn't know how that was possible—or maybe he just felt differently about it now that he was with Carolyn, now that they were boyfriend-girlfriend. Maybe he was jealous, thought he couldn't trust her, didn't know her. We didn't know. Whatever the case, right after he took down the clip, he changed his relationship status from "in a relationship" to "single." And then Gemma posted on his wall: "I used to like you until you got a girl . . . but I still think you are so cute. Text me sometime. ☺"

When people say that Andrew didn't have anything to do with anything, that's only partly true. He wanted to help Carolyn, but not enough, not in the end. He couldn't watch the clip, couldn't watch her come, couldn't watch her body shake, couldn't watch Shane press into her, her mouth open, skin white. He had known before she wasn't a virgin, or at least this is what he said, but the physical proof seemed too much for him. He couldn't have her. Not like this.

We were there the day he broke it off with her—we were walking out of class after English. Miss Simpson had given us a lecture on narrative agency—she never quit—and we had texted each other during class that Carolyn looked thin again. She'd obviously laid off the fried pickles.

Andrew was waiting for her as we left the classroom—he must have run or else gotten a pass to leave before the bell rang, 'cause he was right there, outside the door. He was looking down, examining his phone or his cuticles or maybe even his shoes, but he didn't look up, not even when Carolyn was right in front of him. We said later how weird it was that he didn't kiss her—they were so majorly into PDA—so we weren't that surprised when we heard what happened next. We stayed close behind them—they were going our way anyway. She talked about her dress, about not wanting to take it back, about the money she had spent, about how this dance would be better than Homecoming, more fun, less stress. He didn't care. Or at least he didn't act like it.

"I'm just too busy to go."

"You weren't busy two weeks ago."

"Things have changed."

"What's changed?"

"You have."

"I don't get it."

He waited awhile. And then he inhaled.

"I'm just tired, Carolyn."

"Why are you being mean?"

He let out a breath.

"I'm not being mean. I wish you wouldn't say that."

"Why won't you go with me?"

"I'm just tired. It's just lame."

"It's that clip thing, isn't it? With me in the car."

We couldn't see her face, but we said later that she sounded like she was crying.

"Whatever." He was mad, or depressed or something like that.

"That was, like, forever ago." Her voice had started to shake and she had pulled her sleeves over her fingers and was trying to hold onto his hands. He pulled them away.

"I just don't want to fucking go."

She had her head on his chest. She was leaning her body into him, pushing against him. He lay against a locker.

"Jesus. Stop it, Carolyn."

"Please don't be mean."

He got up. "Quit saying that. Quit it."

"Sorry."

"This is just too intense. I can't do this."

"Are you back with Gemma?"

"What? Who said—? No." He sighed.

"I just saw. On Facebook?"

"What? Are you, like, stalking me?" He said this loudly. People were staring.

He turned to walk away and she called after him: "Drew."

Everything in the hallway stopped. From their lockers, people turned and looked. The teachers stopped talking, they fixed their eyes on Andrew, on Carolyn.

Andrew stood still. His face was red, his eyes bloodshot—he could have been crying.

"What?"

"When will you call me?"

He looked around and let out a breath. He looked up at the ceiling.

"When you calm down." He looked around again. "When this whole fucking place calms down."

April 30, 2011
Carolyn Lessing
Honors English—Miss Simpson

Transcendentalism Final Essay: Persuasive Write

Writing Prompt: You just finished reading "Walden," about Henry David Thoreau's famous two-year stint living in solitude alongside a Concord pond. Consider whether or not you think such an experiment is a good idea. Write a persuasive essay convincing me, your teacher, as well as the rest of your classmates that we either should or should not re-create such an experiment this year. Your essay MUST also include at least 3 of the rhetorical strategies we have studied so far this year.

In *Walden*, Thoreau says: *"I went to the woods because I wished to live deliberately, to front only the essential facts of life, and see if I could not learn what it had to teach, and not, when I came to die, discover that I had not lived."* In his essay, he argues that living in solitude allows a person to live more fully as one can concentrate on nature and one's self. I would argue that such an experiment is selfish and dangerous, because it cuts a person off from others. Connecting with other people helps us feel sympathy and, ultimately, helps us help one another.

As a girl, when I was six or seven years old, my mother, father and I went to live for a summer in a farmhouse in upstate New York. My father was researching a book, and we were allowed to live in the house for three months while he wrote. The house was remote—a twenty-five-minute drive from the nearest town—and did not have a telephone or a television. We were surrounded by rich forest, thick with trees, green as far as the eye could see. My mother and I spent our days going on long walks, taking trails up to the top of small mountains, and sometimes we brought a packed lunch of bread and fruit and cheese. When we finished eating, my mother might read to me or we might take a nap in the sunshine. On days when it rained, we stayed indoors and read and listened to soft music. My family and I were content and fulfilled, comfortable living simply and in nature. Even though I was very small, I have vivid memories from this time, and it was very peaceful.

While we were away, my mother's father became very ill. Because we did not have a telephone, my aunt was unable to contact us and, by the time we returned to New Jersey, my grandfather had passed away. We attended the funeral, but my mother was very upset that she had not had the opportunity to say goodbye to her father in person. My mother and I have spoken about this very little, but I now understand that she must have been extremely angry that she was out of touch during this important time.

As a 21st century teenager, it is hard to imagine living like Thoreau. To me, Thoreau seems like a Scrooge, lacking in empathy and feeling for other people. While his writings point to the benefits that he gained from living in solitude, he does not address how his decision to live this way could be deemed selfish. Living in solitude does not allow one to help another person. Out in the woods, I wouldn't be able to talk to my friend about a problem she's having at home. I wouldn't be able to volunteer at the Salvation Army. I wouldn't be able to watch the news and understand that there are bigger problems in the world than my own. All of these things are part of what it means to be a person and to be humane.

The great thing about living in solitude is that one concentrates only on oneself. The terrible thing about living in solitude is that one concentrates only on oneself. Thinking about yourself all the time is pretty self-indulgent, even if adults accuse teenagers of doing it all the time. In reality, I think it's important to talk to other people, because it helps you understand that you're not alone and that other people have experiences both similar and different to your own. Thinking about yourself all day would be just plain boring.

Thoreau cites the many distractions that we encounter in everyday life, but this seems very limiting. Are other people simply distractions? Isn't it true that some of them are friends? Family? These are relationships that are important to me and, even though they are hard sometimes, I wouldn't give them up to spend more time with "myself" in the woods.

While I accept that we all spend too much time looking at screens nowadays, things like Facebook and Skype are very good ways to keep in touch with people who are far away. How else would I talk to my father? To my best friend Kourtni in New Jersey? These connections help us remember that we are part of a community, and that people rely on us for certain things. Herman Melville was quoted as saying, "We cannot live only for ourselves. A thousand fibers connect us with our fellow men."

All that being said, I would accept that screens and Facebook and iChat can sometimes make us feel more isolated and alone. Instead of meeting up with friends at the mall or for coffee, sometimes we just text or stare at a screen, which isn't the same. An email isn't the same as a handwritten letter. Also, because people find it so easy to send emails and texts and post things on Facebook, it makes it easier for people to be mean to each other. When people are posting stuff online they forget that they are talking to other people, forget that they are still part of a "community."

All in all, I think Thoreau acted selfishly and inhumanely and his is not an example that I think we should follow. We are part of a larger community and everybody plays a role in the community. While it would be easier in some ways to live alone, to not worry what other people thought of us, and to just concentrate on making ourselves better as individuals, I think this is ultimately wrong and not what life is about. Connecting with other people is what human beings were meant to do. The more people realize that this is true, the better off we'll be.

Grade: B-

The writing is still very strong in this, Carolyn but you have received a lower grade because of the misuse (and lack of citation) of quotation. You have misattributed 'you cannot live for yourselves' to Herman Melville (author of Moby Dick?), when in fact this is a quotation from Henry Melvill, a 19th century priest of the church of England. I believe you have relied in a lazy way on the internet and Google for your sources and even the quality of your writing can't overcome this. Please come and talk to me about this. I am disappointed.

may

25

The day it happened, nobody was prepared. Carolyn had been in the library, working on an essay—we had seen her there, head down, three or four books open. When the bell rang at three o'clock, she didn't look up.

Carolyn was special: that's what we'd say later. Some days, she'd smile and laugh and wave at you in the hall, almost skipping as she walked through the buildings. Other days, she looked worried and concerned, black circles under her eyes. The marks on her body were hard to look at and, even though she was thin, some days it was too much to watch—to see her throw away a tuna sandwich at lunch, give her Oreos to some obese underclassmen and nibble on a rice cake for forty-five minutes. She would say she had no appetite, that she was really full from breakfast, that she'd eaten eggs and bacon. But nobody believed her, not really.

She didn't understand the cliques. She thought she could move from one to another and then back again, and not upset anybody along the way. But school was like checkers. Once you jumped over somebody else, they were cleared off the board, and you were topped with somebody else. There were consequences to every jump, and she didn't seem to know this. She didn't even care.

When the bell rang, we waited a few beats, and then we pushed the doors of every building open, punching the metal bars hard to make them bang, and we all came streaming out, in clumps and clusters, in twos and threes and fours and fives. In May, the hot air outside would shock you after a day of raw air-conditioning and we could feel the beginning of a sweat underneath our arms, around the waist of our jeans, on the backs of our necks, hair curling underneath. You would move fast to get out of the heat if you had anywhere to go.

The last week of May, the parking lot was lethal. No tree cover, no wind, just black tar melting under the sun. Car mirrors would blind you. We tried to open our car doors without burning our hands, tried to put the key in the ignition without singeing our fingers, turning the air-conditioning knob to full, windows down. You'd have to wait five minutes before you even thought about getting in.

It was because of this that Shane and Brooke were hanging out in the parking lot, under the shade of an oak tree, trying to stay out of the heat. It was because of this that Shane and Brooke had such a good chance, that there was so much temptation in their way.

Adam Simmons had been smoking up in his car since fifth period, so he was there in his driver's seat, asleep under his Roll Tide baseball cap, seat reclined halfway back, air-conditioning on full blast, his Outback staring at the back of Shane's Explorer. He had the driver-seat window open a crack and when Shane beeped his car door open, the sound melted into Adam's dream, and he twitched awake. He said that in his dream, the cops were shining a light into the driver's seat, making him open the glove compartment and hand over his stash. And the beep was coming from him.

"I had some kind of fucking laser gun in my hand and I was getting ready to fucking shoot the assholes. Only then I kinda opened my eyes and saw Brooke's ass right in my face and I was, like, why the fuck am I dreaming about that bitch? And that woke me up fucking quick."

Brooke was leaning into the trunk of the Explorer, grabbing at something—a cooler, Adam said—and she couldn't reach it, not really, so she had to lower her body in, and as she leaned, her skirt went farther and farther up, so all that Adam could see were her legs—tanned and smooth and long. And then she leaned in to grab again, her arm stretching her body out so that her skirt was nonexistent. She was wearing a purple lace thong, he said, which we found unbelievable—her skirt was white. There was no fucking way.

Adam said he thought it might be beer, and he would have gotten out and asked to have one, only he was completely baked, and he'd get suspended if he was caught drinking or smoking on campus again. He laughed at this, since that day Coach Cox had passed him and knocked on the window as he'd rolled his first joint. Adam said he gave him a thumbs-up and that made Cox's day, so he just walked right by. We didn't believe this either.

Brooke didn't drink beer, obviously, and Shane was in training, so we figured it was Dr Pepper—the kind that you got at Bud's in the glass bottles; they were doing some promotion. Adam testified later that it was beer, or maybe he didn't testify, but that's what he told the cops, and that's what the newspapers said. But we found it kinda hard to believe.

Brooke took a couple bottles out, handed one to Shane, and they sat in the back of the Explorer, Brooke holding the bottle against her chest, Shane rubbing his on his neck. Adam said he was so low in the seat they must not have seen him, 'cause he said he was staring right at them, and he said he could almost hear what they were saying. But he couldn't remember anything.

He said they sat there for fifteen minutes or maybe even more, and Shane had taken out some dip and started to pack it. Brooke had already gotten another drink and had taken out some ice cubes, which she threw down Shane's shirt. They were flirting hard, Adam said, and he thought about starting his car, only now he was worried he looked like a fucking perv, he'd been sitting there so long. It was only that he was too stoned to go anywhere that he hadn't left, that he hadn't gotten out or even waved or honked the horn.

The parking lot had pretty much cleared out—just some teachers' Volvos and Coach Cox's minivan and the band bus, which sat in our parking lot every day and every night—nobody had ever seen it leave the campus. If there had been more cars on the lot Adam said they wouldn't have even seen Carolyn. She could have slipped away and walked home or to the mall or to the movies or to wherever she was going.

Since her car had been keyed, we saw Carolyn walking all the time. We would see her coming out of her subdivision on a Saturday morning, walking along the Stripline on her way to school, walking through the Halls' field at eight or nine o'clock. Nobody was sure why this was—it was just another weird thing that she did. Everything in our town was too far away from everything else for her to *literally* be walking everywhere—but that was how it seemed, and that's what people said. Taylor Lyon said she did it to keep her figure, and we thought that this could be true. She was disappearing in front of us and we came to know her skeletal structure: her collarbone looked thick and we said that if you reached at her chest, you could grab hold of that bone, it jutted out so far it was like a handle. Her elbows were sharp, the small bones on her wrists cut through her skin and looked like they could break her silver Tiffany's charm bracelet if she moved too quick. She was thin before, and she was thinner now—we tried to get the guys to say it was gross, to say that they liked to have something to hold on to. But they didn't say much and deep down, or maybe not even that deep, we wanted her body to be ours. To know what it would be like to be that light, to be that invisible, to be weightless—that was something we wanted to know.

Adam told us that she looked tired, that he could see her through his rearview mirror, and that he felt bad she had to walk the whole way home. "It's a long fucking way to walk—I've done it when I'm too stoned to drive or see my mama." He laughed when he said this. Adam's brother had been four years ahead of us in school—a senior when we were just in eighth grade—and he and his wife moved back to Adamsville straight after college, and they lived two streets over from Carolyn and her mom. People said it was weird that Adam hadn't volunteered to give Carolyn a ride. At first, he told people he hadn't thought of it, and over time, as the story got bigger and bigger, he insisted that he'd been too stoned. Only then it didn't make sense that he remembered all that stuff, all that detail—how far it was, how tired she looked—if he'd really been so stoned, and eventually, he changed that too. "She looked like she wouldn't have taken a ride, anyway. She would've thought I was trying to pick her up." We were never sure which version to believe, but we had an idea: every guy in our class wanted to sleep with Carolyn, from what we could see, but they were afraid of her too. Afraid to approach her, to speak to her directly, to draw attention to themselves, afraid someone might call them fags, or say they had herpes or that they'd wet themselves in the third grade. The newspapers insisted that Carolyn was a loner, that she was "isolated" and "distant." But that wasn't true. She still had her followers—freshmen and sophomores, mostly, at this stage, but still. There were people who liked her, who thought she was amazing and different and funny, who followed her like she was some kind of Twitter trend, wanting to know what she'd do next, who she'd talk to, who she'd sleep with, whose locker she'd be standing by. They didn't talk to her or walk with her, so it was easy to see why people thought she was alone. But lots of us still liked her, even if we didn't come right out and say it. If we were to do it over, we said, things would be different, and we bet that people would be more straightforward, would have been more vocal. We thought that things could have been different. But we didn't totally believe that. Not really.

Adam said it started as an accident, or at least that's what it looked like. Brooke was still throwing ice at Shane, and then he was throwing it back at her, always toward the chest, trying to get the cubes to melt into her tank top or, better still, to make their way down underneath it, in her cleavage, into her bra—a black Victoria's Secret from the Angels' line, probably, something that cost over forty bucks. She spent so much on her underwear that she had to get her money's worth, had to put it out on display.

Shane and Brooke were throwing ice, and the flirting was crazy, that's what Adam said. And they were throwing it harder and harder, reaching back into the cooler and taking out four or five cubes at a time, then handfuls, then Shane was piling it up in his polo, so he could get to it quicker. Adam said he saw a flash of Carolyn's hair in his rearview mirror and then she was in front of his car, walking straight toward the Explorer. In the newspapers, it said she was trying to avoid them, but that's not what we heard. "She was on her way to tell them something, looked like she was gonna tell them off or something."

She crossed in front of Adam's car. Shane and Brooke still hadn't clocked her, they were still in the middle of their game, of their throwing—was this all the fuck they got up to? And then Shane threw a fistful, his arm so strong from baseball, and hundreds of tiny shards hit Carolyn's face.

Adam said he unlocked his doors, he was about to get out, only then Shane and Brooke got up, and they were laughing, and he thought Carolyn was laughing too. Looking back, it seems hard to believe that this would have made her laugh, but Adam said he stayed put 'cause he didn't want to look like a fucking spy, and didn't think they needed anything. Not really.

Carolyn stood still and wiped herself down, the ice melting to water almost instantly. Her T-shirt looked tie-dyed or something as the water spread into rings, into patterns, circles inside circles inside circles.

Then Carolyn spat. This is what we heard. This is what we knew. She got close enough to Brooke that she could spit on her and then she did. Carolyn Lessing spat on Brooke Moore.

And then we heard the rest.

Brooke reached into the cooler and took out a glass bottle and threw it. Adam said she was aiming for Carolyn, he was sure of it, but the bottle missed her, and it smashed to the ground, the brown liquid fizzing, spraying Carolyn, clear shards of glass going everywhere. Adam said Carolyn "stood real still and quiet, like she was fixin' to do something but I couldn't tell what." Brooke and Shane were laughing like crazy now, Brooke doubled over "like she was gonna pee herself." And then Adam looked over at Carolyn again, and she was crouched on the ground, like an animal, he said, like a deer somebody had shot and wounded but hadn't managed to kill. Carolyn stood up, and she was holding the neck of the broken bottle in her right hand. Adam said she looked like she might cry or laugh or something, and then Brooke called out: "What're ya gonna do with that, Carolyn? You gonna cut yourself?"

Carolyn lunged forward and Brooke jumped down from Shane's Explorer. "And she ran over and got all in Carolyn's face, grabbed Carolyn's hand with the bottle in it," Adam said.

He said Brooke's voice sounded like a bark: "You wanna cut yourself? Is that it?"

Carolyn barked back, louder than he had expected: "Get away from me." And Adam said Carolyn pushed the bottle forward and he thought it might scrape Brooke's chest, but Brooke was stronger than Carolyn, so much bigger, and Brooke pulled hard on Carolyn's hand, trying to get control of the bottle or something.

"Let it go!" Brooke was yelling now. Carolyn had turned her body into herself and Brooke got behind her, not letting go of Carolyn's hand.

Adam said he couldn't really see what was happening, only that Brooke was practically wrapped around Carolyn, it didn't look like either of them could move. "I never saw a girl fight before," he told people. "And I thought it was awesome at first, if I'm really fuckin' honest."

Carolyn was struggling to get free—"she was weaker, you know?"—and Adam reckoned they were both still holding on to the bottle, that was what was keeping them together. And then Brooke rammed her knee into Carolyn's back—she was so much taller than Carolyn that it hit her right in the small of her back, "right where it would hurt the most," he said. Carolyn screamed and the bottle smashed to the ground and she fell down, like she was shattering too. Brooke let go, she looked around for a second, and then she ran back to Shane "real fast, like she knew what she done."

Carolyn stayed hunched on the ground for a beat. And then she stood up.

She was bleeding, Adam said, and he couldn't believe how much—and then Brooke looked back and her face fell and went white—she was freaked too. The cut was like a butterfly on Carolyn's chest, spreading out from the center, rivulets of blood making tracks against her skin, like little rivers and from far away, you imagined it could look beautiful, like a henna tattoo, like she'd decorated her chest with red diamanté.

Carolyn looked down at her chest—Adam said she had no reaction at first and then, like a child, "like some kid that doesn't know to scream until her mama turns up," she saw the blood and screamed. And then she screamed more and she started to run. Shane and Brooke hopped out of the trunk and got into the car. Shane started the engine and they waited for two, maybe three minutes—the time it took Rihanna to get to the first chorus of "Umbrella"—and they left. They drove out of the parking lot.

Some of the papers said that they followed Carolyn, with the windows down, shouting at her as she ran home. Brooke and Shane denied this, said they went straight to Shane's house and that Brooke was crying because she couldn't stand the sight of blood.

Brooke told people later the spit hit her hair, just missed her eye. Shane neither confirmed nor denied that it happened. People asked Adam if it was true, if that was what had started it, and he said it was too far away to say for sure, to see that thin and beautiful girl spit on the high school's future prom queen. Taylor Lyon told people it had happened for sure—Adam had told her but told her not to tell anybody—but once the court case began, she pretended she had never heard or said anything.

Brooke told the cops—and the liberal reporters and the local television stations—that it was the spit that had started it. She didn't tell any of us that, mostly 'cause nobody would talk to her after it had all gone down. Who cared what the hell she said now? And the *Adamsville Daily* wouldn't print it.

There were things that were found, things that were printed, things that the cops used, that the district attorney used, to substantiate their charges.

Carolyn's phone. The text feed:

Carolyn: OMG. I'm alone and crying and I can't take this anymore. . . . Seriously freaking out.

X: Oh my God. Are you okay? What happened????!

Carolyn: B & S in parking lot when I was leaving school. Threw glass at me and cut me, I'm not kidding. Bleeding like crazy here.

X: WTF? That is INSANE. They are such assholes, ignore them, she is such a bitch. ARE YOU OKAY?

Carolyn: Everybody hates me here. This cut is gonna leave a crazy scar forever. Swear to God.

X: OMG so many people love you. You know they are just jealous. You need to stand up for yourself. Where are you? Want to meet up.

Carolyn: How can I stand up for myself? It doesn't matter anyway.

We found out later that she hadn't gone home. At least not immediately after. Shane and Brooke hadn't seen where she went, they were too freaked by the blood. But Janitor Ken had seen stuff, and so had a couple of teachers, though they were never named. Carolyn had run out of the parking lot, yes, that much was true. And Shane and Brooke drove out behind her a few minutes later. You could see why some people assumed they'd been following her, that they'd chased her home. But when she ran out of the lot, she turned left, not right, into the football field. We imagined her there, just like the first day we'd seen her, unsteady on her feet, shaking, looking down at her phone. We thought that she had probably texted from there, from the field. Or maybe from the locker room—that's where she went next.

Janitor Ken was cleaning out the toilet stalls in the girls' locker room that afternoon. He didn't see Carolyn come in at first and didn't hear her either. He wore his iPod, he explained later, was listening to Kenny Chesney or something—and so he couldn't say for sure how long she'd been in there before he saw her: standing in front of a row of lockers, shirt off, just her bra. He said there was blood on her chest and that she had blood on her hands too.

He went toward her but she screamed, he said. "I didn't want to hurt her or nothing," he told Mr. Overton later, "I just wanted to make sure she was all right." The school's attorney clarified: "There was a sign saying 'Cleaning In Progress.' She shouldn't have come in." Ken said he backed away and, as he did, she opened the palms of her hands. She was holding something in one of them: "something silver and shiny," he said. The police said later that it was a razor blade. She had cut herself, they figured, and was "involved in self-mutilation" in the hours following the incident in the parking lot.

We wished that we had been there that day, in the locker room. We don't know what we would have done, or what we would have said, but we were sure we would have been able to stop things, to turn things in another direction, change the course of history, or maybe change just a few little things. Only maybe that's not true. Maybe an intervention would have only prolonged it, made everything that followed more painful. We didn't know. Looking back, we saw things no more clearly: at one moment, we would believe she had been on a path we had no control over, like Oedipus following his fate. At another, we would say she was someone in distress and only we had the ability to change things. Either way, we felt such shame it could be hard to sleep at night.

Ken told Mr. Overton, and later the police, that Carolyn ran out after he'd seen her, after she'd screamed, after she'd opened her palms. When they pressed him, he got confused about how she'd gotten dressed, or whether she'd gotten dressed at all, and why she was able to get out without him stopping her. They didn't understand why he didn't call somebody, why he didn't at least tell his supervisor, or one of the teachers still in the school. There were plenty of them around. Ken didn't have very strong explanations, and later, the PTA demanded his suspension. We thought this was sad. But maybe they were right.

Miss Simpson was in her office when everything happened.

She gave an interview to some blogger months later and told them she was there, grading papers, while all this happened outside her window, in the parking lot just yards from her desk.

We could imagine Miss Simpson there. In her office. Alone, with a PowerBar, a Diet Coke, some Reese's Pieces in her desk drawer, her opening and closing the cabinet every five minutes, taking another handful, until all but two she mislaid were gobbled up. She had been working on a paper for the school board and the student alliance for three weeks, a paper on the subject of bullying "in the context of new media" and how the school should respond to this phenomenon. She was using Carolyn as a case in point—she was studying some transcripts from Mrs. Matthew's office, things we would only discover later. She was studying the pieces of text that were public on Facebook, things Carolyn had written in her classes. She had a thesis, and she was determined to get it out there. We knew nobody would take her seriously.

There were so many people who were "culpable," the newspapers said later. And we said it to each other too. There were varying degrees, of course, but we all had a hand in it, we thought, every once in a while, though we never said this out loud. What we said out loud was different, less committal, more defensive, if we were honest. Saying it out loud made it true, we thought, and there was so little that we knew was true. Not in the end.

Adamsville Daily News

LOCAL GIRL FOUND DEAD IN BATHROOM

MAY 27, 2011

Carolyn Lessing (16), daughter of Abby Lessing of D'Evereux Drive, was found dead in her home on the evening of Thursday, May 26, due to asphyxia. Police suspect hanging to be the cause of death and have classified the death as a suicide. Her mother found the body after returning home from work at 5:45 pm. She had received a number of phone messages from a classmate of Carolyn's, who warned her that Carolyn was in a fragile mental state. Police stated that Ms. Lessing left her workplace early in order to check in on her only daughter. Ms. Lessing has refused to comment and has asked the community to respect her family's privacy during this difficult time.

Carolyn Lessing and her mother moved to Adamsville from Haddington, New Jersey, last summer. Carolyn was a junior at Adams High School and had been a part of the Homecoming Court in October. She was a member of the swim team and was on the Honor Roll. Carolyn also displayed a special solo art exhibition early in the year, which featured her paintings and photography.

Richard Overton, Adams's principal, has expressed his deepest condolences to Ms. Lessing and Carolyn's extended family. He said that the death was a "tremendous tragedy for the student body and the faculty" and that "counseling services would be in place for students who wish to avail themselves of these." Overton noted that it would be inappropriate and a breach of confidentiality for him to comment on the girl's mental state during her year at the high school but went on record to state that she was "a popular, bright and friendly girl."

Funeral arrangements will be announced in the coming days.

JUNE

26

We found out stuff about the hanging. There was a thing on the "Today" show and they did a "reconstruction" at a house that was supposed to look like Carolyn's, only it didn't. It was too big and the furniture was too boring and everything was gray and beige and tan. The segment showed some girl sitting in a bathroom, one that looked like it was out of an IKEA catalog. She was texting, then taking off her clothes and examining her arms, her abdomen and her chest in the mirror. They'd put a big fake cut on her chest, like the one that was meant to have happened in the parking lot, and the actress touched it and then made a face as if to say the cut was painful and raw. We imagined it stung. The girl was still wearing her bra and underwear—she wasn't completely naked—but people complained later about her state of undress and how it was wrong of the station to do the reconstruction at all. Ann Curry warned people before the piece started that there was "content of an adult nature" and "images some people may find disturbing."

They showed the girl with a scarf, some crazy long one, like the kind that they were selling in Old Navy before Christmas. She tied it around a lightbulb that hung from the ceiling—nothing like Carolyn's house, nothing like any of their bathrooms, which had light fixtures that looked like they were straight out of Restoration Hardware—and then she stood on the toilet seat and tied the scarf around her neck, like she'd done it a million times before, like she was getting ready to walk outside on a cold, cold day. The camera went to the actress's feet then, just in ankle socks, and she dangled one foot over the edge and then, after a few beats, she slid the other one off too. The camera flashed to black.

They showed another actress then, meant to be Abby Lessing, and we actually thought she looked a lot like her, although the camera never really focused on her face. The woman put a key in the front door and walked in the fake Lessing house, put her blazer on the coatrack in the front hall and walked up the stairs. She called out: "Honey, I'm home." And then, more urgently, she called out Carolyn's name. Again and again, until she reached the bathroom, turned the handle and opened the door. That's when the piece finished. The screen went straight to Ann Curry sitting on a sofa, looking sad and concerned and unsure how to make the transition to the psychologist sitting in the armchair next to her.

We talked later about the *Today* show, how wrong it all seemed, how it was different than almost everything we'd heard, almost everything we knew was true. We'd heard Carolyn had been wearing her bathing suit—her teal and black drag suit—and that she'd done it with her Burberry scarf. We heard this from Blake Wyatt, whose aunt volunteered twice a week at the hospital, helping with paperwork and stuff like that. She'd seen Abby come in with Carolyn, and she told Blake that she thought Carolyn had had some kind of accident at the pool, on account of the bathing suit.

The thing about her scarf—that came from Taylor Lyon, who went around telling everyone she would boycott Burberry from this day forward, that's how traumatized she was by the whole event.

We heard from some seniors that she'd weighed herself a final time before tying the scarf around her neck, and we weren't sure how they could know this, but we thought it seemed true and we almost laughed about it later, but we knew that that was wrong.

We wondered how long she'd planned it, how many pills she'd taken to give her the courage. There hadn't been any note, Carolyn's mother was quoted as saying so later, but we were sure that if somebody looked hard enough, they would find something: a draft in recovered documents, an unsent email, an undelivered text. A note would have helped things, we thought, would have helped us, and everybody else, to understand.

We knew so much, we thought, and everybody seemed to keep getting it wrong and this frustrated us, scared us. Somehow a note would have clarified everything, we thought. Would have put the record straight. Provided closure. Or something.

The funeral wasn't in Adamsville. Her body was flown to New Jersey, and the funeral was there. The school organized a service, though, on our last day, so that we could "have a chance to grieve." Carolyn's mother wasn't there, obviously. She had gone to New Jersey. Nobody was sure whether she'd come back to Adamsville at all.

The service was held in the gym—the theater was being refurbished and, plus, there wouldn't be enough room for all of us. The newspapers said that this was in bad taste, that it should have been held somewhere more "solemn," more "appropriate." The gym was where every assembly was held, though, and it didn't seem weird to us. Or we just didn't admit it at the time.

Miss Simpson led the service and students were invited to give a speech. Nobody volunteered, so Andrew was selected.

We watched him approach the podium, his head down, his shoulders folding into themselves—his spine looked like it had been bent like a pipe cleaner. He wore a suit that must have been his dad's—the shoulders were too broad, the sleeves too long, the pants too short. His face had broken out on his chin—cystic acne we hadn't seen since he'd been on Accutane, and even from the back row of the bleachers, you could see red and purple spots coming up around his jawline. His eyes were bloodshot, tired, weak, watery. He read from pieces of lined paper, the edges torn from a spiral notebook. The pages were folded and worn and his hands shook as he read—he had five or six pages, at least.

"I met Carolyn in the summer before she started at Adams. The first thing I noticed about her was how beautiful she was—really beautiful. I'd heard it from other people already, but she really, really was. And when you got to know her better, she was even more beautiful. Which is hard to believe."

He took a drink of water. His voice was cracking; it looked as if he might cry. Probably would.

"On her first day at school, I helped her get her locker open—I don't know what she was doin' wrong, but I guess the lockers and stuff were different at her old school."

Some people in the back started giggling or crying. It was hard to tell which.

"Carolyn was a friend." He looked up from his paper for the first time. He stared out into the crowd, into our eyes, then lifted his to the ceiling. A balloon from three or four assemblies ago was hanging, deflated, from the rafters. Purple, with a white ribbon, it blew with the air conditioner.

Andrew went on, mumbling, saying things about her background, her childhood in New Jersey, her swimming, her art. Stuff they had put in the papers. Stuff everybody knew. We zoned him out. Just a little.

The gym was cold. Brooke and Shane were in the back row, along with Gemma. Their faces were expressionless. Brooke's face was chalky and her lips were caked with foundation—from a distance, you couldn't make out any of her features: her big eyes, her high cheekbones, her dimples. Gemma was a red version of Brooke—red eyes, red cheeks, red mouth. She looked wind-burned, like after a ski trip or a day on the boat. And Shane's face was only barely visible: his baseball cap—Auburn, worn in—was curved around his heart-shaped face. You could see rim and shadow and the glint of his teeth.

"I got to know her better after Christmas, and she was always tellin' me about stuff up North, and what stuff was like in New Jersey. We were gonna go together, in the summer, for a trip, or at least we talked about it. She had planned out a bunch of days for us, a bunch of things to do."

He took another breath. A cough. Noses blowing, sniffing. The girls in the front row, girls Carolyn didn't even know, had their arms around one another, bodies shaking. The guys looked toward the far wall or the small window over the emergency exit. Taylor Lyon's hair covered her face, we couldn't see what she looked like. Her shoulders moved, so we figured she was crying, but we couldn't be sure.

Silence. Andrew stared at the pages. A minute passed. A bell rang. The teachers whispered to one another. We sat and waited. He began again.

"I thought I'd be able to give a speech here today, and talk about all the things Carolyn was, all the things she said, what she meant to me, and to the rest of us. But I can't." He paused. He looked straight into the bleachers again. "I don't know what y'all want me to say."

He rubbed his eyes, breathing in so hard there was feedback from the microphone, a screeching howl.

"Carolyn was good, you know? And it's, like, like . . ." He was looking for something in the ceiling. His eyes were darting back and forth.

"It's like there's something fucked up about us, you know? Like something really, really fucked up." He was spitting into the microphone, he was crying. "Y'all are gonna say this is lame, now or after. Aren't y'all?

"But I don't give a shit anymore, you know? I don't give a shit." Mrs. Matthew had risen to her feet and was approaching him, her eyes crinkled—she had been crying too. He put his hand out in front of him.

"Nah, nah. I'm done. Sorry, ma'am. Sorry."

He walked away from the microphone. Somebody yelled: "Andrew." He looked up and pivoted back, standing in front of the mic.

"All I wanted to say is I'm real sorry for what happened. I'm real sorry. I really am." His voice was shaking, and he fell to his knees, crumpled. The nurse came over, Mr. Overton took over the mic. The service was over. He told us to enjoy our summers.

Two Sundays after Carolyn Lessing hung herself, we didn't linger around the parking lot at church—our parents wouldn't let us, it was too fucking hot and, plus, we didn't want to talk to anybody. We filed in and sat where we always sat and we were quieter than usual—anybody could have noticed this—and even though the air-conditioning was breathing out a heavy noise, we said later that we could have heard a pin drop. People weren't in the mood for small talk. That's what we guessed.

Miss Simpson led the choir as Reverend Davies came in—there was no accompaniment, just us singing on our own, in four-part harmony.

Amazing Grace, how sweet the sound,
That saved a wretch like me.

I once was lost but now am found,
Was blind, but now I see.

T'was Grace that taught my heart to fear.
And Grace, my fears relieved.

How precious did that Grace appear
The hour I first believed.

Through many dangers, toils and snares
I have already come;

'Tis Grace that brought me safe thus far
and Grace will lead me home.

The Lord has promised good to me
His word my hope secures.
He will my shield and portion be,
As long as life endures.

Yea, when this flesh and heart shall fail,
And mortal life shall cease,
I shall possess within the veil,
A life of joy and peace.

When we've been here ten thousand years
Bright shining as the sun,
We've no less days to sing God's praise
Than when we've first begun.

We had heard the lyrics before, had sung it a million times, and we knew it was overplayed. But it was different now, and everybody knew it. It made our eyes fill up and we looked toward the ceiling to keep from blinking, to keep our mascara from running down our faces. We didn't even know her and we didn't want to look like the poser freshmen who were all sobbing in the bathroom on Monday. But we were amazed and horrified and frightened when we felt the lump in the backs of our throats, the heat rise to our cheeks, the tears start to form behind our eyes. This couldn't happen. Not here. Not now. Not about her.

We finished the song and we pulled ourselves together.

The sermon was standard, run-of-the-mill, all about the evils of drink and sex and impure thoughts. We had thought Reverend Davies might talk about suicide, about dealing with grief, about how to cope with loss. But he didn't. We overheard our mothers, months later, saying that this was "appalling," that the suicide should have been "addressed, at least superficially." We weren't sure what that meant but we were relieved that none of those things had been raised, that we were just carrying on as normal. Looking back, we wondered if Reverend Davies felt in some way responsible—if he was already aware that Gemma had played a part, however small. At the time, we didn't really think about it, and we smiled and waved at Gemma when we left the building. She looked tired, we said. Her hair was greasy, scraped back into a ponytail. It didn't even look that blond. She needed a shower.

Brooke was there with her mother and they both looked pretty and pulled together: Brooke was wearing a cream cotton dress we had seen in the window at Parisians, with turquoise jewelry we knew belonged to her mother. She looked fresh and bright-eyed and her skin was so sparkling we said later she'd probably had a peel. She looked a million times better than she had on the day of the service—she was over the whole thing, we guessed. She had already moved on.

Nobody saw Shane or Andrew. Shane's parents or Andrew's father either. We looked around for them for forever—especially for Andrew—people were still talking about what a weird speech he'd made at the service. It was sweet and all that he cared about her, they said, but it was all a little bit much. Dylan Hall said he thought he was faking. Blake Wyatt agreed. We didn't think this was true, no way, but we had nothing to go on but our feelings, and that wasn't enough to make you want to speak up, not in the beginning. Maybe in the end.

We remembered Andrew at the Homecoming parade, his phone full of pictures, of Carolyn smiling, of Carolyn in the back of the Mustang, of Carolyn fixing her dress. He couldn't have been faking: he had loved her for real.

We went to the country club after service, as usual, and we ate our food on the golf course, on the fourteenth hole, like we always did. We talked about the day that Carolyn had come with us, the day she'd run across the course and jumped the fence and gotten on to the diving board. We talked about watching her dive, watching her glide underwater, perfect and pretty and silent. And then we remembered Andrew again. Him standing and watching her. We wished we had recorded that day, we said. We would have liked to have watched it, over and over and over again.

They called us back into school for questioning, sent an email to parents, "urged them to show complete cooperation with the police and their investigation." The junior and senior class, every last one of us, they asked us to come in on a Saturday in June. The questions would be "routine." They wouldn't have asked if it wasn't "completely necessary." There were a couple of kids in every class who didn't come. Their parents or grandparents were lawyers and when we mentioned this to our parents after the fact, we watched their pupils dilate, their bodies stiffen, afraid they—or we—had done something wrong.

Our parents drove us. Didn't want us out of their sight, we figured, and, plus, they were curious too. We arrived at 7:45 A.M. and as we pulled into the parking lot, we saw them: the reporters, cameras, vans, lights, all of them stationed outside. We wondered how long they'd been there. Wondered if they had catering trucks, like we'd heard they did for movies, like we saw on "Making the Video." What a weird job.

We filed into the auditorium, kept our hands in our pockets, tried to keep our eyes on the floor. We didn't know how to act. Taylor Lyon and Tiffany Port were standing by the bathrooms at the back of the theater, Taylor's face all red and blotchy, her eyes bloodshot. "I'm still, like, so shocked." Tiffany put her arm around her, put her head on Taylor's shoulder. "You are so sweet," Tiffany said. "She was so lucky to have you." Lauren coughed: "Fake." We rolled our eyes and made our way to the middle of the auditorium, took our seats.

Mr. Overton was on the stage with a couple of cops, not local ones, not ones we'd seen around before, but the ones we'd seen on TV. There were two butch-looking women, holding clipboards, writing things down. They had the lights up like they were gonna do a show choir number. Mr. Overton was, like, literally standing in a spotlight.

"I wonder how long this will take." Jessica looked at her watch, then over at Lauren and Nicole. "What? I have a haircut at three." She examined her split ends.

We watched as the student body poured in, saw Brooke and Gemma walking close together, everybody keeping their distance from them. Tiffany and Taylor walked by us, getting seats near the front. "They've a lot of nerve showing up here," Taylor said, looking around to make sure she'd been heard. We thought about telling her to shut up, that she'd a lot of nerve herself, but we kept quiet, looked at our phones, passed around a nail file, a copy of Us Weekly that Lauren had brought with her.

Mr. Overton called us one by one, alphabetical order. They

must have had ten cops asking questions, 'cause they went through everybody real quick. When Lauren came out, she told us what she'd been asked.

They wanted to know who Carolyn was friends with. Who Lauren was friends with too. They had a copy of Lauren's schedule, had drawn circles around classes she had in common with Carolyn. They asked if Lauren had seen Carolyn in the bathroom on the thirteenth of December and if in May she had heard about a plan "to attack Ms. Lessing in the parking lot." If Shane had posted the YouTube video himself, or if it was believed that he'd put somebody up to it. They asked if she'd heard Brooke and Gemma conspiring to slash Carolyn's tires and/or destroy her art project. If Andrew and Shane had talked about having sex with Carolyn Lessing and on how many occasions. Lauren said she tried to tell them about the cutting, the stuff Carolyn did with her protractor, but they didn't want to know about that, they shut her right down. They asked her to try to remember the names that people called Carolyn. Was she called "Yankee slut"? Lauren answered things as well as she could, she said, but there were things she couldn't remember and there were things she thought they wanted to hear. She did her best. And we answered like Lauren did, mostly, though we didn't know what any of it meant.

Later, when we heard all of the charges, we were sorry we hadn't prepared more. Sorry we hadn't tried to give a longer version. We didn't want to protect Brooke or Gemma, or even Shane and Andrew, but we didn't think what they ended up saying about them was true. Not entirely.

We waited for one another. Watched Gemma go in, waited to see how long they'd keep her. Same with Shane, Brooke and Andrew. When Nicole Willis was finished, none of those were out yet. Or else they'd left through the back, some way we didn't know.

Blake Wyatt told people later that all four of them left in plastic handcuffs; the police decided to take them down to the station. We didn't think this could be true, not really, especially since there weren't any pictures of that on the Web. Blake never stopped running his mouth.

Everybody knew the charges were extreme. Or at least that's what we thought, and it was what everybody thought in the beginning. A week after the thing at the school, the district attorney read out her statement on the front steps of the Old Courthouse—a building no longer used for legal proceedings of any kind.

Why the DA used the Old Courthouse didn't seem important to us—but we thought about it later. And we figured out what she wanted: to look positively legal in the eyes of the rest of the state, the rest of the country, the rest of the world. Some of the parents called it cynical. We weren't sure that that was true, but we did think it was weird.

The foreign media—that's what we ended up calling them, in the end, even though we were pretty sure nobody from abroad had ever stepped foot in Adamsville—they were camped outside the courthouse from seven that morning. When Judge Sanders emerged at 11.37 A.M., you'd think the crowd might have cleared. But it hadn't. Not at all. The mob had gotten bigger and bigger as the news—the news that news crews were in town—had spread. And the heat of the morning made them look even thicker on the ground, the whole scene more claustrophobic. We wondered how anybody could breathe.

We watched the whole thing on TV and/or streamed from the *Adamsville News* website. And as we watched, the Twitter feeds went crazy:

Carolyn Lessing's #bullies charged
Carolyn Lesing #bullies & tormenters get what they deserve
Let's hope this sticks to Lessing #bullies

They were going to be tried as adults. That was the first thing. Then they listed the charges: violation of civil rights, criminal harassment, disturbance of a school assembly, stalking, assault with a deadly weapon. Statutory rape for Andrew and Shane too. We were curious about the "deadly weapon." The DA explained that it was the bottle of Dr Pepper that Brooke had thrown at Carolyn. If we hadn't been so shocked, we said, that would have made us laugh. But it didn't.

We didn't understand what statutory rape meant, so we Wikipedia-ed it. 'Cause Carolyn hadn't turned sixteen—"the age of consent"—when she was hanging out with Shane, and the same with Andrew, at least in the beginning: that meant they were rapists. Weird and stupid, we said to each other. You could prosecute the whole high school for statutory rape, we thought, except for a few of the born-agains and the band kids, but even those kids ended up losing their virginity eventually. How they'd prove it became the other topic of conversation—Andrew could just say he'd gone down on her, Shane could claim that she'd just sucked his dick. That wasn't sex or at least we didn't think so, and we weren't sure about the anal stuff, or what it meant if you just let a guy inside you but made him pull out before he came. We remembered the surveys they made us take—some state-sanctioned thing—giving details of what we'd done, how far we'd gone, how often we did what we did, what we felt when we did it. We wanted to get the results of that one, to see what percentile we came out in. Like with the PSATs or any of the other crappy tests they had us take to judge our aptitude. But we never got anything back. We didn't know where we fell, and we wanted to. Carolyn would have been an outlier, we said. All her experience from her old school, the way she flirted, the straps of her bras, the way she sat in class after the weekend. She was different. And she knew how to do things we just didn't. Maybe that's where some of it came from—the way people loved her and hated her. It was always one way or the other with Carolyn. And that was her problem, really. In the end.

There were so many things the news got wrong, so many things we wanted to correct, so many things we wanted to shout about, so many things we wanted to tear up and smash. Only we didn't know how, and we were also tired, tired by the year, by the year that they had created, by our memories, by the things half remembered, half said, half forgotten, half written. We would have corrected things if we'd known how, that much we were sure about, only we didn't know how, and we no longer knew what was true. You tell a lie so many times you forget whether or not you made it up; it starts to seem plausible, tangential memories form around it, giving the lies an alibi, some credibility.

When the journalists started snooping around the school, we weren't the ones they wanted to talk to—they wanted Brooke and Shane and Andrew and Gemma. They wanted the really popular kids, the "bullies," and they wanted the bullied too.

The story about the bathroom was the first one that got out of hand. Brooke following Carolyn in, Brooke calling her a bitch, a slap. They named the date (December 13) and even the time, which made it seem real, we thought, and even though we didn't remember much of it, that kind of thing messed with us, made us not trust our memories—we could have blocked them out, that's what the psychiatrist would say. When we talked to one another, we couldn't remember everything exactly the same, and we weren't even positive it had been Brooke and Carolyn. We said we remembered a hand dryer and a blocked drain. The sound of a hand and ring against a wall. We remembered that two girls talked. They fought. But what exactly had they said? We couldn't remember. And this scared us. All of a sudden it mattered.

USA Today ran it, *Today* replayed its reenactment at least three times, *Good Morning America* brought in a psychologist to analyze the motivations of Brooke, to reveal Carolyn's emotional state. On *Live! with Regis and Kelly* Kelly Ripa related a story of her own from high school, in which she had been afraid to be alone in the bathroom with a bully. People texted in with their stories.

The couple of journalists who spoke to us—there were two young ones, from liberal online magazines—wanted to know first if we were relieved. Relieved about what? About the fact that the bullies were gone, that Shane and Brooke and the others were going to be punished, that they were going to be charged, sent to prison, they wouldn't graduate with us, they'd have to be reformed.

We felt so many things in those days and weeks and months that followed. We were lost, and we were sad, weepy, crying at the freaking "Star Spangled Banner," crying at a long-distance commercial, at the previews for *Grey's Anatomy*. We were angry too, and desperate for everybody to leave our school alone, but at the same time wanting to tell everybody in the world our story, wanting to shake people who weren't paying attention, who were looking the other way. We were mad, mad at our teachers—at Miss Simpson, at Mr. Ferris, at Coach Cox, at Mrs. Matthew, at the teachers we thought knew more than they had let on—why hadn't they stopped things? Were we mad at Carolyn? We couldn't be sure—we cried when we saw her face on the news, begged our mothers to let us stay home from church, from the country club, from the pool, just so we wouldn't have to face a conversation about her. But we may have hated her a little too. She had been popular, she had been beautiful, and nothing that happened to her was that special, nothing that had happened to her made her so unique, made her entitled to die. We couldn't say that to the journalists, we couldn't tell them that we thought she did it for the attention, and that we just thought things went wrong. We couldn't say that, 'cause imagine how we'd look? But we couldn't say it because we didn't believe it, not really.

Were we relieved that Shane was being prosecuted? That Brooke could go to jail? No. No, we weren't. They were victims too, and that's the part that nobody understands. That what went on between Carolyn and those guys, and Carolyn and those girls, that kind of shit happens every day of the week and we just fucking deal with it, you know? And she was part of it. That's what we knew for sure. And we told them that. We told them that again and again and again. And the online magazines, they reported this, and they were discredited, and *USA Today* continued its series, the bullying teens being brought to justice, a school safe at last.

To say we were relieved wasn't true, but that's what was printed, and it was said, and it was printed and said again and again, and before you knew it, you half believed it yourself. The counselors told us "our memories weren't reliable." They shifted and changed and as we swapped stories, things became cloudier, our vision became blurred, we just couldn't remember exactly who was to blame, who started what, who was where and when and why. The reporters didn't help, and talking to them, and to the psychiatrists and psychotherapists and psychologists and social workers, didn't help either. It clouded us again. We were young, that was the thing. We were young. We knew it wasn't an excuse.

{Letter to the Editor, *New York Observer*. Never printed. Obtained under FOIA. June 21, 2011}

Timothy Towers
New York Observer
321 W. 44th Street
6th Floor
New York, NY 10036

Dear Mr. Towers:

I am writing in relation to the article "Mean Girls and Football Fanatics: How Adams High School helped kill Carolyn Lessing," which was printed on June 16, 2011.

The school faculty did not "turn a blind eye" to the allegations of bullying leveled against certain students in relation to Carolyn Lessing, as you suggest. We are currently in the midst of an investigation and review into the incidents involving Miss Lessing and her classmates. We plan to issue a public statement following this work, but in the meantime, we would assert that the implications within your article are defamatory, particularly in relation to the school's attitude to athletics, and I would request that a full correction is issued in tomorrow's paper, accompanied by a robust apology to the faculty, parents and students of Adams High.

If this is not undertaken, the Superintendent's Office has instructed his legal team to begin formal proceedings with your newspaper in relation to libel.

I understand that parents have written to you under separate cover with similar grievances, and I would strongly encourage you to re-examine your newspaper's editorial approach to this subject, which is clearly agenda-driven, reflecting an urban and liberal bias and an overall lack of knowledge regarding the basic facts of Miss Lessing's tragic suicide.

Yours sincerely,

Richard Overton
Principal, Adamsville High School

JULY

27

Our parents were to blame. That's what the papers said later. That was the explanation for a lot of things: our parents. They talked a lot and they met a lot and they cared a lot, but, really, they didn't do a thing. Or they didn't do enough. Not in the end.

The PTA met in the cafeteria on a Tuesday evening, the parking lot full of SUVs and minivans and Volvo station wagons. We weren't sure what they talked about most of the time, but that day in July, three days after our postponed prom, we were pretty sure. We were sure that they would demand stricter codes of conduct, more supervision, fewer bathroom passes, more restrictions on phones, more firewalls on the Web. We were sure they would demand things, and call on the principal to call on the superintendent. Someone might have to resign.

We saw them later on the nine o'clock news, streaming out of the cafeteria into the parking lot, wide-eyed and mouths open, pupils dilated by the flashbulbs and the camera lights. Microphones were shoved toward them for a moment, then a reporter moved to the forefront, as we watched our parents retreat toward their cars. Older and fatter versions of ourselves, wearing Talbots jeans and not Rock Revivals, wearing brown loafers or New Balance sneakers. We watched them: some with their heads down, some with their eyes glazed, others red-faced and veins bulging. Versions of ourselves, only solid, permanent.

Mr. Overton was interviewed—or they tried to—and he just kept saying "No comment," which we thought sounded pretty bad, made him sound even stupider and guiltier than before. We heard later he had a whole legal team telling him what to do. They were crap, we said to each other. If he had just said a little bit more, explained things a little better—then it all might have calmed down.

On TV, Carolyn's class picture came up in the left-hand corner of the screen. We flipped the stations, and Carolyn's image remained the same, only the reporter changed. Kristina Champion for Dothan MCBC, Brent Brinkley for Birmingham-ABC. Carolyn's picture—that picture—would be in *Us Weekly*, *USA Today*, *People*, even the *New York Times*. And blog posts and dedication sites popped up by the dozen in the days that followed. The picture looked different when we saw it there—maybe because it was bigger than the wallet-size photo she handed out two months earlier, writing in pink ink on the back, with hearts underneath her name. BFF, she wrote to some of us. *BFF*.

The reporters summarized the meeting: the parents were "angry" and "upset" and "ashamed." The school board was "shocked" and "undertaking an investigation." They reported on our prom, which had been postponed from June until early July out of "respect." They scanned the inside of the gym: blue and white streamers and a drinks table—the punch looked purple—and the DJ and the airbrushed proscenium arch. Our theme was "A Night to Remember," which we all thought was lame and not really a theme, but the reporters said it over and over and over again. The reporters told us how it was "shameless," "lacking in empathy"—they did a vox pop on the other side of town. People were "amazed" and "disgusted." They showed footage of Shane Duggan getting out of a limousine outside the gym—in black tails with a purple bow tie to match Brooke Moore, who stepped out of the limo after him. They were smiling and Brooke's eyes were like slits—was she drunk? The reporters didn't say that, not exactly. But we knew what they meant.

We drove by Carolyn's house over the summer, more than once. Her mother's Realtor had difficulty selling it, we heard, and we weren't sure if it was just the economy or whether it was all the publicity, or maybe it was both. In any case, Century 21 did an open house that ran for a few weeks. We read about it in the paper. On the Friday afternoons, you could walk around without an agent shadowing you, trying to sell you something when it's obvious you're not even old enough to drink, let alone buy a house.

We went to see it, couldn't not. When we arrived, we were the only people there, and we sat in Jessica's car for ten minutes before we got the nerve to get out and go in. Why we wanted to see it wasn't clear, even to us, but we felt compelled, drawn, driven to the house, to Carolyn and to her mother. We just wanted to look around, find clues, memories, whatever.

It smelled the same, we said. Smelled like new house and chlorine and freesia. It smelled like Carolyn. We stood in the front hall for a couple of minutes, breathing it in, until we couldn't smell anything anymore.

We walked through the kitchen: no food on the shelves like before, no bills lying around the counter, no Abby perched at the breakfast bar eating an almond. We were afraid to touch anything at first, but then Nicole opened a drawer. It was empty, of course, but it made us feel braver, and we began opening everything, just in case. An Adams High School magnet in the drawer next to the dishwasher, a pale green Post-it note with a telephone number in Carolyn's handwriting. We didn't touch it. We left it where it was.

We went to her room. It didn't look like we remembered: looked smaller, somehow, without the furniture inside. We remembered the piles and piles of books and the pictures of her in New York, in New Jersey. And the pictures of her dad. We remembered it all.

In the bathroom, all was clean, sparkling. No Kerastase, no Lancôme, no Sephora candles. Jessica popped the medicine cabinet open. No Seroquel, no Yasmin, no Pepto-Bismol. Just one item—a bar of Dial soap—something Carolyn would never use, we said. Jessica lifted it up and a wide piece of thick yellow tape dangled from its corner. It drifted to the ground. Nicole picked it up: from the crime scene. She had done it here. We backed up and away and out the door of the bathroom. We went down the stairs. We walked out of the house. And we didn't talk about it again.

facebook

Remember Carolyn Lessing

Margaret Grosse

My heart goes out to Carolyn's mother and father, all of her family. I am praying for all of you. Carolyn, you were a beautiful girl who did not need to die. Your killers should be punished with the full force of the law.

Brenda Moody

Those kids deserve what they get.

Geoff Gilbert

Carolyn, you are an angel looking out for us. Your tormentors will burn in hell. This never should have happened.

Tom Stephenson

That whole school should be burned to the ground.

Sandra Sampson

Carolyn, you were so beautiful and kind. May you RIP.

28

There are things that we remember. That Carolyn was beautiful, yes. That she was different, of course. That she came to Adams and she wore California Brand T-shirts and never the same one twice. That she could wear her hair curly or straight. And then there are other things, the things that people may forget, or may want to forget, or maybe they didn't see them. Only that's very hard to believe. She was popular. She wasn't an outsider, at least not in the beginning. She had more friends than we did, at the start, and she had become popular overnight. She was funny, everybody thought so, and she was so pretty, and her clothes were so cool. It was easy to see how it happened.

Brooke and Gemma weren't mean girls, and Shane and Andrew weren't bullies. We said this to the journalists, again and again, and to the guidance counselors and to our teachers and to anybody who said it to us—'cause they said it a lot.

Some people resented the way the story played out. Gemma and Brooke and Shane and Andrew, of course, but there were other people too. Popular kids and band kids and druggies and the Odyssey of the Mind-ers. They bitched about the story, about how Carolyn's family had turned things all around, how the story got reversed—Carolyn could be a bitch too, and the articles never said that, and nobody blogged or Tweeted that—you'd be shot.

But there were others, of course. And maybe they were the majority, in the end. The people that began to believe it all—or maybe they did all along—that Carolyn was a victim, and not a victim of herself, but a victim of those four, and that we were all complicit. That we had watched it all and let it happen. That the four of them should go to jail and then maybe we'd be safe. That they should be punished, and if not by the courts, then by us.

We said later that it was funny how the mood changed—and how nobody said anything about the irony of ganging up on Gemma and Brooke, of egging their lockers and houses, of throwing bricks into Shane's car window, of writing anonymous notes to Andrew, telling him that he should leave town before they made the final arrangements for his funeral. Some girl—from a school in Cullman—came to the high school and waited in the parking lot after school the following fall. She had a knife and some scissors and she and some other girl pinned Brooke down and then cut off a chunk of her hair. Coach Cox got there before they finished and that made it look worse, we said later—her asymmetrical haircut, a penny-size bald spot a few inches from her ear. She went to a salon in Birmingham to try to fix it, but Brooke's hair never grew back the way it used to look. Her hair—which used to be shiny, glossy, swishy—was like hay, in color and in texture, and you'd be afraid to get too close to it. It would scratch your skin, cut you.

We thought it would never feel better, that this would stay around our necks forever. We'd carry it with us to college, and to our first jobs, and into our marriages, and bestow it on our children and then our grandchildren. Not a gift, but a curse, or just a heavy stone that you picked up as a child and never took out of your pocket. Later, when things did start to feel more normal, the guilt would kick in: You did something horrible. And you are too horrible even to realize it.

None of the charges stuck, not in the end. Gemma and Brooke and Shane had to do community service—we'd see them in Harper's Field picking up garbage on Saturdays, or at the Knights of Columbus serving spaghetti dinner—and Andrew, well, Andrew was cleared of everything. There was backlash to all of this too, of course: from the foreign press, the liberal bloggers and from people in the town. Nobody could remember what had really happened but everybody had an opinion. People wanted them to be held responsible. If they were, it meant we were all off the hook.

Andrew and Shane went to college—we'd heard they had trouble getting in, had been wait-listed or straight-out refused from Alabama and Auburn—but when the case finally cleared, they left town. Took them maybe two, three months, but then they were gone. Andrew went to California—nobody could believe it, him going that far away—and Shane to Ole Miss. We wondered if the story followed them around—if their hallmates recognized them from the news, from the footage of them emerging from the courthouse, in their suits with their heads bowed low. We wondered if they ever told anybody themselves. Our parents would tell us that years ago it would have been easier to make a fresh start, but the Web made it all more difficult. There were still Facebook sites devoted to Carolyn's memory, devoted to avenging her death.

It was harder for Brooke and Gemma, that was clear. Gemma's dad requested a parish transfer, but it wasn't granted, and attendance at the church dipped and then leveled off completely. People started going to First Baptist in Cullman so as not to hear him preach. The state convention still couldn't find a new parish for him, so he was forced to step down, eventually. He wasn't prepared to let the whole parish crumble, just because of a bad story in the paper, but things got worse when the church could no longer pay him: he took a job in the Winn-Dixie packing groceries, and Mrs. Davies got some hours at Parisians. They put their house on the market and when it sold, two years later, they moved to another state. Nobody asked for a forwarding address. Gemma was homeschooled the whole time, so we only saw her every once and a while—she looked the same, we thought, only sadder.

Brooke tried to go back to school—she showed up on the first day of senior year and even tried to sit with Tiffany and Taylor at lunch, but they had already arranged the seating. She ate her lunch in the bathroom for the first few weeks and then started skipping classes so often that she was suspended. While she was out, she got mono or Lyme disease or something like that and Mrs. Matthew arranged for all her assignments to be sent home and she graduated with all of us in 2012, but she didn't turn up for the ceremony. We heard she'd be going to Cullman Community the following fall, and a few people saw her registering for classes that August. She'd put on at least twenty pounds.

Taylor Lyon seemed fine over the summer—we'd see her at the country club, at church, in the mall—but we heard later she took it really hard: she never admitted any responsibility, but we thought she should. She cut her hair short and dyed it dark brown, and she got really skinny during the second half of senior year. She turned rexy, we said. And we wondered if her problems were connected to her friendship with Carolyn. We couldn't tell. Taylor was a ditcher, a fair-weather friend. She was Carolyn's first connection to Adams, and she severed it when she got scared, or bored, we weren't sure which.

Ms. Lessing did lots of spots on the news—she was even on *Oprah*—and she looked the same as ever: young, pretty, thin. She seemed more drawn, that was for sure, and tired: there was a blackness underneath her eyes that never seemed to go away, not even when she was on national television. She hardly ever talked about Gemma and Brooke and Shane and Andrew, even when the reporters tried to draw it out of her. She blamed the school, she told them, the administration, for not doing more. When the charges were dropped against the four of them, though, she went on record to say that she was "disappointed" and that "justice had not been done." We never saw her in the flesh again—she had moved back to New Jersey for good—and we never got to see the dad in real life either. He did lots of media too.

He was weird, the dad, everybody said that. He was older than anybody had expected, looked like he could be Carolyn's granddad. He was quoted as saying he "didn't blame the kids" but that he wished the school had done more "for a girl in distress." We thought it was strange that nobody criticized him for living so far away, for not being more involved. But nobody did. They were immune, her parents. And we wished we were too.

She had a special page in our yearbook, Carolyn did. And kids who hardly knew her, we thought, would cry at the mention of her, cheered when they heard about the charges against Brooke and Shane and Gemma and Andrew.

AUGUST

EPILOGUE

At the end of that summer, we went back to Harper's Field. The festival was planned the same as before, though Jessica Grady's dad had said that it might be "scaled down," given all the town's publicity over the summer, the impending trial, the downturn in the economy, everything else. We didn't make big plans around it, but we went together.

We arrived later than usual, around noon, too late to get a balloon ride, we figured. To be honest, we didn't know why we left it so late—we were about to be seniors, it was lame to care about this stuff so much. It was too hot, too humid, too cheesy, all of that. But, really, we had a feeling it had to do with Carolyn. Every place we stepped contained a memory of her—whether real or imagined—and, sometimes, we found it hard to breathe.

As we drove into the parking lot, we could see the balloons, rising and falling, red and purple and green and blue. The band was playing "Proud to Be an American" or something real red-neck like that, and we took our time as we walked into the field. We made our way to the balloons—we could eat and hang out and all that later, if we could bear it—and we saw Jessica's dad in the distance with a balloon, red and white, fire inflating it. He waved us forward and, without thinking, we ran toward him, weaving in and out of the balloons, the baskets, the people. We kept our eyes on him and ran, maybe skipped, and we smiled—this was as it had always been: us together, ready to rise into the air, weightless.

We stepped into the basket and Mr. Grady released the rope. We moved faster than usual, we said, there was a breeze that carried us quickly, carried us high. We looked down at the ground and saw it all change in front of us. People blurred into colors, the ground blurred into shapes. From where we were, the ground started to make sense, appear complete, under control. We were at a distance from it and could see only what we needed to see. From here, we thought, if a car crashed, you wouldn't hear it, and even if you did, it would look like a toy, it wouldn't be real. From here, we couldn't distinguish the adults from the children, the new buildings from the old, the pools from the ponds. We liked it up here, we knew this, to be at a remove from things, to be out of touch, out of control. We asked Mr. Grady if we could stay up for a little bit longer. We wanted a little bit more, we told him, and he smiled. He said that it wasn't possible. They'd be starting the light show soon. Couldn't be in the sky for that.

We looked down again and followed the shapes and instead of trying to identify places, people, buildings, we tried to imagine that it was something else entirely, our town. As we fell farther from the sky, we closed our eyes, afraid to open them again. We saw Carolyn behind a tree a year before, holding Shane Duggan's hand. We imagined ourselves yelling to her, calling her close. But even in our dreams she couldn't hear us; she walked behind the balloons, behind an oak tree and out of our sight. We couldn't reach her.

We felt the wind blow us from the side and we opened our eyes. We didn't look at one another. We looked down and saw the balloons and the fair and the band. Our church and the country club and the pool. We saw our school, we saw Fifth Avenue, the Halls' family farm, the Old Courthouse. We saw a map of Carolyn's year, the year we had witnessed, had observed and recorded, to which we had not objected, laid out in front of us, like a grid. We looked at it and felt the tears form behind our eyes and we tried to blink them away. And then we looked up.

ACKNOWLEDGMENTS

My colleagues at the Arts Council have become a sort of a family to me, and I am deeply grateful to work in an environment where creativity is fostered and encouraged. I am especially thankful to my colleagues Stephanie O'Callaghan and Seán MacCárthaigh, who read my work at an early stage and told me (well, insisted) that I needed to keep going. All of my colleagues have been tireless cheerleaders, particularly Aoife Corbett, Maeve Whelan, Helen Meany, Anthony Glavin, Claire Doyle, David Parnell, Joe Stuart, Jennifer Lawless, Audrey Keane, Fionnuala Sweeney, and Monica Corcoran.

I am eternally grateful to my wonderful, wonderful agent, Sarah Williams. I am grateful that you took a chance on me, grateful that you continue to give me the world's best advice, grateful that you are unstintingly calm and patient and wise and very, very funny. Thank you, too, to Sophie Hicks, for reading my novel early on and giving it your very essential and meaningful stamp of approval. I am also indebted to Ed Victor, Nathalie Hallam, Rebecca Jones, Therese Coen, and Morag O'Brien, all of whom have given me help and encouragement along the way.

I am thankful to my course tutors at the Dublin Faber Academy, James Ryan and Éilís Ní Dhuibhne, and to my fellow writers on the course, especially Anne Learmont. I learned so much from each and every one of you and count myself extremely lucky to have worked with such a talented and generous bunch. Thank you also to Siobhán Parkinson, Elaina Ryan, and Faith O'Grady for giving needed encouragement, and to Rachel Pierce for doing that as well as asking all the right questions.

I owe thanks to many, many teachers and librarians who have deepened my love of reading and writing, especially Jeanne Stroh, John Glavin, and Norma Tilden.

Emily Bazelon's reporting on the Phoebe Prince case in *Slate* was of great assistance to me in researching this book, as was her tremendous book about bullying in the twenty-first century, *Sticks and Stones*.

At Bloomsbury, Helen Garnons-Williams has been the kind of champion a writer dreams of, and her wisdom, insight, and kindness have made everything about this process a delight. Thank you also to Alexandra Pringle, Ellen Williams, Oliver Holden-Rea, Helen Flood, Elizabeth Woabank, David Foy, and David Mann: each one of you has made me and my novel feel special and loved, and it's hard to express just how much this means.

I extend my gratitude to all at RepForce Ireland, particularly Louise Dobbins, Peter McIntyre, Cormac Kinsella, and Bríd Ní Chuilinn. Your company's dedication to promoting great literature knows no bounds.

At St. Martin's Press, I am indebted to Elizabeth Beier. Every note you have given me has made this book better. I cannot thank you enough for believing in the novel and its voice; your enthusiasm and passion are infectious. Thank you, also, to Michelle Richter and Anya Lichtenstein for your efficiency, professionalism, and thoughtfulness, and for answering my endless questions. I am grateful to Dori Weintrub and Ivan Lett for their savvy, skill, and support. And I am indebted to Sally Richardson for allowing me into the St. Martin's Press family.

Thank you to John Boyne and Colum McCann for reading the book when it was in its infancy and for giving me the confidence to submit it to agents. Thank you to the great Roddy Doyle for reading it much later and giving me a badly needed boost of confidence. I am grateful to Paul Murray, Claire Kilroy, and Chris Binchy for their lighthearted and more serious advice about this business of being a writer, and a parent.

I am grateful to have grown up in a house full of books, where reading was a central part of our lives. Thank you to my mother, Ann Dolan Bannan, and my father, William Bannan, for giving me a happy childhood (and adulthood!). In the fifth grade, my mother would read my 500-word themes and give me her notes. You were my first, and best, editor. To my sisters, Elizabeth Placencia and Kathleen Didio, I thank you for reading this before it was edited and telling me you thought it was good. And for being such amazing sisters. Thank you, too, to your families: Doug, Nolan, and Margaret Didio and Rodrigo, Elena, and Thomas Placencia. Thank you also to my cousin Hannah Fandel, who was kind enough to give me insightful notes about being a teenager in the South today. I really needed your help, so thank you!

I extend my thanks to my Irish family: William and Philomena Keegan, Vanessa, Pascal, and Teia Marsh, Christian Keegan, Trish Bunyan, and Gary Keegan, and Laurie, Derry, Hunter, and Wilde Schneider. Never in the history of the world has there been a family more supportive of the arts and creativity. Artistic geniuses, form an orderly queue!

And, finally, but most important, I thank my endlessly

brilliant, supportive, and kind husband, Duncan Keegan, and my daughter, Niamh. The two of you make me want to do something that matters. Thank you for putting up with me, for making me happy and for making me laugh. You are my world. My life.